KENTUCKY NIGHTS

JANUARY RAYNE

Cover Model: Tony Brettman
Photographer: JW Photography
Graphic Designer: Dallas Ann Designs
Chapter Artist: Milkychai

Fang v__v bang on fangbangers

❀ Formatted with Vellum

Also by January Rayne

Shallow Cove Dimensions

The Eternally Series:

Book 1: Eternally Hers

Book 2: Eternally Damned

Book 3: Carnival of Creeps

Book 4: Eternally Cursed

Book 5: Eternally Rare

Book 6: Eternally Lost

Dead Man's Ranch Series:

Book 1: Kentucky Nights

Shallow Cove Dark Dimensions

The Monster Stalker Series:

Book 1: Honeysuckles

Book 2: Snapdragons

Book 3: Hollyhocks

Author's Note

This book is not considered a dark romance but does have a few trigger warnings such as depression, questions of infertility (MMC), pregnancy, period play, and kidnapping.

Scan here to listen to the playlist
of Kentucky Nights:

DEDICATION

To the ones who fight the night
when it enters your mind.
Just know it won't stay dark forever.

And also to Romeo,
You're such a good puppers.

PROLOGUE

KENTUCKY

Year unknown. Somewhere in the south.

There's nothing more beautiful than falling in love with a woman under the night sky. The way the moonlight falls upon her skin spells me into a trance. My eyes drift across her face, appreciating the strands of hair that seem to stand out from the glow of the moon.

Her lips even hold the promise of morning, the thin layer of beeswax reflecting the stars, and soon will hold the warmth of the sun.

Everything about a woman is addictive. The way they speak, walk, the softness of their skin, their body, I can't think of one thing that doesn't invite me in.

Especially when it comes to *this* woman.

Audrey Reese. Heiress to the family fortune her father built after founding Reese Railroads. Audrey is the catch every man wants. The most eligible bachelorette in town, and yet she's spending her nights with me on a blanket in the middle of a field. She must be bored out of her mind wanting to pass time with a cowboy like me.

"You ever gonna marry me, Ms. Reese?"

She pushes herself off my chest, staring down at me with a big smile on her face. "Are you asking me to marry you, Mr. Jones?"

I drift my calloused hand down her arm. She probably hates the way my work-worn palms scratch her, but the softness of her skin is the guiltiest of pleasures. I can't seem to stop.

"Maybe." I push the chestnut colored hair out of her face and behind her ear. "I can't think about anything else I'd rather do in this world if I'm being honest."

Audrey leans down, pressing her finger against my lips. "Do you want to be with me forever, Kentucky?" Her brown eyes are hidden by the darkness of the night. Her nails lightly scratch down my neck, pressing her hand over my heart. "Forever is an awfully long time, Mr. Jones."

I grin, slipping my arms around her waist and rolling her onto her back. The long grass embraces us, and her long hair is spread out under her like a halo belonging to an angel.

"I'm completely in love with you, Audrey. I know I'm nothin' compared to the men your father has lined up for you. I can't offer you the riches you're used to, but I will always do my best to provide you with a life you deserve. I'm just a cowboy, but I promise, I'm good with my hands."

She giggles, rolling me onto my back with more strength than I thought she had. "I don't care about the riches, Kentucky. I think I'd be the richest woman alive if I got to spend every waking moment with you."

I bolt up, squeezing her hips with my hands as she wraps her legs around my waist.

"Then let's get married, Audrey. I'll give you all the kids

you want. I'll be a good father. If you need a bigger house, I can build—"

She silences me with her kiss, taking my face in her hands, and diving her tongue across mine. My fingers curl into her dress, tangling the material in my hands. Our breaths become gasps as we struggle to breathe, not wanting to miss a second of inhaling one another.

Her lips are as soft as snow falling in the midst of winter. Her kiss is peace, a balm coating the chaos inside my bones.

Her fingers unbutton my shirt just enough so that she can slide her palms under, skimming my chest. I inhale a sharp breath when the cold of her hands seeps into my sternum.

"Wait. Wait. Wait." She pushes herself away, her lips swollen and abused from our rough kiss.

My cock aches to slip her dress to her hips and slide home, but I am a gentleman, and a man like me won't ever press a woman to have sex.

"What is it, sweetheart?" I bend down, kissing the edge of her collarbone peeking through the delicate fabric. "Tell me what you need and it will be yours."

"Your blood," she whispers, her tongue licking my earlobe.

I rear back and grin, thinking she must be joking. "Blood? You're already runnin' through my veins. What more do you want?"

Her nails bite into my scalp as she runs her fingers through my hair. "I've been hiding something from you, Kentucky. I need to know if you're serious about wanting to be with me forever, because I can give you that. I can give you immortality."

I'm not too sure what she's saying. The chuckle that escapes me dies when I see the serious expression on her face. I've known Ms. Reese for months now. This doesn't sound anything like her.

"What do you mean, Audrey? You aren't making any

sense. We can stop. I don't want to pressure you into anything—"

"—No. It isn't that. Do you remember what everyone in town is saying? About the monsters coming out at night? Now all the wives put silver crosses on their front doors to keep those monsters away, along with garlic hanging from the doorframe as if it is mistletoe." She rolls her eyes, scoffing at the paranoia that has infiltrated our town.

"Those aren't anything but rumors. Would you be more comfortable goin' inside? If you're afraid, I'll keep you safe, but Audrey…" I cup her face in my hand, my thumb gliding back and forth over the apple of her cheek. "There's nothin' to be afraid of. It's just you, me, and the cattle out here. I promise. Okay?" I slip my finger under her chin, needing her to look at me.

Red flames appear in the endless abyss of her pupils and shock me still.

"They aren't rumors, Mr. Jones. I am what they fear."

I push her off me, grabbing husks of long grass to pull myself away from the woman I thought I loved.

"I'm not going to hurt you. I could have already. Over all these months, have I ever harmed you?" Audrey stands, lifting her dress off the ground so it doesn't drag across the dirt. "Have I ever done anything that would make you afraid of me?"

"No, but I am afraid right now," I admit, my heart hammering in my chest.

She inhales deeply, tilting her head back until she can't suck in any more air. "Your fear is making me thirsty."

Faster than I can blink, she pins me to the ground, and air whooshes from my lungs. Her hand presses against my chest, keeping me down with her supernatural strength.

I can't move.

"You smell delicious." She buries her nose into my neck,

inhaling as if I'm a meal she can't wait to have. "Spend the next one thousand years with me, Kentucky. We can travel the world. You'll never age. You'll never get sick. You'll be stronger than everyone. We can do what we want, when we want. Doesn't that sound beautiful? We aren't fated mates, but I'll love you for the one thousand years we will get together."

Peering into her blood-ridden eyes, I face the woman I wanted to spend the rest of my years with. "That doesn't sound like a life to me, Audrey. I don't want to live forever. I don't want to be stronger than humankind. I don't want to wield that kind of power. I want to grow old one day. I want to die and be buried underneath that big Kentucky Coffeetree in front of my home. Livin' for a thousand years sounds more like a curse than a blessin' to me. I want a human life. I want the life I have, and I don't want it to change." Her fangs gleam in the light as an iridescent tear drips down her cheek. With a shaking hand, I wipe it away. "If you love me at all, you'll respect that. I can't be a vampire, Audrey. I don't want that."

She shakes her head, pressing her lips against my palm. "You don't mean that. You don't understand. That's just your mortality talking. Once you have lived as a vampire, you will want nothing more. You'll wonder how you have lived such a boring human life. You'll be faster, stronger, smarter, and you'll have the ability to mystify. Some even get extra powers like mind reading, healing, taking away pain, but not me. I'm just your run-of-the-mill vampire."

"Mystify?" I question.

She bends down, her hand gliding down my chest. "To alter the human mind and make them believe anything you want them to."

"Have you done that with me?" I dare to ask, wondering if everything between us has been a lie.

Only yesterday were we walking hand in hand in town, popping into the local candy shop to get the saltwater taffy she likes so much. The way she smiled was so human compared to the woman I'm looking at now.

Hungry eyes are the color of a blood moon. Her fangs are sharp and delicate, lethal in a way I'd love to feel them across my skin if she had gone about this another way.

I don't care that she's a vampire. I only care that she made me fall in love with her when we want different things. All I care about is the lie that has been woven between us.

She eases the pressure on my chest, and I no longer feel like I'm sinking into the ground. "You're holding onto a life that is insignificant."

"That's where you're wrong, sweetheart," I say. "I do not see my life as insignificant. I love knowin' all the work I've done, the people I've met, the wrinkles I'll gain, and the pain I'll endure will all be worth it when I'm old and grey. I would have lived a life filled with all the good and all the bad. Why would I want an eternity of that? Why would I want to outlive everyone I love? That sounds like a long time to feel pain, Audrey. Eventually, the good will blur after so long, and everything will feel bad."

She cries, small sobs shake her shoulders, and she cups either side of my face. "Not everything. I've waited a hundred years to love a man like you. You made all the bad feel so good, Kentucky. Please, want this. Want me enough to love you for the next thousand years."

"I don't understand your sense of time." I push her away from me and stand, lacing my hands behind my head as I stare up at the sky.

"You're afraid of me. I can smell it on you."

I drop my arms and turn around, her eyes still the brightest shade of crimson. "Of course I am. You think because I love you that I'm magically going to be okay with you being a"—I lower my voice—"a vampire? People are huntin' you. You've been there with me at the town meetings. Remember William? He's leadin' the damn charge, Audrey. He has half the town convinced, and I didn't believe him. I didn't..." I laugh at myself. "I didn't believe him because I thought it was insanity. It was too hard to believe. You're stories told at bedtime. You ain't supposed to be real. You've killed people." I take a few staggering steps away at the realization that I'm standing in front of a woman who has killed and who could easily make me her next target.

"No. Listen. Listen to me," she continues to cry those beautiful, shimmering tears. Audrey is nothing but a blur as she eats the space between us.

I hardly recognize her like this.

"My kind, we have something called fated mates. You humans would probably know it by the term 'soulmate.' Where do you think the saying 'It was love at first sight' came from? All supernatural creatures know at first sight. It has to do with smell."

"You just said I wasn't your fated mate. Why are you tellin' me this? I don't want that life," I roar, slamming my hand so hard against my chest, I cough. "I don't want this."

"You aren't my fated mate, but vampires, we can choose to mate with someone. It prolongs our two-hundred-year life to a thousand. Vampires who find their mates live forever, but a thousand years? It will feel like eternity, Kentucky. Imagine all you could do. You could be anything you wanted. Take anything you dreamed of. Everything will be easier."

I scoff, looking at her up and down in so much disappointment. My heart breaks realizing that the woman I've loved is a stranger to me.

"I don't want any of that. I'm an honest man. I am who I want be. I am livin' my dream. I don't need forever to promise me what I already have. That's the difference between us."

"You didn't seem to find any differences last night when

my fangs went in your dick and your come heated my hand." Her eyes burn brighter, and her tongue licks over her fangs.

I step forward, tilting my head at the creature I've allowed inside my home and bed. "You mystified me? That's why you didn't answer that question when I asked earlier. You took advantage of me. You claim you love me, and yet you admit to alterin' my mind. You don't do that to someone you claim to love, Audrey. Love isn't selfish."

"That's the human in you, Kentucky. I can change all of that. I promise, I didn't do anything more than feed from you when you were...under my influence. I only wanted your blood, and I knew telling you the truth would lead to this conversation. You started talking about forever, and I thought..."

"Forever in human terms, Audrey. I can't be what you are. I can't do what you do and be okay with it. I refuse. I would never take without askin'."

Silence becomes louder than the crickets chirping in the field. Fog begins to roll in across the surface of the earth. Seeing Audrey standing there in her satin ivory dress, the mist whirling by her feet, the moon full and big above her, while her eyes burn like torches, reminds me of what Death could look like.

"Nothing I say can change your mind?" she asks, taking a step forward into the ray of light coming from the moon. Her cheeks glisten from her tears, and the red pools of her irises seem brighter.

A slight breeze sways the long grass, the blades rubbing together to create a soft static cradled by the night.

"No. It's best we go our separate ways, Audrey. I love you, and there will always be a piece of me that will, but I can *never* be what you want. Even if we continued this, would you be with me until I'm old and grey? When I can't stand or provide for you the way a man like me should, would you want to drink from me then? Would you love me the way you love me now?"

Another fresh tear rolls down her cheeks while mine do their best to break. A part of me is still too angry and afraid to let them fall.

"You still fear me." Her eyes lift slowly from the ground to look at me. "You've never smelled this way before."

"Well, Ms. Reese, I reckon I haven't been so close to death before." I bend down, pick my black cowboy hat up off the ground, and dust it off. "Here. I want you to have it. Something to remember me by in a thousand years."

I hold it out to her, hoping she accepts the olive branch. I almost can't seem to wrap my mind around what just happened. I had the love of my life in my arms not fifteen minutes ago, planning out my future, imagining us growing old together, dying together, and maybe or maybe not have one or two little ones running around.

Yes, it's a simple human dream, but it's mine, and I want nothing more than to live it.

"Don't be silly, Kentucky. You'll be needing it." She smiles at me, throwing my hat like a child skipping a rock across the lake.

Fear doesn't have time to reach its peak before Audrey is on me. Her strength has to be more than ten men. I can't fight her off. Her teeth sink into my neck as her legs wrap around my waist in an all too familiar position we were in not three days ago. Her hand falls across my mouth to silence my scream.

Audrey's force against me is so strong, the momentum flings us backwards onto the wooden fence. The rails break my fall, and at the same time, agony rips through my side before we hit the unforgiving ground. She moans into my neck, her throat moving with every ferocious gulp.

I stare up at the night sky differently. The stars don't seem so far away now that I'm drifting into a place where I'm numb. Audrey releases me at last, giggling as if she's drunk.

Audrey sways above me, my blood staining her chin and teeth. She looks wild and in her element. Her crazed eyes fixate on me, laughter bubbling free from her red-drenched lips.

"Mmm, you are the most delicious man I have ever tasted, Mr. Jones." She bends down, her tongue flattening across the wound on my neck. "Hmm, I could live off the taste of you forever." Sitting up again, she swipes her fingers across my throat and sucks them one by one into her mouth.

A rush of warmth flows from my neck with every pulse of my heart. I slap my hand over the wound, doing my best to stay alive even though I know this night sky will be my last.

My free hand curls around the piece of wood sticking through my side. I wheeze, struggling to inhale even the slightest amount of air.

"Oh, Kentucky. You've gotten yourself in a small situation, haven't you?" She twirls the top of her finger atop the rail piercing me. "I can make it all better for you, baby. I can feed you my blood, and you won't change, I promise. You'll have to die with my blood inside you for you to turn." Audrey grips the stake, ripping it from my body.

A painful shout escapes me, but it sounds like more of a low moan belonging to a dying man.

"You don't have much time until you bleed out, and make no mistake, I will lick you dry so none of you goes to waste."

"I'd rather die," I whisper, the cold beginning to creep in.

With her enhanced speed, she bites into her wrist and shoves it to my mouth. The iron is bitter against my tongue, slithering down my throat like a root growing in the ground. After a few moments, the taste changes to something sweet, and I moan into her wrist, wanting more.

I ache when the muscles, tendons, and flesh begin to stitch

together. My lung inflates again, allowing me to gasp in a much-needed breath of air.

"That's too damn bad, baby. You aren't allowed to die. Not when you're meant to be with me." She bends down, lapping up the blood surrounding my wound.

I was minutes away from death, and now I am invigorated. I feel my muscles becoming stronger. I'm aware of every part of me. The crickets are louder. The scents overwhelm me. I can hear someone laughing in the distance, but no one else is here.

"See?" She rubs her hands up my body, cupping the bulge between my legs. "Doesn't it feel good? Wouldn't you want to feel this way for more than a night?"

"I know it may come as a surprise that some might not want this, but I don't." I spit her blood out of my mouth, wiping my lips on the back of my hand.

"I said the same one hundred years ago, but it ended up being the one thing I never knew I needed."

"Why can't you leave me alone? Just go. Find another."

She's hovering over me again, her knees sinking into the dirt while she runs her fingers through my hair. "Don't you understand, Kentucky? There is no other. I love you, and I know you love me. I feel it even more now that you have my blood in your veins. You hate that you love me. I can sense that too, but in time, you'll wonder how you ever hated me."

"I doubt that, sweetheart."

She smirks, picking up one of the broken rails. "It will only hurt for a second. Death will come fast. Then, you'll be free of the silly little rules of humanity." She rolls her eyes. "Humans righteousness about life is always so aggravating. For example, you think we have only been together a few months, Kentucky, but we have been together for a year. I let you remember what I want you to. It's as simple as that."

I've never felt so violated before. "A year? Why? Why

would you alter my mind to believe we have only been together a few months? What happened in that year that you don't want to tell me about?" Fury, unlike anything I've ever felt, possesses every bone in my body.

It's as if it is amplified.

She smirks, her tongue flicking out to lick the last bit of blood from the corner of her lips. "Someone is mad," Audrey pouts before tossing her head back, and sardonic laughter falls from her lying lips. "But I have the privilege to play with time. I had...business to take care of. I couldn't have you running off to be with someone else. You were all too eager to wait for me, baby." She strokes her finger down my cheek. "Your transformation will be quick. You'll understand, Kentucky. Once you are one of us, you'll see how you even questioned wanting a human life at all."

I've never been afraid of death. I'll happily die under a night full of stars at forty years old, but I know one fucking thing—I'm not dying alone.

I sit up, ghosting my mouth over hers. The shape of her lips has always invited me in. She is beautiful. The most ethereal woman I have ever laid eyes on. A sunset painting the sky different shades of yellows and reds doesn't even compare to her.

I'll never forget seeing her for the first time. I was in town about to walk into the local feed store, when out of the corner of my eye, I caught Audrey walking across the street. Her light blue high heels kicked up dust clouds from the dirt road, and her scarf drifted from her neck, the wind carrying it right to me. I believed the universe brought her to me, and maybe in a way it did, or maybe meeting me was all part of her plan.

"I knew you'd come around, baby."

I ram the stake into her heart, her eyes rounding in shock, and her hand falls to the piece of wood sticking out of her chest. The same broken rail that impaled me.

"You should've listened," I sneer, never taking my gaze from her.

I need to see her die.

Her skin begins to drift away into ash, her beauty finally reflecting her evil intent.

In one last blur, she plunges the stake through my chest. "The same could be said about you, Mr. Jones." My name is the last word that leaves her lips. Her ashes fade into the fog, leaving me alone to die.

At least I have peace as a last luxury.

I was a foolish man to think love could come to me without consequence.

I won't be making that mistake again.

Chapter One

KENTUCKY

Present day

My dead human mate's photo is perched on top of the hand-carved wooden mantle. Daphne stares at me every day while I have my coffee.

She used to make my coffee. Every. Single. Morning. Black and bitter, but she'd always add a few drops of her blood to sweeten it for me.

I miss that.

I miss her.

I miss her kiss on my cheek when she handed me the warm mug before I began my day on the ranch. The memory of her sharing her blood for the first time morphs from her standing in the kitchen to cutting her palm with a knife in the bedroom.

Not once in all my years did I bite her. There were plenty of reasons why. One was because I was afraid I would lose control and kill her. Two, the thought of giving my bite to someone who wasn't my fated mate stopped me. It was this small voice in the back of my head, urging me not to. Three, Daphne didn't want me to bite her because she knew one day she would die, and she didn't want to be addicted to the feeling of my fangs in her vein. She wanted to remain human, and I think she thought the *feel* of the bite would tempt her too much.

Instead, we stocked up on her blood. Even in the bedroom, we were prepared.

I loved that about her—her humanity. I envied her for it too, but it was the biggest reason why my love for her never died.

The worn dark blue recliner squeaks as I stand, continuing to rock back and forth from my absence. I wouldn't be all that surprised if her ghost is keeping my seat warm.

"I miss you. I hate living what I have left of my life without you." I skim my finger down the glass of the photo frame, wishing it were her skin.

I have somewhere between twenty to fifty years left before I finally die. My two hundred years will be up, and I'll turn to ash, ceasing to exist just like I should have all those years ago. I'll finally get to be with Daphne in the afterlife—if a place like that exists for a monster like me.

I've lived too damn long to keep track of all the time I have been alive. The years, weeks, months, minutes, and seconds mean nothing to me. I have an estimate of changes to the world due to the evolution of society—if you want to call it evolution.

This timeline is quite peculiar.

I tend to keep to myself as much as possible now, which is another reason why I can't remember my age. I'm old. I know that much, but I don't look a day over forty—the age I was turned. That I do remember.

After what happened with Audrey, I told myself I was going to fade into existence. I thought that was what she would hate the most. I wanted my life to spite her in every way possible for stealing my ability to die when I was meant to.

The oceans are warmer now. The air is more polluted. The people are angrier. Love for anything in life that brings joy seems to be harder to find.

That's when I had my epiphany.

My maker would absolutely hate it if I fell in love again—like how I wanted before she changed me.

Somewhere between the years of I-killed-everyone-I-came-across to isolating- myself-on-my-ranch, I met the woman in the photo sitting on my mantle.

And her name was Daphne.

The past: sometime in the 1900s

I never left home. I have mystified every single person, not to question why I never age. It takes a lot of work with young couples having babies and growing their families, but I was able to wait a couple of decades before I had to pull out the only trick I have in my vampire book.

If I have to live as this creature, I'm not going to inconvenience myself by moving every few decades. That's not what I wanted when I was human, and it hasn't changed since becoming a vampire.

No, I wasn't about to leave my home when there was a simple solution to fix it, but I'm happy. I love being nestled away on hundreds of acres of land where people can't bother me.

I only come to town when I need more stock in hay, feed, and blood. I keep my head down and my Stetson low so no one will notice me. That's hard to do when a man like me is on a horse like Romeo. He's a large, muscular Friesian with a pitch-black hide and a long, curly mane to match, which ladies often fawn over when they see him.

What no one knows is that Romeo is a vampire too. It wasn't easy making the decision to turn him, but around twenty years ago, he was shot for having an injured leg. The owner had left him to die in agony, and I couldn't allow him to suffer.

I had used my vampire speed to get to him, and when I pressed my hand on his thick neck, I could hear his thoughts. I ended up getting one of those 'gifts' Audrey had warned me about.

"I don't want to die."

His big black eyes stared at me, a tear escaping from the inky pools. I could feel his pain, and it was a feeling I never wanted to experience again.

I was selfish in that moment. I had been alone, learning how to be a vampire on my own, and never coming across another like me. I was lonely for a companion. I sliced my palm open with my fangs, opened his mouth, and squeezed my hand into a fist to allow a few drops of blood to land on his tongue.

I stroked his neck, doing my best to calm him in his biggest moment of fear. *"I have to kill you now if you want to be by my side for whatever time I have left. You like the name Romeo, by chance?"*

I was a big fan of Shakespeare.

"Save me," he begged.

I wrapped my arms around his neck, my heart at my throat. *"It will only hurt for a second, I promise,"* I told him.

Romeo nudged me, almost as if he were urging me to do it.

With my new strength, I snapped his neck, and his limp head fell into my lap. I laid him on the ground and stepped away to give him space. His neck cracked into place, aligning his cervical spine again. He reared back on his hind legs and tossed his two front legs in the air, neighing louder than the thunder rolling above us. The gunshot wound stitched itself back together, leaving him reborn into the monster I've been fighting like hell to accept.

His eyes bled from black to scarlet. His face became sunken and more skeletal. Fangs gleamed in the sun as he reared his head back and neighed, feeling the power of his new life.

The only thing I remember thinking was, *"How the hell do I feed a vampire horse? What was I thinking?"*

Over the years, Romeo and I have learned that his eyes stay red, and he likes to hunt in the woods by himself. He eats other animals, ranging from squirrels to deer, only a few times a week. He's self-sufficient.

I slide off the saddle, tying the reins around the rail above the water trough. Romeo begins drinking, and I pat his shoulder. "Drink up. I'll be back in a few minutes. Don't go biting anyone." I step away, then pause, glancing over my shoulder. "Again."

"He deserved it," he replies without taking his mouth away from the water.

I'm not sure I will ever get used to talking to animals.

My spurs clink with every step on the dusty wooden pathway. The loud thumps of my boots have the locals giving me a wide berth. They must sense something different about me that they can't quite put their finger on. They are smart too. I can smell the spike of fear in their blood when they get too close to me, and I'm too tempted to rip their heads from their shoulders.

The violence I constantly feel—the craving for blood— they never fade.

I open the front door of Hank's Feed Store, the bell jingling to announce a customer's arrival.

"Oh, I am so sorry," an older woman stammers when she bumps into me.

I keep my head down, my Stetson casting a shadow to hide my face. "No problem, ma'am. I insist." I open the door wider, gesturing with my arm out for her to walk into the store first.

"What a gentleman. Thank you."

I smirk, hiding in the casted shadow. "You're welcome, ma'am." My gaze catches the bold vein on her wrist as she lifts her hands, her dainty purse dangling from her elbow.

She walks with sass and attitude, sashaying her hips and demanding attention in the store. I can tell she's married to a wealthy man. She wears fine gold jewelry with a large, tacky diamond on her ring finger. The extravagant-looking older woman is even wearing a stylish light blue hat with a white feather on top of her perfectly styled hair.

I can't remember a time when women didn't have to worry so much about their appearance. It must be a lot of pressure to always feel like you can't be less than perfect. They deserve more.

"Mrs. Bell. How are you today?"

The sugar-laced voice has me stepping inside the store and lifting my head so I can try to find the face it belongs to.

"Oh, Daphne, honey, I hope you can help me."

My, oh, my.

Daphne just became someone I need to know.

"Excuse me," a man's voice pulls me from my stupor.

I blink, realizing I'm standing in front of the door and

people can't get in. "Apologies." I pinch the brim of my hat, giving my chin a small tilt to my chest.

My eyes lock on Daphne, the lovely young woman behind the counter, helping out Mrs. Bell. I don't even try to hear what they are talking about as I slowly walk the edge of the room to get closer to her.

She has strawberry blonde hair that falls to her shoulders. Half of it is pinned back, revealing the delicate features of her face. Her subtle pink lips have a perfect curve to the top, while her bottom lip is just a kiss plumper.

My, oh, my.

Ms. Daphne is a sight for very sore eyes. My spurs still clink with every step until I find myself, unknowingly, standing next to Mrs. Bell.

"Oh, thank you, Daphne. I appreciate your help." Mrs. Bell's eyes lift to meet mine before drifting back to Daphne. "I'll just go. I'll let you know if I need anything." She nudges me before whispering, "She is a very sweet young lady. Don't go messing it up."

I grin, taking off my hat like the gentleman I am, and press it against my chest. "I have no intention of doing that, Mrs. Bell."

She smiles, her cheeks turning a slight pinkish color before she clears her throat. Lifting her hands again, elbows to her side, she saunters over to the aisle Daphne steered her towards.

I stand on the other side of the counter, my hat still pressed against my chest as I get lost in the lightest green eyes I've ever seen.

"Can I help you, Sir?"

"Please, call me Kentucky."

A feverish grin spreads across her face. She tucks her hair behind her ear and glances down. Holding out her hand, she gets the courage to look up at me. "I'm Daphne Reynolds."

Taking her hand gently with mine, I lock our gazes and

kiss the top of her knuckles. "It's a pleasure to meet you, Ms. Reynolds."

"Please," she says breathlessly. "Call me Daphne."

"Daphne," I whisper, completely smitten with a woman I've never met before. "I haven't seen you around Hank's before. Are you new to town?"

"I am. Hank is my grandfather. He needed help around the store."

"Grandfather?" I've been in this town for more years than I can count. I don't remember Hank mentioning a granddaughter.

"Daphne." A hunched-over man on a cane comes from the door behind her. His head is bald, casting the reflection of the sun. "You aren't giving my best customer a hard time, are you?"

"No, Papa. I am just meeting Mr..." Her thin brows pinch together. "I didn't get your last name, I'm sorry."

"Jones. Kentucky Jones." My fangs tingle to breach my gums, wanting to sink into the flawless, smooth skin of her neck.

How would she react to me being a monster? Would she embrace me like I can't embrace myself, or would she run?

"Mr. Jones," she finally finishes her sentence.

"Kentucky always comes in at the same time every week and pays in cash." Hank's glasses are perched on the tip of his nose, the dark hairs a little too long coming from his nostrils blend in with a grey mustache. He scoots in next to Daphne. "Here is what he gets, Daphne." Hank writes down my entire order for proof of purchase.

"Hank, you never told me you had a granddaughter. Is she taking over the store when you retire?" I don't want to be rude, but I need to know where this woman has been hiding. "Apologies if I'm steppin' on business that ain't mine."

Hank waves me away. "You have contributed plenty to my

business, which makes it your business, Mr. Jones. You know my son? William?"

I nod, still never taking my interest away from Daphne.

"Well, God rest her soul, his wife died a few years back. I don't know if you remember—"

"—I do. I was sorry to hear about your daughter-in-law."

"Well, he got remarried. She's a lovely woman who also lost her husband in the war. Daphne is her daughter from her first marriage and my only grandbaby so far. I keep telling them I'm not getting any younger. I want more grandchildren."

I chuckle to hide the sadness that stabs through my chest. His talk of children reminds me that I will never be able to have my own. As I continue staring upon the prettiest star I have ever seen, I wonder if Daphne wants children. If she does, if we ever get to the point where we tell our truths to one another, I couldn't take that choice away from her.

"Do you have Romeo with you?" he asks, Hank's eyes shining bright at the mention of my horse.

I grin, placing my hat atop my head again. "As always. I don't go anywhere without him, Hank. I have your wagon attached to him as well."

It's been years since I've had his wagon. I offered to pay monthly for it, but at this point, I should just offer to buy it. I think the monthly expense helps Hank more when it comes to supplying the store. Until he brings it up as an issue, I'm going to keep my mouth closed.

"Excellent. Daphne. You have to see his horse. He is gorgeous and has red eyes. I have never seen one with red eyes before, and the strongest damn horse I have ever seen, excuse my language, Daphne," Hank snickers.

"He's out front. I can pull him around back to load the wagon. He's tied at the trough," I explain, fighting the urge to contain the vampire nature welling up inside me the longer I stare at Daphne.

"No, no. You're the customer. I'll have another employee bring Romeo around back."

"Remember, Hank. Your employee has to introduce themselves and say they know me, or you won't be able to move Romeo an inch from where he stands." I give him a friendly reminder, not wanting Romeo to kill an innocent worker for doing their job.

"I know. I can't believe that works, but you told me he'd become violent if we didn't take your warning, and I don't want to know what damage that horse will do."

No, he doesn't want to know. Romeo is an anomaly. Most likely, the only one of his kind. I'm sure I broke some type of vampire rule when I changed him, if vampire rules exist, I'm not sure, since the only one I knew, I killed.

"I'll be back. Don't go anywhere, Mr. Jones. I would love to chat."

"Sure, Hank." My obsessed gaze for Daphne falls to her again. "Respectfully, I don't see myself going anywhere."

Hank looks from me to Daphne, then back to me, and a knowing smile rounds his plump red cheeks.

Daphne's blood becomes sweet as her heart rate increases. She twiddles with the locket hanging around her neck, nibbling the corner of her bottom lip.

"Do you mind me asking if you have anyone special in your locket, ma'am?" I take off my hat again, not wanting to be disrespectful while talking to a lady such as Daphne.

"Please, call me Daphne."

"As long as you call me Kentucky. Then, I'll consider us even." I smile, and she places the back of her hand on her cheek as if she is checking her temperature.

"Deal," she says in a breathless way that has me leaning in, wanting to be closer. She opens her locket, and to my surprise, there is nothing in it.

My brows raise in confusion. "Did the photo up and walk away, Ms. Daphne?"

"Just Daphne," her tone is sweet and light like the air in her reply to me.

"Yes, ma'am."

"Not ma'am either!" she giggles. "But no, I don't think I have anything important enough to me yet. You know? Something or someone really special, hanging right here over my heart. To me, a locket isn't just something that holds an image, but it's meant to hold love that's connected to the heart."

"Is that what you want? A love so important it stays with you, like that locket?"

She pinches her lips together, tilts her mouth sideways, and pretends to think. Her finger taps her lips before she snickers in sweet, bountiful giggles. "Yeah, Kentucky. Just like that."

We lock eyes, not saying a word, and I can't help but wish I had met her in a different time, in a different life, where I couldn't kill her because of my need.

❦

I slip her locket off the corner of the picture frame, my eyes pooling with tears as I open it like I do every morning. A slight click opens the delicate silver. It burns my fingertips, but I don't really care about the slight pain when I know I can heal.

Pushing the oval face to the left, the first tear falls when I open it to reveal a photo of me on the left and a picture of us on the right.

She got what she wanted, and I wish it were enough to soothe the ache of missing her. I'm only content because I know she was happy in the end. I remember her wrinkled, spotted hand taking mine. She was always so cold at that age. Her long, strawberry blonde hair had turned white. Those light green eyes I fell in love with were cloudy. Daphne couldn't see in the end, but she knew I looked the same as the day I met her.

"Always so handsome," her voice shook with age.

I leaned into her touch, bringing her hand to my cheek so she could feel me. I didn't care that she was old or that she didn't look as young as when we met. I wanted to die with her, but she didn't let me. She wouldn't allow me to die.

"Promise me, Kentucky. You'll live another full life and love another. Your heart is too good and too full of love to give. You might meet your fated mate."

"I don't want her. I want you, ma'am. Just you."

"What did I tell you about calling me ma'am?"

I couldn't laugh at her joke when I could hear her heart slowing. It was subtle. She couldn't feel it yet, but I could.

"—Kentucky. Promise me."

"I can't do that, Daphne. I won't break a promise."

"You gave me what I wanted. It's time for you to have what I've had all these years."

"I did. I got you, didn't I?"

"You know what I mean, Kentucky."

"What did I give you? I could have turned you—"

"—It's not what I wanted, and it isn't what you wanted. You gave me love important enough to stick with me. It's your turn."

"Daphne, your love will stick with me for all eternity, fated mate or not."

She died a moment later with a smile on her last breath.

I didn't bury her right away. I couldn't. Fifty-ish years of us being together, and all I had left was her shell. She was mine in that lifetime. I just wish the world weren't so cruel and could have given her to me for all my lifetimes.

The locket is fisted in my hand when the scent of blood infiltrates the air, ruining my morning routine. With tears still wetting my cheeks, my vision turns a predatory shade of red, and my fangs breach my gums.

I reach for my 1847 Colt Walker Revolver hanging on my hip. Blurring out the front door to see who my intruder is.

That blood doesn't belong here, and no one is allowed on my property but me.

Even if the scent of this blood is the best I have ever smelled in all my years of living.

DEAD MAN'S
RANCH

CHAPTER
Two
DRUSCILLA

The jolt of my head bobbing down awakens me. My vision blurs, struggling to focus on my surroundings. Parts of my body ache that I didn't know could. I groan, squeezing my eyes shut from the pain throbbing in my cheek.

I blink a few times to clear my vision. I sway left and right as I continue to get my bearings. Sunlight pours in through the window, causing me to wince. Dust particles come to view first before my blurred environment finally makes itself known.

An aged leather couch is to the left, flush against the living room wall. The TV is on, but the volume is so low, I can't hear what the actor is saying. Not that it matters, but I wouldn't mind a little trash TV under the circumstances.

The wooden plank floors are old. Wide gaps between each slab allow me to see the dirt the cabin is built on. To the left is a small kitchen, and to the right is a hallway that I assume leads to my kidnapper's bedroom.

"Fuck," I whisper to myself when I notice I'm naked.

I wiggle in the seat, blowing out a relieved breath when I

realize I'm not sore between my legs. The relief is short-lived when I notice large bite marks on my inner thighs.

"What..." The simple word dies from my dry lips.

Confusion adds to the throb on the side of my head. I try to follow the dried blood on my body, noticing more bite marks.

Deep wounds decorate my torso and arms. When I move my neck, I hiss from the sharp stings radiating from either side. Warmth drips down my throat from the movement. I'm very aware of the slight tickle of the rivulet sliding down until it stops at my right breast.

"You're awake."

The unexpected voice has me looking left, then right, but no one is there.

"That's good, Druscilla. I like that you have so much life in you after I took so much of it last night."

I don't say a word. I'm not stupid. The more I say, the more he can twist my words and use them against me. My entire body trembles with fear. Tears threaten to break free, but I can't let them fall. Men like him enjoy that too much.

"You can pretend all you want, Druscilla—pretty name, by the way—that you are brave and strong." He grips my shoulders from behind me, bends down, and inhales so deeply, he moans. "But I can smell your fear, and you smell so fucking good." His finger swipes the fresh blood drip, following the trail up my chest.

His other hand slides across my shoulders as he walks with heavy steps to stand in front of me.

He sucks his finger into his mouth, groaning when he tastes my blood.

"There's just something about you. I can't put my finger on it. You aren't my mate or anything like that." A chaotic, mad laugh fills the dusty space. "Wouldn't that be terrible?"

"I don't know what drugs you are on, but I won't tell

anyone what happened here. Just let me go, and you can go back to whatever drug-induced stupor you enjoy."

He bends down, gripping each arm of the chair I'm sitting in. I smell the metallic taste of my blood on his breath. A maniacal smile spreads across his face, and I gasp as a new wave of terror quakes my body.

Blood tints his teeth. The red sinks into the nooks and crevices, painting a predatory picture that I will not be able to forget. He will be the reason for my nightmares, but I will be the reason I overcome them.

Two sharp cuspids protruding from his mouth can only be one thing.

Fangs.

I've heard stories like everyone else. Vampires, werewolves, elves, fairies, and whatever else parents tell their children growing up. They can't be real, but the logical part of me is wondering where the stories started.

Isn't there truth to everything, even if it seems unbelievable?

My intrusive thoughts turn to cannibalism. I'm not sure why, because being drank dry is just as terrifying as getting eaten, but I'd rather have a vampire drink my blood than a cannibal add me to his ingredients list for his stew.

He tilts his head, his eyes flashing a bright crimson. He lifts his hand for me to see, and one by one, each nail lengthens to a sharp claw.

"Ah, I hear your heartbeat. It's quicker with fear." He combs his fingers through my long, wild, red curly hair. "There's no need to fear me. I don't think I could ever kill someone as beautiful as you."

"Fuck you." I gather the spit in my mouth and launch it in his face, where it lands right on the corner of his mouth.

He snarls, grasping each of my legs and spreading them

apart. "Do not tempt me. Remember, it is you who is helpless. Not me."

"What...do you...want?" My teeth chatter. Not from the cold, but shock.

"You. Do you not remember the fun we had last night?" He continues to brush his fingers through my hair, his claws catching on the tangles. "We danced. We drank. You were all over me."

My brows pinch together in thought, trying to remember anything from last night. I'm drawing a blank. I can't remember how I met him, talking to him, or how I got here in this rundown cabin.

He pretends to be sad and frowns. "Aw, that's okay, Druscilla. You wouldn't remember because I made you forget everything. We met on that dating app and met for drinks." He kisses my cheek, and I pull away, not wanting him anywhere near me. "I told you my name was Louisville, but everyone calls me Louis. Ringing any bells? You said you loved how unique my name was." Louis smiles as if it were a fond memory. "I could make you submit to me right now, but where's the fun in that?" He flattens his tongue on my cheek and licks the tears that I couldn't hold back any longer. "This is so much more fun when you fight me."

"You're sick," I hiss. "You're insane. Vampires aren't real. You're sick. Please," the word is a broken sob. "Please, let me go."

"That's not going to happen." Louis grips my chin, forcing me to look into his scarlet irises, and my stomach turns. "I suppose that would be an easier explanation for your puny human mind to comprehend, but no, I am perfectly sane. Come on," he urges, playfully knocking my chin with his fist. "You know what I am. The truth is screaming at you, clawing at your gut." He pats my stomach. "Come on, Druscilla. Come on," he urges, his voice becoming higher as he antagonizes me.

Again, he licks me, only this time he gathers the dried blood on the other side of my throat. "Tell me and I'll heal the bite marks on your neck. The left side is still oozing. I wonder if I sank my fangs in too deep. I'd apologize, but"—he sighs, clicking his tongue—"I just don't care."

"You're a vampire." I hold my head high, staring into his eyes because no matter how scared I am, I will never cower. "Or you *think* you're a vampire."

"Think?" he repeats.

With a smile, he is nothing but a blur until he is on the other side of the living room. "What about now?" Louis speeds across the room, standing in front of me again. He unties one wrist, my hand tingling with the new blood flow, and he stretches my arm.

I hate that I groan because it feels so good.

I sway again, a dizzy spell weakening any fight I had in me.

"I might have taken a little too much blood, but now I have to show you the truth, so you'll believe me."

My eyes droop, wanting nothing but to go to sleep.

His hand slaps my cheek, and my eyes snap open to see him glaring at me. "Watch me."

I don't know why, but I feel compelled to listen to everything he has to say all of a sudden. "I'll watch," I reply, witnessing him bringing my wrist to his mouth.

"Are you watching?" he asks.

"I am." My voice is dull and monotone, the urge to follow his command stronger than my will to live.

His fangs rip into my flesh, the pain burns, igniting a scream that sears my throat.

Removing his cuspids, he groans, tilting his head back, keeping the grip on my wrist as he licks the corners of his mouth. "So delicious."

He drops my arm, and it hangs limply by my side.

"Do you believe me now?" The bright embers bear into my soul.

Adrenaline surges through me, awakening my weak body. "I do."

I have my arm freed. This is my one chance to get away. Not that I have a chance to survive a vampire, but I have to try. I'm not going to warn him. I'm not going to ask any questions to prolong this conversation because while I know in my soul, he is a vampire, there is a small part of me that doesn't believe a damn word he says because how the hell are vampires real?

I can't think about that right now. All I need to focus on is making it out of here alive, and if he is a vampire, then my chances are slim to none.

"Now that we have that out of the way, I'm thinking a few things. One, you can be my human blood bag because I really do love how you taste, or—"

I slam my fist into his crotch, then grip and twist.

It was the closest part of him to me and the easiest. I wasn't sure if it would hurt since he is a "vampire" but with the roar that is coming from his chest and ringing in my ears, I'd say it does.

"Fuck you and what you're thinking."

He falls to his knees, cupping himself, and then I rear my arm back, punching the middle of his throat.

Louis's eyes widen as he struggles to gasp for air.

I don't know how much time I have, but I use my free hand to untie my other wrist. When I stand, I stumble, catching myself on the chair that's held me all these hours.

With newfound anger, I flip the chair over, kicking one of the wooden legs off. Taking the stake in my hand, I use all the might I have left and shove it into the middle of his throat.

His blood spills onto the floor, mixing with mine, and I

don't wait another second to see if he dies, lives, or pulls the stake free.

I run.

My vision darkens around the edges, but I can't pass out now. I have to keep going. No one is going to save me but myself. That's how it has always been, and that's how it will always be, because depending on others has gotten me nowhere in life.

Ripping the front door open, the sun shining through the trees blinds me, and I fall down the rickety porch steps. The cool earth cushions the hit of my shoulder. My knee hits the grass. Dirt flies into my mouth when my chin smacks the ground.

Pushing myself up, I stagger and stumble for a few seconds. My legs are finally under me, and I sprint, my life depending on my will to live.

The air is humid, causing my skin to become hot and sweaty. Twigs break and stab the bottoms of my feet with every stride. I bite through the stings, but a pain-filled whimper falls from my lips.

I don't know how much strength I have left.

I slip on the debris and leaves on the ground, catching myself on a nearby tree. The bark is harsh and rough against my sensitive, wounded skin, but at least I know it doesn't mean to harm me. That alone brings me peace.

After inhaling a few deep breaths and not bothering to wipe the tears from my cheeks, with weak legs, I run again.

The deeper I go into the woods, the more my path darkens. The sun's rays are eaten as the canopies of the trees become thicker. Shadows win against the bright light of the sun, encompassing me in cool, much-needed shade.

The further away I get from Louis, the more my memory pieces together. I'm still missing large gaps that he says he took from me on purpose. I don't know how or why. I'm not sure if I'll ever fully understand the power he claims to have.

What if I can't remember because I drank too much? What if he slipped something in my drink? What if the blood I saw him drinking was a scheme, somehow?

I sway again, my foot twisting in an awkward position, and this time, when I fall, I stay on the ground. I stare up at the sky, the blue peeking through the small breaks in the branches, wondering if this will be my last day here on earth.

Choking for breath, my stomach rolls from running, from having not nearly enough blood in my system, from pushing myself when Death was already knocking on my door.

The last light stops peeking through the fingers of the trees from a quickening of clouds. Each gasp of air I struggle to inhale reminds me of five years ago, when I watched my dad die. He had an allergic reaction to a bee sting, and we had no idea he was allergic. It was terrible. I don't think I had ever been so afraid in my entire life. The way he desperately gasped for air, croaking, needy for the smallest amount of hope.

There was none.

It was only him and me for the first twenty-three years of my life. Every picture and every memory I had was with my father. My mom died when I was a baby in a car accident.

It's just me now.

I do have my best friend, Carmen. She comes from a huge family and always has me involved in all their get-togethers. When I didn't come home last night, I can bet she called the cops. It isn't like me to stay out all night or not text or call.

I'll miss her.

Thunder rolls up above, and the cool touch of rain begins to hush around me, a soft drop against the ground. My naked body begins to shiver from the sudden decrease in temperature paired with the rain. I have to get up. I have to keep moving.

The ground becomes mud, and it slickens against my

body. My palms and feet can't get traction. I'm still so weak from whatever has happened, my head swims, and my soul has finally reached its brink.

I slip down to the edge of a small cliff...and gravity wins. The rain must be pouring harder than I thought because I slide down through the mud with ease. I spin, slamming into a tree trunk, and fire spreads up my side from the agony. The incline is too much, and I fall into the rushing river below.

Plunging into the cold water, unconsciousness pulls me under its spell while the current takes me to my final resting place.

Because my god, let this fucking day be over.

CHAPTER

THREE

KENTUCKY

I stand at the edge of my property line, analyzing the woods for any sort of movement. The scent of blood still hangs in the air, yet it has faded, almost like the person the delicious fragrance belongs to is further away than they were minutes ago.

Certain words keep playing over and over in my head, words I'm trying to ignore, but the pull to find the source of the person responsible for the chaos in my soul is too strong to ignore.

Beloved.

Fated mate.

Mine.

I remember Audrey teaching me about fated mates before she turned me. On top of the researching vampires on my own to learn who I am and how to be, I know having a mate is not something I want. I didn't want it then with Audrey, and I don't want it now.

Being born to live and die is the beauty of being a human. You have a certain amount of time to fulfill all your wishes, hopes, and dreams. That's the wonder of being alive. You're under a time constraint.

To love, to fuck, to laugh, and to cry.

There are only so many moments one can have before the peace of death takes over, making room for another soul to have their chance at the world.

The curse of living forever leaves no room for moments to be cherished or treasured. In my almost two hundred years, time has melted together.

What makes living forever so fucking special?

Even with all the negative emotions I have about living for eternity, I still can't turn my back on my mate. It's not the kind of man I am. It's clear she is hurt, and I can make sure she is okay before sending her on her way to live the life she deserves.

Even the thought of not having her here has my eyes morphing red.

The heavy hooved steps of Romeo have me turning my head to see him meandering toward me. He has blood on his snout, and his thick tongue flicks, licking the liquid free from his top lip.

"Romeo, we have a human to find," I tell him, staring out into the forest again.

The wind sways the branches, causing the leaves to rub together. In the distance, there's a river rushing with cold water, which has me wondering if that's why her blood is becoming so faint. She had to have washed it from her body.

"I smell her," he says, trotting up to stand next to me. *"Why do we need to find her?"*

"She could be my mate, and she could be hurt." I take off my hat and run my fingers through my dark hair, doing my best to come to terms with my new reality before placing the Stetson back on.

"You don't want your mate. You've made that clear."

Romeo stomps one hoof on the ground, slinging his head up and down to make his point.

I grind my teeth together, not liking how much the truth hurts. "I can't leave her hurting. It's not right." In the little bit of time I spent researching vampires, I didn't find too much information about fated mates. Some books said the two destined can deny the bond, sever it, and live how they want. Other resources said, death was the only option if they did not mate.

I should know more than I do, but it's not like I've made it my life's mission to find any other creatures like me. I came to terms with what I am a long time ago, and I'm happy living in my corner of peace without being bothered.

The arrival of my fated mate might change all that though. I'm going to have to come to terms with dying sooner than I thought. She's going to ask questions. She's going to want answers to those questions that I don't know.

This is the last thing I need. Why can't the universe leave me the fuck alone? Why can't I live and die on my own damn terms? Something or someone always gets in the way of those plans.

The universe is fucking with me.

"Shut up, Romeo," I grumble, patting his neck before I grip his mane and sling my leg over his back to get settled. "I want to follow the scent. Let's see where it leads."

He neighs in response. I'm happy he isn't a big talker. I'm not either. I prefer silence. With a sharp whistle and a very gentle nudge to his sides, Romeo begins to gallop using his vampire speed.

I stay low to his neck, careful to miss the low-hanging branches that would easily take off my head. There would be no healing from that.

He leaps over a fallen log. The sound of his hooves is thunderous, shaking the leaves from the trees with the strong force of his strides. Anyone could feel the rumble beneath their feet, not knowing that it isn't an earthquake or a storm, just a horse that could sling the flesh from their bones with one small kick.

Romeo releases a high-pitched neigh before sliding to a stop near a cliff. The blood is heavier here, weighted with iron, and the perfume of it has my eyes rolling to the back of my head. My fangs lengthen again, wanting nothing more than to feast on her jugular vein.

I've never had the pleasure of giving in to the ultimate urge. My mouth waters from the thought of it. Her body against mine, my hand splayed across her stomach to keep her close to me, the other cupping her cheek, while her back is nestled against my front, and my cock is lodged deep inside her while I feed.

I slip from Romeo's back, my spurs spinning when I land on the wet ground thanks to the storm that just passed through. There's still a slight mist in the air that clings to my skin. My boots sink into the mud as I follow the scented path.

My body buzzes in a way I've never experienced before. I'm thirsty for someone I've never met.

Literally.

"Anything?" Romeo's question infiltrates my mind.

"I smell her." The mist turns to a heavier pace. Water gathers in the curve of my hat, dripping down the front when I tilt my head down to see inconsistencies in the mud. I squat, tracing the grooves of what looks like a handprint. "She was here." I stand, my heart pounding in my chest with horror and excitement.

I'm scared of how badly she is hurt, given the amount of blood sticking to the air, even after the rain has washed most of it away.

"Stay here."

Romeo chews on the weeds, not paying me any mind at all.

My vision stays cloaked in red as I study the tree line, walking slowly to the edge of the cliff where I spot broken twigs and blood swiped against a green bush. The leaves must have been protected by the trees' full canopies as it rained.

I'm tempted to taste it. The thought has my cock hardening in my jeans, pressing into the zipper. The thirst, the need, the lust to try the simple red swipe almost controls me.

I want to swim in her blood, drench myself in the one thing that's meant to be mine.

Oh...to indulge in such fantasies will ruin any plans I've made for myself.

Damn, I should have brought my lasso just in case she was in the water and trapped. I could pull her free. I wasn't fucking thinking. All I have is my gun.

A worn path is made from her slipping down the hill, the mud holding the imprint caused by her body. Touching the leaves she touched brings me closer to her somehow. She was here. Right fucking here. So close yet so far.

Anger wells in me, knowing I've made peace with wanting to die when I'm meant to, and now...

And now, I don't know what to do.

All I know is I can't let her die out here. My heart hasn't gone that dark and cold.

Crouching, I leap to the bottom, my boots sinking in the soaked clay by the riverbank. My brows furrow when I trace the blood staining the bark on the tree trunk. She tried to hold on.

She's a fighter.

I like that.

I stare out onto the waves in the river, a new fear clenching my breath as I watch the water rage. It smashes against large rocks, the current swift and unrelenting.

Sniffing the air, a low, aggravated growl rumbles in the

back of my throat. I can barely smell her now. The rain, the river, they've washed her scent away.

All I can do is follow the current and hope I find her alive. What happens to me if she is dead? Do I die too? I grind my teeth together, growling like the storm above. My breath lulls from between my lips in a slow, cold fog.

I punch the nearest tree, the wood splintering and snapping. The large pine crashes across the river, causing a new makeshift bridge to get to the other side.

The temperature has dropped faster than I expected. It was hot and humid only an hour ago. If she is alive, she won't be for much longer.

With a snarl, I leap to the top of the cliff. Romeo is soaked. His mane is sticking to his hide, and the end of his tail is dirty with mud. The neon red orbs pierce me through the rain. Blowing a raspberry, he trots his way over to me.

"We need to follow the river. She could be anywhere now that the current has her."

He shakes his head, the spray of water slinging from his mane. *"I'm hungry,"* he huffs, not caring at all about my mate.

Typical.

I scoff while hopping onto his back. "You can hunt later. I need to find her, and I need us to be on the same page, or you can go back to the barn."

"We will find her." He turns his head and bumps his nose against my leg. *"I can sense your worry. I don't like it."*

"Yeah, me neither. Come on, head down to the riverbank. We will follow it."

"Fast or regular pace?"

"Regular. I don't want to miss anything."

He neighs in response, rearing his legs into the air when lightning cracks across the sky. I grip a fistful of his mane, tightening my legs against his sides. His hooves slap on the mud, flinging it over my boots. He bolts down the cliff using his enhanced speed, stopping at the riverbank like I asked.

"Follow the current, Romeo. Let me know if you smell her or if you see anything."

"I will. I promise, Kentucky."

I pet his neck, giving the muscle a few light slaps.

He trots the best he can, given the circumstances. More mud flings behind us every time he lifts a leg. I scan every inch of the river, hoping I don't see her body floating or stuck in between rocks.

I check for drag marks along the riverbed, hoping she found enough strength to pull herself to land.

I'm not seeing anything. The unique scent of her blood almost can't be smelled anymore, and if it goes away completely, I'm worried I won't be able to find her at all.

"It's okay, Kentucky. We will find her. We will look all night if we have to."

"I hope you're right, Romeo. I hope you're right." The familiar feeling of hopelessness turns my stomach into knots. I've felt like this only a few times in my life.

When I died and when Daphne died, I never expected to feel this way again, not after everything. I keep to myself because my entire family is dead. The friends I had growing up...dead. It's why I'm a loner. Life isn't easy when you're the only one left in a world that no longer makes sense.

A squirrel jumps onto a nearby rock, and Romeo's ears perk up. He stops in his tracks, and I let out an annoyed sigh, tossing my head back to allow the rain to hit my face.

"Don't even think about it."

"It won't take long. Just to hold me over," he begs. *"We have to walk right by him anyway."*

We have rules for when he hunts. No baby animals and no females, as they could be pregnant.

"Don't kill the squirrel," I grumble. "At least not with me.

I'll give you a few bags of blood at home. Just hold out for me."

The squirrel is too damn cute. I have a soft spot for the tiny little creatures.

"Fine," he growls.

We walk by the fluffy thing, and I can't believe this, but I'm holding my breath. I watch Romeo's head turn, eyes locked onto his prey, and he stays in that position until we are too far away.

Finally, he looks straight ahead.

"He lives to see another day."

I chuckle at the tone of his thoughts. He is pouting.

"And so will you."

"Barely."

"Don't be so dramatic. We ain't got time for that." We've been searching for hours and have come up empty-handed.

I can't smell her anymore. I can't stop now. I've come too far. Being able to move on with my life would be impossible. I already know that I would be restless and spend the rest of my days searching for my mate.

It's an instinct I can't turn off or run away from. My vampire nature would never allow such a thing. My blood sings for her. Only she can ease the chaos in my veins since she is the cause of it.

"Wait."

Romeo follows the command, freezing mid-step.

I tilt my head back, inhaling to figure out what foul scent is bombarding me.

"What is that?" Romeo rears his head back, disgusted.

"Smells like wet dog. Follow it and fast." I know a little about shifters. A friend, if we want to call him that, educates me when he pops in every now and then.

What little I know is due to him, books, and the internet. The internet is by far my most favorite advancement since I have been alive. Anything and everything exists. I don't ever have to leave my home, which works out for a man like me.

The only way the internet could improve my life even more is if blood could be delivered.

Romeo's speed is much faster than my own, and we are able to cover more land. Huge chunks of wet grass are dislodged from the ground as he runs up the hill, leaving the river behind us.

The horrid scent of dog and something else I can't put my finger on brings us to a rundown bar. I've never been here, but I suppose I haven't seen a lot of places that resemble a shack like this one.

The business, if we want to be that generous, is barely standing. The foundation is slanted, and the wood that creates the walls is dark grey, rotted to the core. Debris clogs the gutters, and moss hangs over, stretching to reach the ground. What once were windows are just holes.

I take that back. There's one that's cracked, but it has cobwebs all over it, telling me it hasn't been opened in quite some time. Don't get me started on the porch. The middle of the damn thing sags. Whoever built this needs to find another job.

"I hope she isn't here. I can't smell anything over whatever rancid scent that is."

"Me neither." I slide off Romeo's back. "You can stay or go. Whatever you prefer is fine by me."

He pushes me, slugging his head against my shoulder. *"I'm staying. I'd never leave you alone. You saved my life. I'll continue to save yours."*

"Who says I need saving?" I smirk, scratching under his jaw.

"You do." He flicks his chin out, hitting me square in the chest. *"Right there."*

My playful smile fades, and I swallow the frog that's

somehow found itself in my throat. I try to pretend I have no idea what he is talking about, but I do. I forget animals can sense things others can't.

"I'll call for you if I need help. If things go south, run, and don't stop until you find another vampire to take care of you, okay?"

The droplets of rain gather in his black lashes. With every blink, they drip into the corner of his eyes, sliding down his nose. It almost looks like he's crying, but why would he miss an old grouch like me?

His ruby irises narrow at me, the top of his lip curling to show a long, thick fang. *"Nothing will happen. I have your back, Kentucky. End of story."*

I know when to leave well enough alone.

My clothes are soaked to my bones at this point. I turn, staring at the front of the bar. The rain clings to the rusted metal roof, reminding me of the days I chewed tobacco and I'd spit it in a tin. The clink alone takes me back to the taste, and I can hardly stomach it.

Howls of laughter echo from the bar, returning my focus to the matter at hand. I dip my chin, and water rushes off my hat and down my nose. An abusive amount of rain begins to pour. Humans with regular vision wouldn't be able to see in this. The bar would be out of sight for them.

Not me.

Even with the sheets bearing down from the sky, I'm able to see the bar just fine. Past the static of the storm, eight heart-beats stay in tune with every spin of my spurs as I charge towards the door.

The bottom step is broken in two, and the middle has a hole just to the right of the center. A loud creak vibrates under my boots from my weight against the old slabs while I survey the deck to see a few sets of rocking chairs still and empty.

I do appreciate the saloon-style doors, even if the bar is one gust of wind away from crumbling to ruins.

With a sly grin on my face, I keep my head down, hand on my gun, and my fangs at the ready. Licking the sharp point, I push myself through the doors and stop right in the entryway.

The bombarding scent of wet dog almost staggers me. That might be the worst thing I've ever smelled, and I've cleaned a barn for over a century. The next smell is smoke, and it's coming from the bar to my right. Spilled beer, piss, sweat, and most definitely sex hang in the air.

But it's the scent of what is buried underneath all the putrid aromas polluting this space that lets me know I am right where I need to be.

Her blood.

The roars of having a good time die when they sense my presence. Only the country music blaring from the neon blue and red jukebox sitting in the corner interrupts the silence.

"What the fuck are you doing here?" my new friend growls without manners.

I can't stand people who don't have manners.

His black boots fill my vision. I tilt my head, impressed with the silver lining at the very tips. One quick kick from my buddy here and I'll be in a lot of pain.

"I'm hoping you can help a fella like me out, regardless of our differences, I ain't here to fight."

His friends become closer by the sound of their own shoes scuffing against the ground.

"Why would you walk into a rogue wolf shifter's bar asking dumb fucking questions like that?"

"I smell someone that belongs to me here, you see, and I'm going to need that person by my side when I leave. That's all I want."

"That's too bad," he says, taking a step forward. "I don't make deals with bloodsuckers."

I smirk, cocking the hammer on the Colt. "That *is* too bad, isn't it?" Quicker than he could muster up a pathetic bark, I draw my gun.

The bullet leaving the barrel is loud. Smoke drifts from my gun, and I lift my head, smiling from ear to ear. "You should have made the deal, pup." I smack his cheek twice, the force of that simple act causing the wolf shifter in front of me to fall over.

I use him as a step, cutting his throat with my spur. "I would say all that blood smells good, but"—I sigh —"you really do smell awful. It must be embedded in your DNA."

A burly shifter wearing a white, stained tank top charges me, claws drawn. In a blur, I aim and fire, shooting him right between the eyes.

I step on him too. "I am a gentleman. If any of you want to leave, now is your chance before I kill you, and I will if it means getting what belongs to me. Either you understand or don't."

"How are you killing them?"

Too many sets of glowing angry eyes are on me to see who is asking the question.

"Silver bullets. Made them myself after learning that little trick from a book. Now, give me what I want before I kill you."

"I don't think so. That pretty little thing belongs to me now since she wandered onto my property." A tall, skinny man with light brown hair sits in a chair, his feet up on the table. A match strikes, the flame lighting a cigarette he has between his lips, and the smoke that hangs in the air becomes more dense when he blows out a cloud. "She owes me for her life."

I snarl, blurring to his side and ripping out his spine, the cigarette still hanging between his thin, paper lips. "My patience is gone." I whip the spine through the air like a lasso, wrapping it around another's neck.

With a hard yank, the man's head is ripped from his shoulders, tumbling across the room. Another charges at me in shifted form, his pack close behind him. I leap to the left, my trigger finger blurring with how fast I shoot and reload. Each wolf falls to the ground, leaving no one else but the bartender.

I aim my weapon, and he raises his hands in the air, the white towel a flag of surrender.

"Are you going to kill me if I tell you what you want to know?" he asks.

In one swift distortion, I'm in front of him, gun pressed under his chin. "Unlike your friends here, I'm a decent man. I like the truth. If you're honest, you can go. I swear on my fangs."

"They have her in a shed by the river. Rogue shifters aren't the best company. I heard them talking, and they had horrible plans for her. One said he was going to pass her around—"

"—Enough," I hiss, my fangs aching for violence.

I struggle with the need to kill him. I don't want his blood. I only crave the one I've been scenting. I want him to die because he wasn't going to do anything to try and save her. He should face the death penalty for that, but unfortunately, I am a man of my word.

Shoving the hot barrel against his chin, I let him go. "Go," I order.

He jumps over the bar, shifts into his wolf, and bolts out the door. Swinging my gun around my finger, I tuck it in the holster and take one step to the back door.

"Kentucky, I didn't take you for the killing type. Color me impressed."

I groan when I hear his voice. I did not miss this man at all. "I don't have time for this, Lorcan. My mate is on this property somewhere, and I have to find her."

"Your mate? Last I checked, you didn't want one. I've known you a long time, Kentucky. This changes all your little plans." He grins, wiggling his fingers at me playfully.

I blur through the back door, needing to get away from him. Lorcan and I have an odd relationship. I wouldn't call him a friend, but he is the closest thing I have to one. He came to take my maker's soul the night she died. He's a Void, a grim reaper who works for Death.

I thought he was there for me, but when I lived, Lorcan didn't take my soul. Over the years, I know he has done his best to heal me, as a good friend would do. He let me know the basics about being a vampire. Told me how there were other creatures too. He helped me when I didn't have anyone, and I'm grateful for that.

But damn that Void for his poor timing. He is always good at interrupting. Always.

He pops up in front of me. "Usually when another paranormal kills another, I have to let the Hell Harvester's know. You know, the paranormal cops that keep order. The Four Horsemen."

"Let them know, Lorcan. I do not care. I have business to attend to, so if you don't mind."

"Well, you've put me in a spot—"

I sneer, pressing my gun between the abyss's he has for eyes. "I don't care about the position you are in. Do your job. I don't care if Death comes knocking at my door and sends me to the pits of hell." I whistle for Romeo, needing him here for when I find my Beloved. "But I will find my mate. I won't let her die here."

"Don't you know? You don't want to live forever, Kentucky. You have two choices now. Mate her and live forever, or don't and you both die. So if you don't want to live forever, I say leave her here, and you can finally die the way you have always wanted."

I snarl, launching at him, but he vanishes into thin air.

"You're so moody for a cowboy. You know I'm telling the truth. Oh, oh, can I pet him?" He claps his hands when Romeo stops beside me.

"No."

"He isn't interested, Lorcan, and I need to find my mate. Stop bothering me."

"Why? You want to die. I'm only doing what you want." He snaps his fingers. "Shit, I have to go. The boss is calling, but you need to think about what I said. You can finally have an out, Kentucky. You can finally be free. This conversation isn't over, but I have to take these souls to Hell. Lucifer is pissed. Alright, bring it in, give me a hug." He spreads his arms, curling his fingers in a gesture that says, 'come on.'

"Don't make me shoot you."

"I'd live." He's gone, leaving me irritated like always.

I'm frozen in place, his words sinking deeper into my soul. I *do* want to die. This is my chance. I could turn my back, walk away, and be gone forever.

The scream I hear ruins any of those thoughts. No matter how much I want to die, I could never leave my mate behind without telling her the truth.

With a held breath, I bolt downstream. I'm almost half a mile away from the bar when I catch sight of an old shed nestled in the darkened part of the forest.

She's in there. I know she is. I feel the pull, the rope that ties us together, tugging at my soul harder. The desperation in the muscles of my heart is something I've never felt before. I become more frantic in the need to get to her.

Her blood is easier to scent the closer I get.

Mate.

Mine.

Beloved.

There are the words again, echoing in my mind. The

reason why I've lived when I wasn't meant to is for this moment. All these years, all this time wondering why I've survived, makes sense now.

I've lived to save her.

I bust the lock, rip the door from its hinges, and fling it to the left, the wood smashing against a tree. The inside of the shack is dark, but with my vision, I'm able to see the woman who has caused my soul chaos in my very stagnant life. Iron hangs in the air. Blood is dripping in tune with the rain outside. She's lying in the middle of the floor, barely breathing, the strong scent of drugs coursing through her system.

"What did they do to you?" I stare at my fated mate in horror, a rage of violence building in my chest.

I'm glad I killed them all, and I'd do it again if it meant finding her.

In another swift motion, I'm wrapping my arms around her to lift her from the filthy ground. She's limp, falling into my hold without a fight. Her eyes continue to stay closed even after jostling her around. She's unconscious.

Good.

I don't want her waking up to see a stranger holding her naked, bruised, and wound-ridden body.

She's alive.

And naked.

I can't help my reaction since she is my beloved, but I can control my actions. I turn my head, tug my shirt off, and gently put her head through the hole, then her arms. Pulling the shirt down, I swallow the lust, trying to possess my ability to string a thought together. Her soft skin brushes against my century-or-so-old calloused fingertips, and I am already craving to explore her body.

Now is not the time for those sensations.

My shirt falls to her knees, giving her privacy and keeping

her wounds covered. Her body should only be revealed if she wants to reveal it.

Slipping my arms around her, I pick her up and hold her to my chest. My eyes water when her scent buries itself in my lungs. I inhale deeply, pressing her harder against me, and bury my nose into her hair. She was so close to death that I might not have been able to hold her in my arms. I almost didn't get to experience how good it is to hold the one who is fated to me.

My tear drips into the gash on her cheek, and I lean down, pressing a gentle kiss on the middle of her forehead. "Come on, My Darlin' Beloved, let's get you home."

Maybe dying can wait another day because living doesn't seem so bad now that I have her in my arms.

DEAD MAN'S
RANCH

CHAPTER FOUR
DRUSCILLA

The bites sting in the rushing water. Dirty river floods my mouth, choking me. Every few seconds, the rough waves take me under as if hands are pushing down on my shoulders in hopes I'll drown. I struggle against the force, using my arms to bring me to the surface. I inhale water and air, the river teasing me with its promise of death.

The wild current smashes me against a rock, my head taking the brunt of the impact, and it knocks me out. I'm face down in the water and have no more energy left to fight.

It's sad that I'm waiting for a waterfall to put me out of my misery. The bites all over my body burn from the filth I'm submerged in. Just as I have given up, someone clutches my arm, dragging me out of the water.

There's hope.

"Well, well, well. Look what we have here, fellas. All that pretty just for me."

I scream myself awake, bolting up to see a man sitting on the edge of the mattress with a rag in his hand. I scream again, scurrying away from him until I'm at the edge of the bed. My mind is playing catch-up. I have no idea where I am, who this man is, or how I got here.

The bed dips from his weight as he stands, and he lifts his arms. "I don't mean you no harm, ma'am." He takes off his hat, holding it against his chest. "I know you're confused, and I'm happy to answer any questions to ease your mind." His smooth, velvet, classic southern accent wraps around me. I could listen to him speak all day. "There's no need to be afraid of me. I'm not going to hurt you."

"Where am I?" I croak, my hand flying to my throat when I hear how hoarse it is. My stomach grumbles too, and I can't remember the last time I ate

"You must be dyin' of thirst. Here." An antique white pitcher with painted blue and orange flowers along the sides seems a bit ridiculous in his large hand as he pours the water into a vintage blue glass. "Before you go drinkin' that, make sure you can keep this broth down first. You have to be hungry, but I want to see if you can handle this broth, okay? Then, you can tackle the breakfast in the kitchen. I made it myself," he puffs out his chest with pride.

One hand holds a cup of water and the other holds a mug with broth. He holds out the glass with broth in it first and the amount of fear I felt eases.

There's something about him that puts me at ease, and I'm not sure if I like how defenseless that makes me feel. No one should have that kind of power, but he does. The immediate safety is all too consuming, sitting here in this bed, wrapped in a warm blanket, and not faced with someone who wants to use me.

He waits for me to take the glass full of broth from him, but I cock my left brow, rearing back.

He smirks, my heart fluttering from the simple expression. "You don't trust me. I understand. Does this make you feel better?" He presses the rim of the glass against his firm lips, gulping down half of the contents. Wiping his mouth on the back of his hand, he holds it out towards me again. "See? It isn't poisoned."

It's hard not to notice how handsome this stranger is. He has thick black hair with the sides cut short, but the top is long with natural waves. His beard is just as dark, reminding me of a starless night sky. I lick my lips as I look him over, my interest locking on the width of his chest and broad shoulders.

Even under the beard, I can tell he has a strong, square jawline. He has firm lips, not too thick, but also not too plump. He has high, rounded cheeks and a strong, straight nose. His skin is golden from being out in the sun so much. Every part of him screams 'hardworking man' and there isn't one soft thing about him that I can see—other than his eyes when he smiles.

And yes, while his body is sculpted, muscles tightening the cotton shirt, it's his eyes that announce kindness. They remind me of burnt pools of honey with brown and golden hues joining together to create their own personal, unique color.

I could watch this man all day without saying a single word, and I'd consider it time well spent.

Snatching the broth from him when my stomach growls again, I take a giant gulp. I hold it in my mouth when the flavors burst across my tongue.

Oh, god.

This is terrible. It might be the worst thing I've ever tasted in my entire life.

The broth tastes like days-old sock water. It's the only thing I can compare it to.

"Good, right?"

His thoughtfulness is too sweet to shoot down. Add in the little smile he has watching me drink the broth he made me, and all I can do is swallow.

I cough when the broth threatens to come back up. "So good. That was so nice of you to make it for me."

"Drink the rest in the cup, and then I'll give you some water. I'm sure you're dehydrated."

"Right. The rest. That's important." I peer up at him over the blue cup, watching him smile so big, I have to smile in return.

The broth even smells like socks.

Here we go.

Holding my breath, I chug the warm liquid down, forcing myself to swallow. While it does taste horrible, I already feel better with having something in my stomach.

"Good girl," he praises me.

That causes my stomach to flip with excitement. I want him to say it again.

"Here. I can drink the water myself too, to prove it isn't poisoned," he offers.

I trust him. Plus, I need to wash this sock-water down with something.

Wrapping my fingers around the glass, I finally take it from him. I guzzle the cool, refreshing liquid down until I'm lifting the glass in the air, sticking out my tongue to get the last few drops.

"Whoa, now. No need to scrape the bottom of the barrel. There's plenty more where that came from. May I?" he questions, instead of just removing the glass from my hands.

He is leaving the choice up to me.

I lick my lips, gathering the few droplets of water remaining. "Thank you," I whisper.

He fills the glass without taking it from me. I'm focused on that. He is showing me I can trust him. After the nightmares I've been through, the simple kind gesture is something I have missed.

"I'd like to introduce myself to put you more at ease." He

sits down on the edge of the mattress again, and the entire bed dips from his weight. He seems too large of a man to fit in this room. "I'm Kentucky Jones." He holds out his hand.

"Kentucky? I'm sure there is a story behind that. I like it. I'm Druscilla Whitley." I eye his hand, wondering if he is someone I can trust to touch.

"Druscilla. I like that too. It's pretty." The way he stares at me has me wondering if I'm the only woman he has ever seen.

Flattery gets him a handshake. I slip my palm into his, a warm buzz awakening every nerve ending. I pinch my lips together to swallow the gasp. Kentucky's calloused thumb drifts over my knuckles. A slow back-and-forth rub. His black eyebrows pinch together in thought, and even though he is a stranger, I am curious what is going through his head.

Lifting my hand to his lips, he presses a soft kiss across my fingers. "It's very nice to meet you, Dru."

The answer is no. I cannot trust myself to touch him.

I clear my throat, tugging my hand away when the connection between us becomes stronger.

The silence is awkward. I don't know what to say, and I'm not sure I want to speak. I can't tell if this is reality or not, and I'm too tired to know.

Clearing his throat, he stands, snagging his hat off the top of the dresser. "You're safe here, at Dead Man's Ranch. You don't have to worry about anyone hurting you or coming to get you."

"Dead Man's Ranch?" The high-pitched break in my question should be embarrassing. My palms begin to sweat and slip across the glass filled with water. It tumbles right out of my hand, bumping the bed before heading to the floor.

Water spills all over the sheets, but before the loud crash of the glass shattering, Kentucky is there.

Quicker than I can blink, he catches it before it hits the ground. He freezes, his shoulders rising and falling in a way that lets me know he didn't mean to reveal his secret. He peers at me from the corner of his eye, waiting to see if I've reacted.

Oh, he hasn't seen nothin' yet!

"It's an inside joke considering I'm a dead man." He straightens, setting the cup on the dresser, continuing to give me my space.

"You're one of them." I slip from the bed, my feet landing in a puddle of water on the wooden floor. Naturally, I take a step back from him. My eyes are round in shock, and I can't catch my breath. "Please," I beg as terror begins to take hold and memories of being bound naked to a chair assault me in every corner of my mind. "Please, don't hurt me. Just let me go. Please, just let me go. I don't know what you want, but I don't have it, okay? I can't give you anything." I snatch the vase sitting on the table closest to me and launch it at him.

He ducks, the vase shatters against the wall, and a shard lands in his cheek. A big white chunk of pottery sticks out from his face. Meeting my eyes, he tugs it free and drops it on the dresser.

Before my eyes, his skin heals, the blood sinking back into his body.

Not once does he lose his temper. I expect him to charge, for his eyes to change, for his fangs to flash, but he remains calm and collected.

That only confuses me more. There's nothing else I can throw at him unless I try to pick up this chair nestled in the corner.

I'm trapped.

I peer around the room for another exit, spotting a window to my left. I hold my breath, plastering my body against the wall as I scoot closer to my only route to freedom.

His gaze drifts from me to the window. "You're upstairs, Dru. If you fall, you'll hurt yourself. It's best if you don't do that." His eyes morph red, reminding me of a ruby gem catching the sunlight.

I try not to get lost in the catastrophic color of his eyes and remember they are the color of murder. "Why? You're going to kill me anyway."

He takes one step forward to try and stop me. "Dru, Darlin', hurting you has never once crossed my mind. You're safest with me. I'm not sure what vampire you ran into before, but they aren't like me. We can talk about that if you want, but remember this, I could have left you in that shack. I could have done a lot worse. I could have finished you off and drank what little blood you had left. I killed all those shifters to save you. The wounds on your body were pretty bad. You had lost a lot of blood and...I healed you."

The hesitancy in his sentences tells me he isn't telling me the entire truth. Do I care about the truth, or do I need to be thankful that he saved me?

"You are still weak from the blood loss. I've made you breakfast to help get your energy up. You need to eat."

I inch closer to the window, still not fully believing him. "Did you play with my mind like the other vampire did?" My fingers curl around the window frame, the adrenaline pumping in my veins, shouting at me to risk my life and jump.

The muscle in his jaw ticks from clenching his teeth together. "When you're up for it, you'll tell me all about this vampire who took advantage of you so I can kill him. To answer your question, no, I did not use that trick on you."

The slight click of the lock has Kentucky inhale a sharp breath. "Don't, Dru. After all you have survived, you're going to risk your life jumping out of a window? I won't allow it."

He's right, but the closer he gets to me, the more my knees tremble, and it isn't because I'm afraid. It's because, for some reason, I want to leap into his arms. Why would I want that? The thought alone has me opening the window.

"Just tell me who hurt you and I'll prove it, Darlin'. I'll bring you his fangs if it means you will rest easier."

"You'd kill your own kind?" The breeze swaying the curtains can't hide the surprise in my voice.

"They aren't my kind, Darlin'. I'd kill them all for you if it meant your heart got to beat for another minute. I smell how afraid you are, so I'm going to give you space. I'll go if you promise not to jump out the window." He steps around the foot of the bed, and I lean against the windowsill to get as far away from him as I can.

He points to the heavy wooden door to the right of me. "There's a bathroom there. You'll find everything you need. There are clothes folded on the vanity. I'm afraid I don't have anything in your size, so hopefully what's in there will suffice."

My nails dig into the windowsill to strengthen my grip. "I should want to kill you," I say out of nowhere, tears brimming in my eyes when I think about the way that vampire bit me, the way the shifters clawed at me in the shed. "I should want you all to die."

"I agree. You should." He backs away, opening the bedroom door with iron hinges, the top of it arched and wide to fit his body frame. The design in the wood is intricate, with a beaming sun casting down on a large amount of land. A few cattle graze the pastures, and a horse stands guard with them.

His brutal honesty takes me by surprise.

"Now, I'm trusting you, Darlin', but I'll save you again. I'll save you every time, even if it means saving you from yourself." He eyes the window, gripping the tip of his hat with his wide fingers, he tilts his chin to his chest, and walks out.

I'm left staring at his strong back and the way his muscles flex when he grabs the door handle to shut it. With a soft click, I'm alone in the massive room with a heart that aches, and I have no idea why.

I'm not sure if I would have jumped out the window. I do

know it was a dumb thought because that's a farther drop than I imagined in my head. I would have broken a bone, at least.

Another door slams in the house, followed by loud thuds going down the steps. Spreading the charcoal-colored curtain to the side, I lean out the window to see Kentucky walking towards the barn.

Even though I'm in a stranger's home, I will say it is a stunning property. The house is rustic and made out of thick logs and stone. Kentucky must have added to it over the years. Some areas are a little more outdated than others, giving them more character than your typical cookie-cutter home.

I continue to peek at Kentucky walking away from me. The further he gets, the more my soul hurts.

He must sense my eyes on him because he stops mid-step, turns his chin to his shoulder, and even from here, I can see the rise and fall of his muscular shoulders.

Kentucky locks eyes with me, and the sun breaks through the rain-filled clouds. The bright rays reflect off the red irises, reminding me of what lurks underneath the cowboy.

Thunder clashes above, the clouds suffocating the sun with the promise of a storm, and the bright red glare coming from his eyes is gone.

A large tree with long, zig-zagged and misshapen branches hangs over him, protecting him from the light rain that has started to fall.

As I take him in, my eyes fall to his jeans that fit him in all the right spots, cupping his bubbled butt and bulging thighs. I shouldn't notice his body. I shouldn't notice the sharp edge of his jaw. Even with the thick black beard, I can tell this man is carved out of the material all women want.

He places his fingers on the brim of his hat again, giving it a tilt.

I hate to say this, considering the circumstances, but it might be the most attractive gesture I've ever seen a man do.

He turns, walking out from under the canopy of the tree that was protecting him from the rain. One thing I notice about Kentucky is that he is never in a hurry. He is still walking like I would or how any person would.

Why isn't he using his vampire speed? He could get everything done in seconds and do whatever he wants for the rest of the day—whatever vampires do.

Wait, how is he in the sun? Actually, how was my kidnapper in the sun too? I thought vampires caught fire in the daylight? Vampire questions convolute my mind, and I want to know their truths.

I close the window, locking it in place, and lean my head against the wall. I take a large deep breath and blow it out slowly to calm my anxiety. It's fine. I'm fine. I can leave whenever I want and go home. I can't say I was held hostage by a vampire, then shifters, and then another vampire saved me, but I'll think of something.

Anything is better than the truth.

Carmen is probably losing her mind with worry right now, and hopefully, my job is still waiting for me. I'm a dentist back home, and I've worked too hard to get that job for it to be taken away from me like this.

I have to find a way home.

My fingers play with the hem of the shirt I have on to relax me. Only to realize the clothes I'm wearing aren't mine.

It's Kentucky's.

If I'm wearing his shirt, it means he saw me naked. Heat tempers my cheeks with embarrassment. Until now, no man has seen me naked. I haven't dated or had sex. I have never wanted to. I'm not ashamed to admit that.

Most men do not meet my standards. I don't know Kentucky enough to say what kind of man he is, but he had the respect to cover me with the shirt from his own back to give me privacy. I think that speaks volumes. It should be what every person would do, yet this world isn't as kind as I wish it to be.

Bringing the material to my nose, I inhale, getting the faintest hint of coffee and pine.

"Yeah, I need to shower." I glance down, wondering how Kentucky could manage to be in the same room with me, given how dirty I am.

My left arm is clean, while the rest of my body is caked in grime.

Wait a minute. The rag he had in his hand.

I crawl over the bed and stare at the cloth in a bowl of murky water. He was bathing me. What kind of vampire does this? He can't be this gentle or good. I've seen what they can do.

What is his endgame?

And what did he mean when he said he'd killed them all for me?

My head swims with confusion, hunger, and dehydration. I can't think about Kentucky like this. He is the enemy. He probably wants to suck me dry like the other vampire who tied me to a chair.

No. I will not be fooled by his lush, charming accent, muscles, or cowboy hat. It's all a rouse, somehow; his kindness, his patience, and even his honesty are in question.

All the stories I heard growing up tell me vampires are soulless, and so far, my own experience proves that.

Yet past my fear, past the doubt, and in the deepest part of my heart, something is telling me Kentucky's soul exists, and it doesn't compare to anyone else's.

I'm not sure how to trust him, but I don't have to.

I'm leaving when I have the energy, and Kentucky will be in my rearview.

CHAPTER FIVE

KENTUCKY

I pride myself on being a good man, a decent man, the kind that would do anything for anyone if it meant they got a better life. Free will is the most important for anyone, human or paranormal, and Dru thinks she has it.

She's probably in her room planning a way to escape, wanting to go home where she belongs.

I'm afraid I can't allow that to happen.

I can't let her go. She's meant to be here with me. If she leaves, I'll have to hunt her down and bring her back. If I kidnap her, that will set me back even further when it comes to gaining her trust.

Everything I felt about dying has changed because of her. Dru can be mad at me for being a vampire; she has the right to be afraid of me after what happened, but I'm also angry.

Her arrival in my life has changed all my plans. Death can no longer be an option because I refuse to let her die. I'm not that cruel. My life has always been controlled by outside forces.

My free will has always been abused, bent, and molded by someone else.

I thought I had finally taken control back, living my life by sunsets and sunrises. I was ready to die under the night sky, the stars beckoning me into their space to welcome me home.

Yet again, the universe has other plans.

I'm starting to realize that home isn't a place.

It's a person.

And she's inside the house right now, probably planning my demise.

I'm going to give her the space she deserves. I'll let her come to me when she's ready. Even with my own turmoil about our situation—I'm hopeful—I could scent her interest.

The fear was strong and bitter on my tongue as it filled the space of the bedroom. Behind that and the anger—and there was a lot of anger—I smelled desire.

Whether she likes it or not, she's attracted to me.

"You are going to get me fired."

I hang my head, my hand gripping the twine bundling the hay bales. "You're going to make me commit murder if you keep popping up unannounced."

"How else am I supposed to talk to you, Kentucky? Do you even have a phone?"

"Of course I do." I'm learning how to use it. It's dead in a drawer somewhere. All the technological advances over the years can be hard to keep up with.

I'm working on it.

"We will circle back to that and talk about why you didn't give me your number. Have you thought about what I said?" Lorcan jumps on the bales of hay and sneezes. "This barn is dusty. Do you clean it?"

How does someone kill someone who is already dead? Maybe the internet can tell me when I'm done working for the day.

"I clean it, but it is hay, Lorcan. You might be allergic."

"I'm a paranormal entity. We don't have allergies, Cowboy Dracula." He sneezes again, and this time, his head pops off, rolling across the barn in quick bumps.

His mouth is smashed into the stall. "Hey, can you bring me back to my body?" Lorcan mumbles. "The dirt tastes so bad."

His body falls from where he sits, his arms stretched out, looking for his head.

"I don't know. Seeing your skull rolling around brings me more joy than it should."

Lorcan manages to roll his head back and away from the stall. His mouth parts on a gasp, inhaling more dust. He sneezes, the force causing him to roll down to Romeo's stall.

"Oh my god, it reeks over here. What do you feed him?" He gags. "And where is my damn body!" he cries, but the body in question rams into a beam.

I grin, knowing damn well I wouldn't laugh at all if it weren't for Lorcan.

Tossing the bale of hay over my shoulder, it lands with a loud thump in the bed of the old truck I have parked in the barn. My plan was to fill the feeders out in the pasture for the cattle, but with the rain steady, I'll have to fill the row barn instead, where most of them will be huddled anyway.

A few creaks and groans have me turn to see Lorcan twisting his head back on. He cracks his neck left and right, then shakes his body.

"Okay, that's better. That was rude. You could have helped me."

I shrug a shoulder. "Seems like you had it under control, Lorcan. Who was I to interrupt your process?"

He holds a hand to his chest, offended. "I'll remember that when I have to take you to Purgatory."

I toss another bale of hay into the truck. "What's that?"

Lorcan knocks his head into the beam a few times, groaning. "You really don't know much, do you?"

"Only what you tell me." I grunt, throwing two more bales down from the loft. "Other than that, I don't care, Lorcan."

Lorcan takes a seat on a bench, then screams at the top of his lungs when one of the barn kittens scurries across his legs. I don't think I've ever seen him move so fast.

"What is that *beast*?" He hides behind me on the loft, leaving the little kitten down on the main level.

The grey kitten sits down, peering up at us with big blue eyes. *"Meow."*

"So vicious. You should be afraid. He probably smells your bones and needs a good chew."

"Feed me," the kitten says into my mind.

"Go to your mom. She'll feed you," I reply. *"You aren't ready for big kitty food yet."*

"That's terrible. Why would you keep such a creature here when you know that all I am is bones?"

"That's exactly why I keep him here, Lorcan." I school my features, doing my best to seem serious.

The kitten hisses at us before running away and slipping under an unused stall.

He shakes his bony finger at me. "This is why I'm taking your ass to Purgatory if you ever die. And before you ask"—he places his hand over my mouth to silence me— "Purgatory is the place all paranormals go. Consider it the next town over from Hell."

"Sounds like a vacation," I say, my tongue dry and my attitude uncaring.

"It isn't so bad. I really like it there."

"So go back and let me do my job." I grip the twine again, launching it through the air.

Lorcan dodges to the left to miss the rectangle charging at

him. "I know when someone is trying to get rid of me. We need to talk, Kentucky. And it can't wait."

"Yes, it can." I throw another bale through the air, and to my surprise, Lorcan freezes it mid-air and gently places it down with the rest.

"Surprise. I'm not a complete wreck. You don't know much about the paranormal life. I have respected your choice to remain a loner, to not give you the knowledge that you need for survival, but since you never cared about survival before, I gave you space." He snaps his fingers, and I'm forced to sit down.

I can't move.

"Yeah, don't even try to use your little vampire speed. You don't have shit on me, bucko." Lorcan dramatically flaps his black robe just when Romeo lets out a large neigh. "Hush. I'm not going to hurt him or anything. I don't have a mean bone in my body." He smiles, raises his brows, and waits for me to laugh. "Get it? Because all I have are bones that make up my body. Get it, Kentucky? Get it?"

I roll my eyes, wishing I could blur away from him. He can be annoying when he is determined. "I get it, Lorcan." Rain clatters against the roof, proving how much longer my day is going to take, especially with Lorcan here. "I can't wait for a lecture all day. I have shit I need to do. Romeo needs new horseshoes, the cattle need to be fed, and I need to make sure I don't have any other injured animals on top of needing to do a perimeter sweep of the fences. If any posts are broken, I need to fix them. I have a few cows that are due to give birth any day now. I might need to help them with that. So get on with it."

"I understand you are busy. You have been running this ranch for a very long time, and you should be proud of yourself and your success. This is the best ranch in the south. People pay a high price for one of your cattle. You should be proud of that, but I'm not here to talk about your ranch,

Kentucky. You don't have a long time before you start to wither away now that your mate is here. You know of her existence now. She's in your home. The scent of her will fill every room, taunt your control, tug at your will, and I know you have a lot of control. You are unlike any vampire I have ever met, but you can't wait to make a decision when it comes to her. You don't have that kind of time."

I try to lean forward, but his magic stops me. "What kind of time frame are we talking about? Months? A year?"

Lorcan frowns, followed by a long sigh. "You might have a week before you start to go mad from hunger. You won't be able to feed from anyone else. All the blood bags you have? That's all over now. You will throw up anyone else's blood. Your body will reject it. I know you're already feeling the need for her blood. It will just get worse. You will spiral. If you don't complete the bond, you will die, and that will kill her. You can't live without one another now. You have to decide what you want more. Her or death."

"A week?" I know I sound confused and in disbelief. I knew there was a chance we could die from what I've read, but a week? I thought I had longer to wrap my head around living for all eternity.

And Lorcan is right. She has only been here a day, and I'm already craving her blood. I want to know if the taste of her will be the end of me. Will I succumb and give in to the undying need of her blood in my veins?

The thought alone has my mouth watering. My fangs lengthen, and I bend my head down to keep my reaction private. Any reaction Dru ignites from me belongs to her.

"I'm sorry, Kentucky, I—"

A knock on the barn door interrupts us. I try to stand, but Lorcan's magic still has me frozen. By the aromatic scent cutting through the musk of the barn, it's Dru, and for some reason, she has come to see me.

I narrow my eyes in warning at him if he doesn't let me go.

"Oh, fine." He snaps his fingers, freeing me from his damn invisible prison. "This conversation isn't over." Lorcan vanishes, leaving me alone at last.

I stand on the edge of the loft to see Dru standing there with a glass of—I sniff the air—lemonade in her hand. She drops the umbrella on the ground and sets the glass on the truck.

"I don't know why I'm here," she says, tilting her head up to speak to me. She's drowning in my oversized shirt and sweatpants.

I have to swallow a growl of complete need as my want for her warms my blood.

Damn, they look much better on her than they do on me. She's already in my clothes, and all I want to do is rip them free so I can worship her body the way she deserves.

Even with Daphne, the lust was there, but it was never like this. My skin feels tight, and my gums hurt to the point of tears as I hold in my fangs.

I jump down from the loft, my spurs spinning when I land, and I straighten to my full height. Lifting my hat off, I take slow and deliberate steps towards her, stopping a foot or so away so she doesn't feel like I'm invading her space.

She already seems so lost. I can smell how wary she is just being this close to me.

"If you don't mind me sayin,' I'm glad you are here." Our eyes meet, and I'm finally able to see her since she has showered and washed away all the dried blood, dirt, sweat, and whatever else had dried on her body. "My god," the words are spoken on a slight growl. "You are beautiful, Dru."

Out of all the stunning things I've seen in my life, Dru is and will always be the most beautiful. Prettier than a sunset fading on the pasture horizon with fireflies burning the night and the stars out by the billions.

She has brown skin that I'm dying to feel under my finger-tips. Her eyes are big and round, filled with innocence and fear. Lashes surround hazel irises. Brown begins on the inside of the black ring, then forest green, and yellow just around the pupil. A few dark brown freckles pepper across her high cheekbones and nose. She has a heart-shaped face with a delicate, soft jawline. Even her eyebrows are full and perfectly arched. There isn't one detail of her face that I'm not obsessed with. I could stare at her all day, every day, and the time spent still wouldn't be long enough to get my fill of her beauty.

I'm not proud of where my thoughts take me, but I'm still a man, and I'm wondering if there are any freckles on her body. I'd love to find out. I'd want to take my time, searching for every spot so I can lick and kiss, have her gasp and moan in ways that she'd thank me for.

My awe of who Fate has deemed my mate doesn't stop there. Her hair is light red with beautiful, bouncy curls that almost touch her shoulders. I already feel the urge to run my fingers through it while her head is on my chest.

Maybe one day, my touch can put her to sleep instead of scaring her.

All the talk with Lorcan about dying again flies out the window when I have her in my sights. Death no longer exists in my future when she's standing in front of me. It's when I'm alone with my own thoughts that I remember the plan.

"I brought you a lemonade when I saw you working in the barn and thought you might be thirsty, but then vampires don't drink lemonade, do they? I'm sorry that was so—"

"—Thoughtful," I finish her sentence, reaching for the glass she didn't have to bring me at all. "I don't know much about other vampires, but I love a home-cooked meal and fresh lemonade." I take a large, generous gulp, downing half of it. "Ah." I lick my lips, wanting to get every drop. "Thank you, ma'am. You didn't have to do that."

She looks down, toying with the hem of the shirt. "You don't have to call me ma'am. Call me Dru, please. I should go. I don't know why I'm here. I'm bringing a vampire fucking lemonade," she mumbles as she turns around, snagging her umbrella.

I reach for her, my hand clutching her arm, and the rotten stench of her fear has me release my hold on her.

"Apologies. I didn't mean to scare you."

"You-You didn't." Her voice shakes with the inability to cover her fear.

I grin, scratching the back of my head. "You don't sound too convincing, Dru. Plus, I can smell your lie." I tap my nose.

"I'm sorry." She turns around to face me, and her beauty steals my breath.

"Don't ever apologize for being afraid. You have every reason to fear me after what you have been through, but I promise, I am not going to hurt you."

She crosses her arms and rubs her hands across them. She's cold. Goosebumps arise across her flesh, a sensation I haven't felt since I was turned.

"What's crazy is that I believe you won't hurt me. I don't know why. You could at any minute. You could snap my neck when you decide you're done with me. I just need a few more days, and I'll be out of your hair. I need to call my friend, Carmen. She can come get me to take me home."

I step forward, placing the half-drunk lemonade on the edge of the truck. "You don't have to leave so soon. If you haven't noticed, I'm the only one who works this ranch—"

Romeo's high-pitched neigh interrupts me.

"—Apologies. My *horse* and I work the ranch. I could always use another set of hands." I know she needs the truth of why she can't leave, and I'll tell it to her. Soon. I just need more time to figure out what to say.

What do I say to someone who is afraid of me? I have a

feeling she isn't going to be too keen on being destined for a vampire.

She quirks a brow. "I have a job. I haven't been there in a few days, and they are going to fire me if I'm not already. I have calls I have to make, and then I need to get back. You understand, don't you?"

I swallow, hating that everything in her life is about to change. I've been there. I know what it is like to have plans and then have them ripped away from you.

"Of course I do. I can't help that I enjoy your company is all, Miss Whitley."

"Miss Whitley?" She shakes her head. "Sometimes you talk like you're from another time."

"I am, but I don't really keep track of time, so I can't give you an exact date of just how long I've been around."

She leans against an empty stall, eyeing me as if she's trying to figure out if I have another angle. "Just Dru, Kentucky."

I tilt my chin in acknowledgement, unable to stop myself from grinning. "Yes, ma'am."

That causes her to smile, and I know parts of my soul are tethering to her regardless of whether I want it or not.

"Why is it that I don't want to be away from you?" she asks, rubbing her arms again. "Make it make sense because I can't."

I'm not ready to answer that. I'm not sure if I'll be able to by the time this week is up. I open the truck door and grab my black coat. "Here, Darlin'. There's no reason for you to be cold. May I?"

She nods, pushing herself off the stall. I drape the jacket over her, helping her with both sleeves.

"There. That ought to keep you warm, Dru." I love seeing her in my clothes. Her hair against the dark black of the jacket reminds me of the sunset, the reds painting the night sky with the last breath of daylight.

"I think it's a little big." She holds out her arms and laughs when it falls to her thighs, the sleeves covering her hands by many inches.

I lean against the truck, my thumbs hooking in my belt loop, and say, "I think you look just right."

"You sound like you're flirting with me."

I scoff, placing my hat on my head. "I suppose I am, but it has been a while."

"How long is a while?"

"Years. I've lost count." A small stab of guilt penetrates my heart when I think of Daphne. She wanted me to meet my mate. She never wanted me to not exist anymore. For some reason, she thinks the world needs me because it needs kindness.

I don't think I'm kind at all. I'm resigned, and that's a whole lot different than kindness.

Dru steps forward, and she doesn't understand that the closer she gets, the harder it is for me to control myself. Her scent wraps around me like a blanket, warm and comforting like a hot day after being so cold.

And I've been cold for far too long. The bitter winter nights don't even compare. Dru is melting all my reserves in just a matter of hours. What could she do with me if I were to give her eternity?

The closer she becomes, the more our bond strengthens.

There's no way out of this for me. I know that no matter how much I've wanted to die over the years, staring into Dru's hazel eyes, all I see is forever.

And that scares the hell out of me way more than Death ever will.

DEAD MAN'S
RANCH

CHAPTER
Six
DRUSCILLA

"You better answer me, Kentucky." I must be an idiot for threatening a vampire, but I need to know why I'm drawn to him in ways that make no sense to me.

My eyes begin to water from the sheer frustration of wanting to throw my arms around him and kiss him within an inch of my life. That's so foolish to want when I know in the blink of an eye, he could kill me.

His eyes lose their light as his smile fades into a frown. "I don't know what you're talking about, Dru. You should go rest. I'll find my phone and charge it to make sure you can give your friend back home a call."

I scoff, invading his space when the urge to slap him twitches my palm. "Oh, don't you dare even think about telling me what to do," I hiss through clenched teeth. "And don't change the subject. You know exactly what I am talking about." I poke him in the chest, ignoring how firm his pecs are. "You're choosing not to tell me. I deserve to know after everything. I'm absolutely terrified of being here, being in front of you, being so close to someone who could kill me quicker than I could even think about screaming, but I am.

You are the very thing I fear, and for some reason, I am here. I refuse to back down or cower away from the very thing that is bound to kill me."

"I'm not going to kill you, Dru. I don't know how many times I have to say it."

"Until I believe it." I shove him again. That was useless. He doesn't even move an inch.

Kentucky could have pretended to give the slightest sway. It would have done wonders for my self-confidence.

"I could stake you in your sleep," I grumble under my breath, annoyed by this vampire.

"You could try," he smirks. "I admire your courage to confront me, Darlin'. It's admirable, given what you have been through." He taps the side of his nose. "I smell it."

I clutch his jacket around me and step back, losing any vibrato I had. "Smell what?"

"How scared you are. That's what makes you confronting me sweeter than ice-cold blood on a hot summer's day."

I swallow, touching my throat in disgust at the thought of tasting blood.

"And yet—" He stretches his arm, his hand near my face, and I flinch. I expect a harsh touch. Maybe a grab to the face or a slap across the cheek. Instead, he tucks my hair behind my ear. The rough callouses on his hand awaken my nerve-endings, the slight stroke of my flesh causes my heart to stammer. "Your bravery still overcomes the bitter aroma of the terror you're feeling."

Panic surrounds me like a tornado, whirling, spinning, and twirling all around me. I have to put more distance between us. The pull to him is strong, so much stronger than any amount of fear in me.

It's almost enough to let me forget he is a monster.

Almost.

Taking another step back, my foot catches on a dip in the

ground. I spread my arms out, reaching for something, anything for me to latch onto. My fingers slide against the driver's side door of his pickup truck, barely missing the handle.

Can't a girl catch a break?

Kentucky is nothing but a mirage in front of me, moving so fast I can't tell where he is until his arms are wrapped around me. My body is pressed against his, and every hard ridge of his muscles seems to hold onto me. His face is so close to mine, I can see the small freckle on his left cheek.

The entire time he holds me, I'm holding my breath. If I move, if I breathe, I might forget how I ended up here and do something I might regret.

Like kiss him the way my soul is urging me to.

His dark cognac eyes fall to my lips, then up to my eyes. I watch the struggle he has not to give in, to not take the kiss I know I wouldn't fight him on. Even though I'm in the arms of a predator, I've never felt safer.

"You're starting to make saving me a habit." This time, it's my gaze that falls to his lips.

"Saving you is a habit I'll never break." His hand cups my jaw, his thumb stroking the edge.

"Why?" The short, simple question has been burning in my mind since I arrived.

Why save me? Why bring me here? Why does he want me to stay? Why isn't he like the other vampire? I have so many questions.

Kentucky rolls his lips together, lifting me to my feet to help me stand. "Are you okay, Darlin'?" he kindly asks, pushing my hair behind my ear again as if he is transfixed.

"Why can't you answer a simple question? I don't understand you, Kentucky."

"Because the answer I have, you don't want. It's easier for you not to know." He grabs the lemonade I brought him, downing the rest of the cold liquid. A few drops of condensation fall onto his beard from the glass as he has it tilted. I'm entranced by watching his throat move with every swallow.

Time slows right before my eyes as I become transfixed on Kentucky.

The muscles in his neck are so defined, and with every contraction of muscle, my mouth becomes drier, and an urge inside me becomes hungrier. I lick my lips, witnessing the condensation fall onto his beard. I hold my breath and hope he can't hear the catch with every inhale.

His lips are still wet, and his tongue flicks out, tracing his mouth to gather all the goodness I wish I could taste. His hand rises, and just when I think he's going to wipe his mouth across the top of his knuckles, he dips into the front pocket of his T-shirt and yanks out a handkerchief.

Of course, he has a handkerchief.

Still, I'm spellbound by how he wipes his mouth. Kentucky runs the cloth down his beard to gather the droplets my dry throat had been thirsty for.

Why do I find myself wishing I were that damn handkerchief?

He tucks the used cloth back into his pocket and pauses, his nostrils flaring as he scents the air, and his eyes shift to the brutal, unrelenting red.

Crossing my arms over my chest as I watch him, my infatuation grows, and I forget why I was getting angry at him. I'll remember eventually. How can anyone expect me to remain level-headed when he has his damn cowboy hat on, shirt stretched tight across his torso, and leather chaps over his jeans?

He makes it very difficult to focus and remember that I hate vampires.

His fangs descend, and the sudden urge to feel them break the tender flesh of my neck has heat pooling between my legs.

"Apologies, Dru. I can smell..." He clears his throat and turns away, walking toward a stall. "Doesn't matter."

"My blood?" Flashes of the bite marks all over my body remove any lust that had possessed me for that minute.

"Amongst other things," he growls, cutting those glowing eyes at me. "I think it's best if you go inside, Dru. You need to rest. The vampire who kidnapped you is still out there, right?" The hinges to the stall door creak when he opens it.

"There you go, thinking you know what's best for me. Again. I decide that. Not you."

"Darlin', I've been around these parts a long time. I think I know what's best and what's not." He whistles to the horse in the stall.

"You have been alone out here for way too long to know what is best for someone. Typical man thinking he knows better than everyone else." I place my hands on my hips, debating if I should stake him right through the heart to end this back-and-forth nonsense.

"Come on, Romeo. We need to change your shoes." Kentucky grabs the lead, a long black rope, and tugs. Large steps send vibrations through the ground before a giant horse comes walking out of the stall.

I inhale, rushing backwards when I take in the size of the beast. That's the biggest horse I've ever seen. His coat is a glossy onyx, deep as the night is long, with a long, wavy mane. How big and gorgeous this animal is, isn't what has me shaking in fear.

I'm not sure what happens to my body. Everything freezes. My entire body is locked in place, trembling in absolute terror from the sight before me. The horse's large, scarlet-burned coals bear into me. The entire eye is encompassed in red, no white corners, no pupils, just endless pools of blood.

He neighs, his top lip curling up, and that's when I spot the fangs.

"He-he-he has fangs!" I stammer, pointing my finger at the creature as if I'm accusing him of a crime. "He's...he's..." I can't finish my sentence because I can't seem to catch my breath. "Can't be possible," I whisper in disbelief.

"Dru, it's alright," Kentucky tries to soothe me with the horse by his side. "Hey, look at me. Dru." He cups my cheek, his thumb swiping away the tears as I stare at the towering demon. "My Darlin' Girl, look at me." His voice is soft and gentle, smooth like silk dragging across my skin. The baritone of his timbre speaks into veins and finds the very part of my mind where the fear lives. "You're safe. I'm not going to allow you to be hurt. I will never put you in harm's way. You're safe with me. I'm going to protect you, Dru."

The horse hangs his head, almost as if he is trying to appear smaller. The motion breaks me from my trance, and I cautiously slide my gaze to Kentucky.

His worrisome brown eyes awaken me as I look into them. How could someone so kind have danger lurking under their skin?

"There you are," Kentucky smiles, showing straight white teeth. "How are you feeling? Do you need to sit down?"

I shake my head, clearing my throat. "No. I'm fine. I'm so sorry. I'm still wrapping my head around the fact that vampires exist, which means other paranormal creatures exist, and it's a lot to take in. He looks like Lucifer's pet."

The big demon neighs, pawing the ground in protest.

Kentucky chuckles. "This is Romeo." His horse bucks his head, shoving Kentucky's shoulder. "And he really didn't like you saying he was Lucifer's pet and"— he quiets as if he can hear what Romeo is saying—"and wants you to take it back. Are you kidding me, Romeo? You're acting like a child who didn't get his way. You have better manners than that." Kentucky scolds Romeo, and the horse's ears flicker left and right in response. Turning to me, the vampire grins. "He apologizes, Dru."

"I-I don't even know what just happened. You're talking to him like he can understand you." My words are glazed in confusion. "I might need to sit down, actually."

Kentucky's grin fades. He drops the rope in his hand, blurring to drop the tailgate. My cowboy swings me into his arms and sets me down on the truck. The second his arms fall away from me, I miss the safety his embrace brings. My soul awakens the loneliness in the marrow, and I yearn.

I yearn to the point of hurt, to the point of despair, that if I don't feel his touch, I'd beg Death for peace.

What is wrong with me?

"You doing alright, Dru?" Kentucky asks, peering inside my soul with how deeply his gaze penetrates. It's as if he feels what I feel.

"Yes. I'm so sorry." I hide my face in my hands, wondering when this nightmare will finally end. I'm making a complete fool of myself.

Large hands wrap around my wrists, tugging my arms down. "Don't be sorry. Romeo's appearance can be terrifying if you don't know him. He's twenty-five hands tall and a thousand pounds. He's a vampire. If you weren't afraid of him, I'd be worried, Dru."

I peer down when his thumb drifts over the top of my wrist, trying to soothe the panic. "He won't hurt me?" I ask, choosing not to ask him to remove his hold on me.

The more I'm near him, the more I find myself in need, and his touch, his grip on me, it satisfies the craving that's building for him.

"He won't hurt you. I promise. He's gentle until he is in a situation that causes him not to be. I know it's shocking. Even in my world, vampire horses aren't common. I saved him because he asked me to." Kentucky scratches Romeo behind the ear. "He's been by my side for a very long time, and he will protect you."

I hold up a finger. "Okay, I have a few questions. What do you mean, he asked you? And why would he protect me? I'm someone new to him."

"When I was turned, I was told sometimes vampires get a gift. Mine is talking to animals. I don't know how it works or why. To answer your other question, he'll protect you because I told him to. What's important to me is important to him." He takes my hand. "Come on. Let's start slow, Darlin'."

"You know I only have more questions now, right?"

He scratches his chin, smiling. "If you didn't, I'd be worried. We can talk about it later if you like. For now, take my hand. I'll never guide you to anything that will bring you pain."

With Kentucky by my side, we reach for Romeo, and he moves to be closer, wanting us to rub his neck. He is softer than I thought he would be. His tail flicks, and a muscle on his back twitches when I graze it.

"See? He likes you. There's nothing to be afraid of." Kentucky grins at me from the side of his mouth. "I admire how you push through your fears, Dru. I like that a lot. You still trusted me when you had no reason to."

"You make me realize that maybe there's nothing to be afraid of," I say so quietly, I can barely hear myself over the harsh beat of rain coming down on the roof.

The barn darkens as the grey clouds thicken, the red hues of Kentucky's eyes glowing in the shadowed barn.

"What's the meaning of the color of your eyes? Why red?"

He growls, the twin flames brighter the closer he gets to me. My heart hammers against my chest, beating like a wild drum when he becomes so close, I can smell his scent over the rain.

"Hunger."

CHAPTER
SEVEN
KENTUCKY

She tests every ounce of my self-control. I have a fire building inside me, crackling with furious rage as it becomes hotter. I cage her in with my arms, each hand gripping the edge of the tailgate on either side of her legs. The metal crunches in my grasp, leaving indentations of my fingers and palm.

I'm fighting every urge not to steal her lips in a heated kiss. If I do, I'm not sure I'll be able to control myself any longer. I'm afraid of what I'll do. I'll want to bite and feed off her blood.

I know the moment I taste the sweet nectar, I won't be able to stop. I'll want more. I'll want her to clutch onto me while sliding my cock deep inside her, pumping into her in tandem with every long drag I take from her vein.

What would her blood taste like during an orgasm? Would she beg for more? Would she like it if I fed from her?

I can't believe I'm entertaining the idea of having her in the way I'm dying for, but if I don't allow myself to indulge for even just a second, I might lose my mind.

With nervous, trembling fingers, I dare to risk any progress we have made to touch her legs. I wish I could feel the softness of her skin, but the material of the sweatpants she is wearing stops me. The barrier only makes me hungrier. We both inhale from the electric shock pulsating between us, the gravity of Fate pushing us together.

My head becomes dizzy with need. I can no longer hide my want. My cock is hard and aching beneath my jeans, the ridge pressing against her leg. I know she can feel it. Whether she realizes it or not, she presses herself harder against me.

I hang my head, closing my eyes to hide my nature. This isn't fair to Dru. She shouldn't be fated to me, not after what she has been through. All I can do is prove I'm not like him. I'm not a vampire who loses control. As long as I can do that, I might be able to earn her love.

I might be able to get her to stay.

Our breaths become heavier the more we deny the inevitable. The space between us sparks as we fight the gravity pulling us together. I can't resist. My palms drift up, traveling to her arms, goosebumps pebbling her flesh. What a gift to know she reacts to me in such a way, even though it goes against everything her mind is telling her.

I lift my head, allowing her to see the real me, the one who's constantly hungry for her. It's only been one day. *One* day of having my fated mate near me, and it's like a million fireflies lighting up my soul. I'm nervous, excited, and I wouldn't be the kind of man I aim to be if I didn't admit I'm also afraid.

I'm afraid of what this love means for me. How it changes everything I've had planned. How I *want* it to change everything I've had planned. How I can't even see my future without her being the center of it. This had to be what Lorcan meant by going mad. I don't know if I can take this for a week.

I want Dru bound to me. I want her claimed with my mark. I want her blood in my veins, giving me life.

Her palm rests on my cheek, her eyes darting across my

face to try to make sense of what is happening. Her heart rate increases, the beat becoming faster as I lean in a slow, careful motion.

"Kentucky," she whispers my name in uncertainty.

And that's when I smell it again. Underneath all the lust, there's a small bitter twinge of fear.

Closing my eyes to regain some self-control, I push away from my beloved to get some needed space. I can't look at her. If I do, I'll break. I'll throw caution to the wind and kiss her the way she deserves. Long, slow, and deep with hints of tongue. The kind of kisses that last all day and leave their mark. Anyone would be able to tell what we were up to by our swollen lips because we wouldn't be able to get enough of one another.

The scent of her being afraid of me hurts more than any challenge this world has given me. It hurts more than Audrey's betrayal and even more than Daphne's death. I'm not sure what kind of man that makes me admitting that, but this is my fated mate, someone meant *for* me.

"Kentucky, I—"

I lift my hand to stop her. "—It's okay, Darlin'. The last thing I want when I kiss you is for you to be afraid." I inhale a deep breath, gaining control of my body. The red tint fades from my vision, and my fangs sheath themselves. Even my claws retract. "But make no mistake, Dru. It isn't *if* I kiss you, but *when*."

"When do you think that will be?"

I hope in less than a week. The truth is on the tip of my tongue, wanting to break free, but I swallow it. I don't want her to kiss me because she feels doomed. I want her to come to me because she wants to feel me against her. That will mean more than the seven-day timeline ever will.

"I can't believe you almost kissed her in front of me. Yuck."

I cut my eyes to Romeo, who is staring daggers at me. *"Mind your business."*

"I couldn't if I tried since you're in the barn."

"I don't have time for your attitude right now, Romeo."

Romeo huffs, stomping his left hoof onto the ground as he begrudgingly accepts the harsh tone of my voice.

"I should go."

I spin on my heels, watching as she slides off the tailgate. Even in clothes that are three times her size and with the wariness of her expression, she's breathtakingly beautiful.

Even when she fears me.

"Yeah, that's probably a good idea." I bring my fist to cover my mouth as I clear my throat. "Go rest. I won't be in until later. I still have a lot of work to do."

She nods, opening her mouth to say something, then decides against it.

"Dru?" I stop her before she leaves.

"Kentucky?"

I take her hand in mine, wrapping my fingers around her hers to pull her knuckles to my lips, and kiss them softly. "Have a pleasant evening."

Her smile threatens her lips, suddenly a bit shy. "I hope you do too, Kentucky."

Against every urge and want piling inside me, she takes her hand away, her fingers slipping away from me.

Turning around, she bends down to pick up the umbrella. The rain is unforgiving at this point, coming down in punishing bullets. Lifting the black canopy above her, Dru walks out of the barn into the storm.

Lightning sparks across the sky, and she jumps from the loud, audible crack.

"Come on, Darlin'. Turn around for me, let me have a little hope," I mumble to myself, never taking my eyes off her. "Come on, come on," I beg the universe.

I've never asked for anything from this world other than to leave me alone to die, but now, I'm desperate like a drought thirsting for water.

As if I've summoned hope itself, Dru stops, her shoes becoming ruined with mud. The rain beats against the umbrella, mimicking a drum that fills the silence between us.

She peers over her shoulder, her brows furrowing together in thought. That hazel gaze graces me while she nibbles on her bottom lip.

"You're going to let her go?" Romeo asks.

"I have to," I reply, wincing in pain as if she's slapped me across the face when she removes me from her sight to continue towards the house.

"Go get her!" Romeo nudges his nose against my shoulder, shoving his vampiric strength into my shoulder, and it sends me forward.

"I can't," I snarl. "She's afraid of me. I won't kiss her knowing that. She'd be kissing me because she'd have to because she felt coerced."

"Or maybe you'd show her there is no reason to fear her fated mate," he says.

"Life ain't a romantic comedy, Romeo. It doesn't work that way."

"How would you know? You've never tried."

"Maybe tomorrow."

"There are good vampires and bad ones. It's the same for humans. There are ones with morals and ethics, and then there are ones that thrive off pain and fear. You are still a man, Kentucky. A vampire, yes, but a good man. They are one and the same."

I give Romeo a pat on the side of the neck with a forced, tight-lipped grin. "Thanks. I appreciate that, but it's only been a day. She deserves her space. She deserves to make the choice to come to me after what she has been through."

"Don't let her leave or you'll be signing your death certificate."

"This isn't about me, Romeo. It's about her and if she'd rather die than be with me, then I need to respect that."

He shoves me again. *"How would she know those are her options when you haven't even told her?"*

Guilt settles in my gut. I know he's right. I need to be forthcoming, but that's hard to do when dealing with a human mate, especially one who was kidnapped and tortured by someone who is a vampire.

Somehow, I need Dru to fall in love with me in seven days and decide this is the life she wants. Forcing her to accept me won't do either of us any good.

"Don't be so complacent or accepting of this situation. Are you still hoping to die? Is that why you aren't running after her in the rain? I hear that's romantic."

"What do you know about romance?"

"Enough to know that Dru isn't the only one with fears they are holding onto."

I cock a brow at my horse. "You're sounding more like my therapist. I don't need you giving me life lessons."

"Apparently, you do, considering you don't know what you're doing with your extended life. You're waiting to wither away when a chance of happiness is knocking at your door."

"Don't make me use silver on your shoes," I mutter.

I want to clarify that I would never do that. I only like to give him a hard time.

He exhales through his nose. *"I'd like to see you try."*

"Alright, jokes aside, it's time for a trim. Give me your leg."

"No."

I sigh, a throb building in my temples from annoyance and hunger for Dru's blood. I have to push that aside. Her blood is something I might not ever have the pleasure of tasting, and the sooner I wrap my head around that, the better off I'll be.

Hope is by far the most deadly emotion there is. It's dangerous. The pesky feeling lifts your soul so high that you begin to build confidence that life will go your way—and then, like the ruthless bitch hope is—it pulls the rug from under you until you're on your back.

Hope and Karma have to be related because both are cruel mistresses toying with a man's emotions.

"Romeo, give me your damn foot."

"No."

I yank my hat off and toss it in the bed of the truck, getting unreasonably frustrated with his antics. "I said give me your damn hoof, Romeo," I snarl.

He blows a raspberry, his lips vibrating together before he backs up, turns, and has the audacity to walk himself to his stall. He bites the rope attached to the door and tugs it closed, leaving me standing in the middle of the barn alone.

"Really? Really, Romeo? You're going to be mad at me for not running after her?"

Silence.

"Romeo!" I belt, knowing damn well he can hear me.

Again, silence.

"You really piss me off more than a raccoon is when it's wet." I huff, knowing I have other chores I need to do.

"That doesn't even make sense. Raccoons love water and know how to swim," he finally responds, and of course, it is to correct me.

I throw my hands up in the air, completely done with this conversation. "I don't know how you know that."

"Animals talk."

I pinch the bridge of my nose, not knowing what to say to that. Romeo is obviously done with my company for the day, and I need to get the hay to the row barn for the cattle.

"Okay, fine then. I'm getting back to work. Stay here in

your stall then." I jump onto the bed of the truck, snag my hat, and cover the hay with a tarp.

Hopping to the ground, I lift the tailgate and slam it into place. My fingers trace the indentations I've left behind. Her scent lingers, the warm spice of her lust clings to the air, taunting me.

Hanging my head, I clutch the same spots dented into my truck. This woman is going to test me in ways I never thought were possible. I remember thinking that Audrey was the biggest event that ever happened to me. Being with her was a test in itself. I understand now that she never loved me but was using me, and I allowed it.

My entire life leading up to the day I got turned had been unremarkable. I was alone. My mother died giving birth to me, and I never knew who my father was. My uncle raised me, and when he died in my early twenties, I figured the rest of my days would be spent alone.

The ranch would have had to be sold if I got too old to manage it, since I had no one to pass it down to. The more I think about how truly alone I was, the more I think Audrey knew that no one would miss me if I were gone.

She had hoped turning me would be the answer to my lonesome nature. I'm giving her too much credit. She wasn't that kind. She had hoped it would give her more purpose than she had.

The thing is, there's a difference between being alone and being lonely. Being alone is peaceful and resonating. There's nothing like being in the pasture and watching the sunset after a long day. The soul becomes healed staring at a fading horizon promising another early morning will come.

Loneliness is deeper than that. When your own company is no longer enough, your heart begins to ache for love that hasn't seemed to find you yet. It's a heavy burden to carry, a tragic ailment that will eventually kill. Loneliness is a murderer who takes its time to suck every inch of life out of you before you come to the decision that you've had enough.

In a way, it's a vampire, taking every ounce from your heart until it finally stops beating.

Is that what's wrong with me? All this time, I've been alone, but have I been lonely instead?

I stare out into the pouring rain, wishing Dru were still standing there looking at me over her shoulder. She's in the house now. The porch light is faint in the haze of the weather, acting like a beacon to bring me to her.

As much as I would love to walk through my front door and spend the evening trying to get to know Dru, I think it's best if both of us have a little space tonight. I know she's confused, and I don't trust myself not to feed from her without permission.

The more time we spend together, the hungrier I become for her.

I climb into the truck and grip the wheel, leaning my head against the headrest to take a moment for myself. I don't know how she takes her coffee, and I love her more than I want death.

I loved Daphne as much as I could, but what I am already feeling for Dru? It's so much deeper than love. The notion of love doesn't come close to the enamored infatuation that is heavy within my body, in my stomach, clawing its way to what's left of my humanity and latching on.

I'm completely desperate for her in ways that are beyond comprehension.

The more I focus on her, the more I can sense her. I feel her in my home. I can't tell which room she's in because our bond isn't strong enough yet for me to track her in that way, but she's there.

If we were mated, I would be able to perceive any and all emotions she has. In turn, it means she would be able to feel everything I feel, and that might scare me more than dying ever has.

She'd be able to finally have the weight of the loneliness I've been bearing for all these years. She'd know intimately the most vulnerable part of me—the part that has been aching for *more*.

Dru would be able to feel how much I wanted to die. There would be no escaping that. Not wanting death is so new to me, I'm not sure if I believe it yet. I've convinced myself that living isn't important for more years than most will ever live.

The old pickup truck grumbles to life. The thick purr reminds me of when the first automobile was invented in the 1870s. I remember being in awe of such technology. I never thought I'd live to see the day cars were invented.

And now there are too many types of vehicles to keep track of.

Never thought I'd be alive for that either.

The squeak of the windshield wipers brings me back to reality, staring out of a cracked windshield being pelted with rain. I can't see two inches in front of me. Luckily, I could drive the path in my sleep. The brakes squeak when I come to a stop, pressing the button I have for the tall metal gate to swing open.

When I'm through, the mechanical door swings shut, locking the bar in place. The road dips from the uneven path, causing me to bounce in my seat as this old girl trucks up the hill, tires slipping and sliding every few feet.

"Kentucky!"

"Kentucky's here!"

"Come on, ladies!"

I grin when I hear their thoughts slamming into me. "Hey, everyone. Meet me at the row barn. Get out of this storm," I shout out the window, rain pouring into the cab and soaking my pant leg.

Pulling into the barn, the rain finally stops beating the rust off my truck. Lightning dances gracefully through the ominous dark clouds, a ballerina performing a powerful show for all to witness.

Slamming the truck in park, I do something I don't typically do; I use my enhanced speed. Ripping the tarp off the hay bales, I stack as many as I can before blurring to the rows and filling the feeders. Dispersing the hay is easy with my claws, dividing it up perfectly amongst the cows.

"Thank you, Kentucky."

"Thank youuuu," is mooed from another corner.

"Thanks!" a smaller voice chirps.

"You're welcome. Try not to go outside, okay? It's getting nasty out there, and some of you are about to give birth. Play it safe, ladies."

The entire group moos in unison.

"Great."

I pop the tailgate down and take a seat, staring down at the house that holds my fate. Thunder shakes the ground, causing the truck to slightly quake. Bolts continue to shock the sky with their anger, a blinding white shooting through the clouds.

Rain fills the gutters, and small creeks drain across the yard. In all my years, I've never seen the climate so mad before. The storms are worse, devastating entire states, obliterating people's homes. I haven't seen a tornado rip through these parts in at least a decade, but it wasn't anything serious. Lately, I've been wondering if that streak is coming to an end.

I'll have to keep an eye out tonight and guard the house. I refuse to let anything happen to Dru, storm or not, her life will never be at risk.

The wind howls, reminding me of a wolf signaling his pack. The memory of those shifters hiding Dru comes to mind, and I snarl, wishing I could kill them all over again.

My eyes focus on my new lasso hanging on the side of the barn. I might have taken a few shifter spines and fused them together, creating the most lethal weapon I've had besides Romeo.

They're my trophies.

And if Dru wants, she'll be able to hold her abuser's spines in her bare hands, proving who the weak ones really are.

Anyone who dares touch her again, I vow they will be a wonderful addition to the lasso.

I jump off the truck, my boots scuffing the ground as I walk to the edge where the roof stops. The pull to her is strong. Heat warms my body, sweat soaking through my shirt, and I tug it over my head. God, I feel like if I don't get to Dru, I'll rip out of my own fucking skin.

I want her.

I need her.

She's mine. She's all mine.

Why can't I have her?

I can't. I can't take away her will.

I won't take away her will.

One step into the rain and the cool touch of water extinguishes the wild fever I just had. I take a deep breath, my cock still stretching the denim jeans. I've never felt this kind of want before. I ache.

I fucking *ache.*

I crouch, leaping onto the second story of the barn. I keep a room up here for when I want to sleep closer to the stars.

Ripping off the chaps, I toss them on the small cot in the corner.

"Come on, Kentucky. Snap out of it." I grip the edge of the barn door, leaning out the window to allow the rain to hit me again.

The water soaks my hair, drenching me until it slips over my lips like a beverage after a hard day's work.

The need barely eases. But my skin isn't on fire like it was before.

Fuck, my fangs throb in agony from wanting to sink into her. I reach to touch one, and the threat of my finger ghosting over the point causes another wave of pain to pulse through the tooth.

"Fuck!" I roar so loudly, the monster inside me grips my throat, turning my shout into a guttural howl, and I fall to the floor.

My nails dig into the floorboards, engraving long grooves as I fight the need to jump out of this window to take what is rightfully mine.

I rip my pants open with my claws, free myself, and fuck my fist. It will have to do.

For now.

DEAD MAN'S
RANCH

CHAPTER EIGHT
DRUSCILLA

I know I shouldn't be spying on him. It isn't right. He deserves his space just like I deserve mine, but when I walked into the empty house, I missed him.

That's ridiculous, isn't it? Missing someone I barely know. I don't understand this need to be close to him at all times. Most of me believes he isn't the monster I thought, yet, there is another part that is screaming to run and never look back.

The mere thought of turning my back on Kentucky has pain searing through my heart. Kentucky is so much more than I originally judged him to be. I thought he was a monster, a killer, someone who was playing with his food. Even though it has only been one very long day of being here, the truth is, I'm not sure if I do want to leave.

I don't understand why, but he knows the answer. I'm not the kind of woman to leave when I don't have all the information. I refuse to have anyone else make decisions for me. No one has ever had that power over me, and they never will. I've always listened to myself. My instincts have never steered me wrong. I only want to understand why I'm so drawn to him and why the thought of leaving makes me sick to my stomach.

He's different than what I thought a vampire was. He's a gentleman. He has manners that I've only seen in old romantic movies. He cares to have self-control if his fighting his vampire urges in the barn tells me anything. That means more in this world than he knows.

Most human men don't even try that hard.

The rolling baritone of thunder has me blinking away my inner turmoil. I glance around the rustic living room, knowing I shouldn't peek into the telescope again to peer into the pasture where Kentucky is. I need to get my mind off him.

It's an impossible task when I'm surrounded by him.

The living room is open to the kitchen, surrounded by floor-to-ceiling windows, and there are more of them than drywall in this house. I wonder if he likes natural light or just likes being able to see outside. Whatever the reason, I love it.

There's a worn leather sectional couch sitting in front of the fireplace, and a coffee table that looks handmade with the same designs as the bedroom door. There is simplicity to the decor. I can tell he hasn't really made himself at home. Usually, people have personal touches like art hanging on the wall, pictures of friends or family, books lying around, but the house is almost stale.

Clearly, he only rests here.

If I lived here, I would change that.

Why am I thinking like that? This isn't my house. I don't live here. In a few days, I'll be home in the comfort of my own bed, surrounded by books, movies, records, pictures, and everything else that makes me, *me*. That brings me peace like the dozens of blankets I have that I love to wrap myself in while lying in bed and watching TV.

I dart my eyes around the room, twisting and turning my body to see if I'm missing it.

Nope.

Kentucky doesn't have a TV.

The wind howls outside, causing the trees to smack against the glass, and I jump, startled by how loud it is.

The rain is bulleting against the windows too, and in the distance, the trees sway and lightning strobes in the clouds. With every burst of light, the sky illuminates the pasture, the long grass swaying back and forth.

It's serene.

Unable to stop myself any longer, I lean down and place my eye against the telescope, guiding it left, right, up, and down to find where Kentucky is. He was by his truck, but he isn't there anymore.

"Where did you go?" I ask no one other than myself.

My sights finally land on him, and a breath catches in my throat when I take in his bare chest. I straighten, knowing I can't look at him without him being aware.

That would be wrong. So very wrong.

I nibble on my thumbnail with anxiety, staring at the telescope and debating if I should walk away.

The temptation is too strong.

He doesn't need to find out.

Bending down again, I rearrange the focus on the lens to get the clearest view of Kentucky I can. He is gripping the top of the window frame, leaning out to allow the rain to drench his body.

"Damn," I whisper to the empty room, thankful that I'm alone or I'd be embarrassed gawking over him.

The water slicks his torso, defining the hard ridges of every muscle. His chest and shoulders are wide, built with large muscles that only come from working on a ranch his entire life.

He slicks his hair back, away from his eyes, the twin crimson drops glowing in the chaos of the storm. His mouth opens, the low light from the barn shines against the pointed fangs, and his roar is so loud, it causes a picture to fall from the mantle.

I'll pick it up in a minute.

In response, my blood heats, and a light sheen of sweat causes his shirt to stick to my back.

I straighten again, fanning myself from the overwhelming sudden warmth that not only has my cheeks burning, but my underwear drenched. My clit throbs with need, my nipples tighten under the shirt, and the material lightly scratches against them. The slight sensation causes me to pinch my lips shut to hold in a gasp.

I can't look at him again. It isn't right. It's wrong. Everything about me lusting after him is hypocritical. He should be everything I'm against.

I can't help it.

I have to. I *need* to see him. If I don't, I might scream until I die, until I run out of air, and don't care to take another inhale because living for another second without seeing him wouldn't be worth it.

Peering into the telescope, my mouth becomes dry from what I see. Kentucky is kneeling, eyes once again the color of a predator, frustration and pleasure snarling his face, and his hand stroking his thick cock.

"Oh my god," I gasp, licking my lips as if I need to quench my thirst by licking the rain off his body.

His head is tossed back, one arm leans against the barn, while his other hand is busy fucking his cock. Kentucky's sculpted muscles are tense, the veins in his arm defined by the stern grip he has on himself.

By how his nails have lengthened to claws and his facial features seem a little sharper, more cut and angled, he is in full vampire form. Another roar rips from him, the vibrations tickling the pads of my feet. He's staring at the house through the storm, his free hand slamming against the ground. His claws create grooves in the wood as if he is holding himself back from launching himself in my direction.

The longer he stares at the house, the more I begin to wonder if his struggle is due to me.

And for some reason, I *really* love the sound of that.

Watching Kentucky lose himself to me has my hand drift down my chest, stomach, then dip under the waistband. My fingers graze over the trimmed hair I keep, caressing over my throbbing clit. A rush of heat pools into my panties, my hole pulsating for more.

"Ahhh," I groan, slipping two fingers inside my pussy to try to ease the agony of not having *him* stretch me.

Knowing he doesn't *know* I'm watching him fuck himself has me so wet, I have to insert another finger. Rocking my hips against my hand, all I can think about is how I wish I were fucking him instead.

I moan when he lies down, whimpering when he wraps both hands around himself. His thumb swipes over the wide head before tracing the crown. I love the expression taking over his face. His mouth is parted, those sharp fangs on display, and his eyebrows furrow differently with every tight stroke he gives himself.

Tracing the crown again, he arches his back, and he slams a fist through the wooden floor. Another growl rumbles the windows, adding more sensations and bringing my orgasm closer to the surface.

"Oh, god!" I cry, taking my fingers until I reach my knuckles. I need more. I need so much more.

He arches his back again, exposing the defined grooves on either side of his hips. I wonder what those gasps falling from his lips sound like. What makes him moan and shout? Would he whisper how good he feels into my ear? Could I make him feel that good?

I shouldn't be doing this.

Oh, god, I can't stop watching him.

He's beautiful.

His hips begin to move, thrusting into the air, and the thought of me on top of him, taking him, being stretched by him, calling out his name, my orgasm slams into my bones.

I cry out, wave after wave of pleasure sweeping through my body. My head becomes dizzy with how intense each spasm is. My knees buckle, and I catch myself on the telescope, the cool metal pressing against my heated flesh.

Tugging my fingers free, I suck them into my mouth, licking the proof of how good Kentucky makes me feel away.

When the room stops spinning, I peer into the lens again, spying on him once more. The head of his cock is a blushing red as a bulging vein fills the length. Blood pumps into the impressive shaft so much, he looks so hard it seems painful.

Right now, I'd love to be the one to take his pain away.

I can't believe I just thought that about a vampire. Kentucky isn't just *any* vampire, though, is he?

He's mine.

I'm not sure where that thought comes from. He isn't mine. I don't plan for him to be. We are too different. What kind of life could we have if I'm a human and he is a vampire? I'd grow old and die while he gets to live forever? No. That's cruel.

It's best if we both realize that any type of pull we experience with one another, we ignore.

You can't.

The voice in the back of my head whispers another useless statement to me.

Yet as I watch Kentucky bringing himself closer to climax, I know the voice in the back of my head is right. All I can do is ignore it the best I can until I can go home.

You're staring at your home.

Kentucky clamors one last time, and the lightbulb in the

lamp to the right of me bursts, plunging me into darkness. The need for him is still there, a need that I can't seem to fix by myself.

If I watch him this one time, I'll be free. It will have to be enough to give in to this tiny fantasy of him before the real world creeps in again.

Just. This. Once.

Convincing myself is easy, but believing is another issue for another day.

I find the perfect angle of Kentucky. I get to see *everything*. From the strong muscles in his thighs bulging, to his long cock with girth that would cause me to lose my breath, to his handsome face pinched with lust, to the tensed tendons in his neck as white streams paint his chest—I get to see every sin.

It's the name that falls from his lips as he continues to orgasm. I can't hear him, but I can see the word forming as he spills his passion, over and over again.

Druscilla.

Druscilla.

Druscilla.

My name is on repeat with every pulse that flexes his cock. A jet of white lands on the side of his mouth, and saliva floods my tongue, wishing I could be the one to lick his mess clean.

I inhale a sharp gasp, covering my mouth with the hand that still carries the scent of my orgasm. Then witness him take his finger, wipe his come clean, and suck it into his mouth.

Oh, god. I moan internally, knowing if he and I ever fell into bed together, it would be explosive.

He lies there on his back, completely spent. If we were together, we could fall asleep, only to wake up to make a mess of each other again.

"Dreaming of things you shouldn't," I scold myself, yet don't remove myself from this telescope.

Kentucky sits up, wiping his chest with his shirt, then

tucks himself into his jeans. He leaves the button undone and the zipper down, revealing his happy trail that leads into a groomed brown bush.

Snagging his hat, he places it on top of his head, staring right into the lens as if he can see me on the other side. There's no way he can see that far, right? That amount of distance with the naked eye is impossible.

He hand walks forward until he is on his knees, gripping the edge of the floorboards. His knuckles turn white, and the pouring rain slams against him in abusive sheets, soaking him.

Dipping his chin, he hides his eyes, but it's the crooked smile tilting the left side of his lips. He shows a flash of fang that has me staggering backwards and falling onto the couch.

He knew somehow. He knew I was watching him. Embarrassment is a fever taking over my body. I bury my face in my hands, wondering when the exact moment was that he knew I was spying on him. This is so unlike me. I have never acted this way before in my life. Kentucky brings out a side of me that I didn't know existed. And I'm not sure how I feel about that.

"Damn it, Dru." I groan in frustration.

All I can do is hope he doesn't bring this up to talk about. I fan my face again, another brutal heat wave causing my body to betray me. I have no idea what is going on, but this isn't summer heat. This isn't because it's warm in the house and I need air conditioning. My blood feels hot. There's a constant sheen of sweat cloaking me from head to toe. My arousal is still high. A pulse stays in the sensitive bundle of my clit, causing more lust to pool in my panties.

I'm not hungry or thirsty. The only thing I find myself wanting to sate my needs is Kentucky.

"He's a vampire," I tell myself through clenched teeth. I'm sick of this. I'm tired of feeling like I have no control when it comes to how I want to feel about him.

My mind says one thing, yet my body and heart say another.

"You can't want him. Remember what Louis did to you, Dru. Remember, they are hunters. Kentucky doesn't care about you. You're just a means to an end." Hearing the words helps ease the fire boiling in my blood, the feverish need lets its strangled hold on me go, and I'm able to breathe.

I stand, waiting to see if the dizziness will cause the room to spin again. My surroundings stay in place, and I let out a breath, relieved I have control of myself. In the last few days, with the chaos of being kidnapped by a vampire and then lusting after one, a demonic possession of my body seems to be the only answer that could make these events have any sense.

Stretching over the faded recliner nestled in the corner, I flip the switch on the wall, and the light comes on, blinding me for a nanosecond. I rub my eyes, blinking away the spots floating around in my vision when I catch sight of the picture that fell off the mantle. It's lying face down on the emerald, green rug.

"Huh," I say with curiosity, glancing around the room to see if I missed other photos hanging on the wall when I looked the first time.

There aren't any.

Whoever is in this picture frame must be very important, and I am too nosy not to know who it is. I'm careful when I pick it up, not wanting to jostle the glass in case it is broken.

I flip the photo over, the polished golden frame shines so bright, I can see my reflection. There is a crack from the upper left corner that travels across to the bottom right, cutting directly in front of the image.

For reasons I can't explain or understand, my heart fractures when I'm faced with another woman. She's beautiful too, the kind of beauty that only existed in another time. I can't tell from how faded the image is, but her hair is blonde or maybe a light red, and her eyebrows are thin, but considering the era, that doesn't surprise me. Thin brows were the trend for the longest time.

Her eyes are bright, shining with a happiness that matches her delicate smile. She seems kind and gentle. Just by looking at her, I can tell she must have been soft spoken.

A tear drips from my cheek and onto the glass. I wipe it away before it has a chance to get into the crack. I have no idea why I'm crying or why knowing Kentucky loved someone before meeting me bothers me so much. I shouldn't care that he had a life. He lives for so much longer than a human being. I would be surprised if he didn't love multiple women throughout the years.

I don't blame him for that.

"Why do I care? This doesn't make sense! This is maddening!" I growl in frustration. "I shouldn't care," I say to the woman in the photo. "I don't understand why I feel the way I do about him. A part of me hates that you got to his heart, that you got to him first, but I also know that wouldn't be fair of me." I set her down on the mantle again, trying to remember the exact position she was in.

My legs hit the couch when I take a step back to see how she looks above the fireplace. The living room light reflects off something small to the left of the woman in the frame.

Nosey me, I step forward to see a silver necklace. The chain is thin and light between my fingers as I hold it up in the air.

It's a locket.

I press the small piece of metal, keeping the locket closed, then flick it open.

All the air is sucked from my lungs. More tears flow down my cheeks the longer I stare at what the locket holds inside.

Kentucky is on the left, and a picture of them together is on the right.

They are so in love. She's looking up at him with adoration, and he's laughing. I didn't know he could laugh. I don't think I've seen him smile. The scene captured looks like a candid moment more than a planned photoshoot.

He had an entire life before I met him.

I have no answers as to why my heart is broken. Kentucky has nothing to do with me. He's allowed to love who he wants to love. He's allowed to have other experiences.

Then why am I so hurt?

If I don't get answers soon as to why I feel like this, I'm going to lose any and all ability to have any rational thoughts. The longer I'm here, the more confused I become. He's starting to infiltrate my being, the part that makes my soul free, and I don't know how to untangle myself from him.

Sniffling, I hang the necklace on the corner of the frame, wondering how this woman loved a vampire.

Maybe it was because the vampire in question is Kentucky. Maybe that's the difference.

Lifting my shoulders, I wipe my cheeks on the Dead Man's Ranch shirt, getting the faintest hint of Kentucky's scent. Another ache adds to the fractures splintering across my heart.

I become exhausted the longer I stare at her photo and being wrapped in his clothes. Needing space, I dash down the hall to get away from her, from him, from it all, and into the room I'm staying in.

I jump onto the soft bed, burying my face in the pillow.

And I sob.

I'm breaking into too many ways to be fixed.

I miss him.

But I'm not allowed to because Kentucky Jones' heart belongs to someone else.

CHAPTER NINE
KENTUCKY

I can't sleep.

I lie wide awake on this bumpy cot, staring up at the ceiling to see I need to clean the beams. With my enhanced vision, I zero in on the large spider creating an intricate web. I'm always fascinated by spider webs. They are so beautiful and strong, yet deadly to a spider's prey.

I relate all too well. In this case, I'm the web, and Dru is the unfortunate soul who is trapped in it.

I sigh, rolling to my side to get comfortable.

Then, the other side.

Finally, I roll to my back, staring back up at the filthy beams.

"Damn it," I say to the empty space, my restlessness getting the best of me.

Who am I kidding? I'm not going to be able to sleep another damn day until I know what will happen between Dru and me.

"Need me to sing you a lullaby?"

The irritating sound of Lorcan's voice has me snag my hat

and place it over my face, hoping the Void takes it as a hint to leave me alone.

"I know a great Purgatory song. It will definitely help you fall asleep, but you also might never wake up again. You have a fifty-fifty shot. Do you like the odds before I start doing my voice exercises? I need to warm up."

"Lorcan, what do you want?" I drowse, interlacing my fingers across my chest to get comfortable.

The bottom edge of the cot dips from him making himself at home. "I'm here to check on you. That's what friends do, Kentucky. I know you wouldn't know that because you're a loner, blah blah blah, and whatever other bullshit you say."

I take my hat off, exhaling with aggravation as I stare at his cloaked figure. "I'm fine, Lorcan. No need to check in so much. I've been fine for all these years, I'll be fine for more."

"So you're agreeing to eternity, then? You're agreeing that you can't fight Fate, no matter how much you want to."

I sit up, swinging my legs over the edge of the cot and placing my elbows on my thighs. "Lorcan, I'm not fighting Fate. I'm just not completely accepting of it, considering Fate hasn't necessarily dealt the best cards for me."

"You are so maddening." He stands, drifting over to the door. His long black cloak drags across the floorboards, disrupting the dust. "You have no idea how many paranormals would kill to be in your shoes, to have a mate, to know they won't be spending the rest of their days alone. I'm included in that. I am..." He tries to find the words as he stares out of the loft. "I am envious of the gift that has fallen on your doorstep. I don't understand, and I will never understand why you are resisting. You infuriate me."

With a sharp turn on his head, Lorcan's glare bores into me, the once blackened holes now shine a furious orange—the same color I imagine Hell's flames would be. "You have a gift in your home, and yet you are here," he spits with disgust.

"Withering away in a fucking barn that reeks of cow shit, by the way. If anything, I wish Dru could be free of you so she can have a love that is worthy of her."

Like smoke, I'm in front of him in less than a second, my hand wrapped around his neck, snarling. I draw my gun, pressing it under his chin, and pull the hammer, the click audible in the silence of the loft.

"You better watch how you speak to me, Lorcan. Friend or not, I have no issue trying to kill you even if every attempt fails because every fucking attempt will bring me joy. If you dare, for one fucking minute, think you can come onto my property, speak of wanting my mate, and wishing her away from me. If you weren't already dead, I would think you have a death wish."

His bony fingers circle around my wrist one by one. The orbital sockets of his eyes ignite into fire, the orange flickering and swaying the more anger takes hold. "That's hilarious coming from you—a man who has wished for nothing but death since the moment he was turned. Poor pitiful you, Kentucky. If it is death that you wish for"— like a phantom, his hand disappears into my chest, and the sharp points of his fleshless fingers latch around my heart—"I can give it to you. The peace that you have been longing for, the silence you have been dreaming of, the moment of your life finally coming to an end—it can happen right now."

I choke for breath as his grip tightens around my heart, the bones threatening to puncture the delicate tissue.

"Isn't this what you want, Kentucky? To be free of this world, this pain that you are always feeling, the bitterness, the betrayal? You can have everything you have wanted at last. I'm only offering this opportunity one time."

"That would mean Dru dies," I croak, doing my best not to move in sudden motions.

"I didn't think you cared about that."

I thought I had him by the throat, but Lorcan is much stronger than he has let on. An invisible force pulses from him, pushing me away until my hand is free from his neck. The Void still has his forearm deep within my chest, toying with my life.

"Seems like you've been waiting to do this a long time, Lorcan."

"I haven't," he admits, the brow bones pinching together as if he is hurt I have asked that question. "You are my friend. When you were turned, it was me who took your maker's soul to Purgatory. I freed you from her. I have stayed by your side all these years to see if you would make a change in your path, because Kentucky, your struggles that you have experienced, do not end in death. They follow you to the afterlife. Free her from your fucking misery, Kentucky. Let me take her to Purgatory, and I will give her a fresh start, a new fated mate in a new dimension where you will never be able to find her."

Growling, I grab onto his arm and tug it, forcing him deeper into my chest until his fingers touch my spine. "Fucking try to take her from me when I haven't had a chance to have her to myself, and I will drag you to the pits of Hell myself, Lorcan. I will only exist to torture you. Take me to Purgatory, fine, but it won't mean you will be rid of me. I will be your shadow, the noise you hear in the dark, and you'll wonder if it is me." I lean in, smelling the scent of smoke and flame off his cloak. "And it will be. It isn't up to you to decide what she wants, and it isn't up to you to decide what I need. Dru and I will work this out together because this is between her and me. If she wants a new life, a new mate, a new beginning, then I will gladly let you rip my heart out that day."

Drawing my weapon again, I press the barrel between the endless pools of fire. "Let me go, or it will be your spine I add to my lasso, Lorcan."

He tilts his head, the warmth of the blaze flickering inside the coal caverns, heating my face. "You think I'm scared of you haunting the night? You have no idea what being afraid is until you are a Void, slithering from dimension to dimension, taking souls of the foulest beings known in the universe. And you think a vampire like you could ever put fear into me?"

He pushes his forehead against the weapon, and a clicking sound that I've never heard before comes from the back of his throat. "It's laughable that you think I would fear a creature such as a vampire. Especially one who knows so little about his kind or abilities or lore or fated mates or anything else related to the issue. You have isolated yourself due to fear of who you are. I do not share that emotion because I like who I am. Can you say the same, Kentucky? Can you admit that you are at peace with your life now, or do you still ache to be put out of your misery?" The words are spoken from a villain, not the friend whom I have known for more years than I can remember. "I will give you until your week is up before you or Dru begin to experience agony so unbearable, you will beg for me to stake you."

Tired of hearing him speak, I pull the trigger. His head jerks back from the force of the bullet penetrating his skull. Lorcan straightens, a mad cackle leaving between his teeth. He snags my wrist, guiding the gun to his nose, and he inhales the smoke drifting from the barrel.

He exhales through his mouth, blowing the gunpowder-filled cloud into my face. "Mmm, it's been so long since I've taken a hit. Smells good." Lorcan plucks the bullet from between his eyes and lifts it into the air, examining it. "You make your own bullets. That's impressive." He flicks the flattened piece of metal across the room and steps closer. "Don't ever shoot me again, Kentucky, or I'll stake you and make your afterlife worse than the life you thought you had here. You might be powerful, but there are always creatures more powerful than you. I am one of them."

"Don't test me again, and I won't."

"I can't promise that," he says. "Testing you seems to be the only way to get the truth. I won't ever stop doing that."

I groan, holstering my gun. "You make me madder than—"

"—No." He places his fingers against my lips. "Shhh. No. We don't need another Southern allegory that paints a picture of your anger. I get it. You're mad. And you know what, you're not really good at the allegories."

I pick up my hat that fell onto the floor, dusting the soft material off with my hand before placing it on my head. "Are we good, or do I need to shoot you again to leave me alone?"

"Well, that won't work. I love the smell of gunsmoke too much. So that's just foreplay for me, baby."

"Don't call me baby. Don't make me..." I almost say shoot you, but remember he likes it. "Don't make me go get the barn kittens."

An audible gasp escapes him, a hand flying to his chest. "That's so rude."

"You make no sense, Lorcan. A gunshot is a whole lot ruder."

"Everyone has their preferences. Friends? I forgive you for shooting me." He holds out the hand he had inside my chest, strangely, it isn't covered in blood.

"Friends." I grip his hand for a firm shake. "Maybe I need to try to get out of my bubble."

"You should try. If you choose death, that's devastating, Kentucky. You think your world is dark now? You haven't experienced pitch black. Sure, you're weighed down by emotion, but you can't have that in Purgatory, or it can get you killed. You have five days, give or take a few, because every couple is different. I'll be here to take your souls if that's what you choose, but please don't make me reap a friend." His hand lands on my shoulder, giving it a tight squeeze.

"I'll do my best, but I won't make any decisions for Dru. She has to want this as much as I do. I won't force her."

The orange illuminating in the caves of his eyes vanishes, leaving me to stare at an empty abyss. "I understand," he says. "Very honorable of you. You've always been the most respectful vampire I've met. It's finally time to enjoy your life, Kentucky. Give it a chance. I doubt it will disappoint you this time."

An owl hoots nearby, probably perched on a low-hanging branch of the tree next to the barn.

"I have to go. Souls are calling for me." He turns to walk away, flipping the back of his cloak in a drama-filled fashion, and it fits his personality.

"Do you reap humans too?" I ask before he leaves.

"All souls that exist. I don't work alone. There are thousands of Voids. I have a ton of brothers and sisters."

"Must be a heavy burden to carry."

He frowns, a sudden sadness filling the air. "It is. We feel everything. The pain, confusion, fear, sadness, and we even see their deaths. For new Voids, it can be bad. There's an adjustment period, but the burden never fades, not really. We just learn to live with it."

And then he is gone, nothing left of his presence except the bullet that is on the floor.

My spurs spin with every step I take to the edge of the loft, needing to feel the breeze against my face. There isn't a star in the sky. The galaxy is covered in sardonic clouds promising more rain. Moisture hangs in the air, the earthy scent of wet dirt has frogs croaking in the distance and singing in the rain.

Crossing my arms over my chest, I stare down at the house I've built with my bare hands, and there's something so satisfying in knowing my mate is there, safe and sound within the walls I've built.

After all this time, maybe I've been waiting for a reason to turn this house I've spent my entire life perfecting into a home. All of it, every door and window, every add-on, maybe it was all for my mate.

Am I really entertaining this idea of living forever?

I rub my eyes, blowing out a pent-up breath. It is easier said than done to change the course of what I thought was the rest of my life. For more years than Dru has been alive, I've had a plan. From the moment I was turned, I knew death was the only acceptable answer, but only when my vampire life came to a natural end.

I don't know many people who get so many chances to live. Is Dru supposed to be "The third time is the charm" kind of deal? Why now?

A whimper pulls me from my self-inflicted confusion. I zone in on the house below, waiting to hear the noise again.

A few seconds tick by without another sound. "Losing your damn mind." I wonder if hearing random things is a side effect of not having the bond complete. It has to be.

I press my palms against my eyes and yawn, spinning on my heel to head back to the cot when I hear the whimper again.

And again.

Red colors my vision, my fangs lengthen to prepare to attack. "Dru," I growl, leaping from the loft. Mud splashes all over my jeans when I land, my boots sinking into the wet ground.

Blurring through the front door and to her bedroom, I pause at the doorway. She's restless in her sleep. Dru has kicked the quilt I hand-stitched down to the edge of the bed. Sweat pebbles on her forehead while a tear breaks free, sadness rolling down her cheek.

I kick off my shoes, not wanting to get mud all over her bedroom floor, and then realize I have mud on my jeans too.

Fuck.

I blur to my room to get a clean pair of sweatpants, then speed back into her room.

It's hard to take a breath in here when the air is thick with fear. It's suffocating, like breathing in a room full of cigarette smoke.

Dru screams, "No! No, please, don't. No!"

As gently as I can, I lie down next to her. The sheets are damp from her sweat, and the shirt she's wearing sticks to her skin. She's burning up. Swallowing my own trepidations, I wrap my arms around her waist and pull her close to me until my bare chest is against her back.

Brushing her hair behind her ear, I whisper, "You're okay, Dru. You're with me. You're safe. Come back to me, Darlin'. Come back."

She whimpers in response, her lashes fluttering while she fights to break the hold this dream has on her.

"I'm right here. You're safe." I stroke my knuckles up and down her arm, hoping touch lifts the nightmare from her mind.

Another fresh dose of terror fills the room before her eyes open. She turns to me, eyes wide, pupils blown, and she screams, pushing me away by shoving me in the chest.

"Get away from me! Get away!" she shouts, but she doesn't recognize me. "Don't hurt me. Please, let me go!"

She's still dreaming.

I snag her in my arms, placing my fingers under her chin, and force her to look at me. "Wake up, Dru. You're safe with me. It's Kentucky. You aren't with him anymore. Come back to me. Come back." I kiss her wet cheeks, tasting the salt in her tears. "I'm not going to let him touch you again, Darlin'. If he ever tries, I'm going to kill him. I'll add his spine to my lasso, okay? I need you to follow my voice. You can do it." I stroke my calloused finger down her cheek, appreciating how someone so beautiful could ever exist.

Dru is prettier than any sunset, sunrise, or shooting star I have seen in my old age. I love the freckles dashed across her cheeks and nose, a map showing me where to kiss.

"Kentucky?"

I blow out a breath when she says my name. I hold her close, cupping the back of her head, and press her against my chest.

"I'm here, Darlin'. You were having a nightmare, that's all. I have you." I press a kiss to her forehead, loving how she sinks into my embrace. "You're safe. I'm not going to let anything happen to you. I promise."

"Kentucky," she murmurs half-asleep. "So glad it's you." Those are her last words before sleep takes her again. She gets comfortable, lying her head on my chest, her palm lying over my heart.

But you know what makes me happiest?

Fear is no longer a ghost in the room. The air is clean with relief.

She isn't afraid of me, and damn, that alone puts me on top of the world.

DEAD MAN'S
RANCH

Chapter Ten

DRUSCILLA

A strong scent of pine and coffee wakes me up.

My eyes blink open in sluggish flutters. The cool drying of drool has me wiping my mouth, only for my hand to hit a body.

A very firm, large body.

Oh, no.

I jolt into a sitting position, my vision still blurry with sleep. Sliding my eyes down, my mind begins to whirl with possibilities as to why Kentucky is in bed with me. He isn't wearing a shirt. I'm able to see every square, sculpted inch of his abs, and the wide detail of his chest.

A chest that has dried drool on it.

The familiar heat I felt yesterday begins to build, but it isn't as bad since Kentucky is next to me. The fever is more like a low simmer preparing to boil over. That's fine. I need to buy more time to fight the way I'm beginning to feel about him.

His black cowboy hat is hiding his face, and his legs are crossed at the ankles. His feet hang off the four-post bed, showing he is too big for this queen-sized mattress.

"You're thinking awfully hard, Darlin'." His voice is deep and smoky with the edge of morning.

I scoot away from him, needing to give myself a small amount of breathing room because I am too close to throwing myself at him. He smells so good. His being so close to me has my heart racing, but there's no way I'm having a conversation with him with morning breath.

He lifts his hat from his face, his tired gaze finding me.

I've never seen him so attractive. The way his eyes hood, the faintest hint of red in his irises from either hunger or waking up, the way his lips seem still yet full, waiting to be awakened with a kiss.

Oh, I can't think like that.

"You're still thinking so loud, I can almost hear your thoughts. What's on your mind, Dru?" he asks, his voice rough as if he just took a shot of whiskey.

"What are you doing in my bed?" I scratch at the dried drool on my hand.

What the hell happened last night? I can't string two thoughts together until I have a cup of coffee, then maybe I'll be a functioning adult.

Maybe. Depends on how good the coffee is.

"You were having a nightmare last night." He sits up, lifting his arm to hang his hat on the bedpost. "I came in here and held you to calm you; that's it. I promise. I didn't pull any funny business. I'm not that kind of man," he states, crossing his arms over his chest.

"But—" I scratch the side of my head, remembering he wasn't in the house last night. "But you were in the barn. How could you hear me?"

He taps his right ear. "Part of being a vampire, Darlin'. I have enhanced abilities that include strength, speed, and hearing. I heard you. I came here as quickly as I could, but I jumped into a mud puddle and had to change, as you can see," he chuckles, then yawns, showing straight white teeth.

As a dentist, I can't stop staring at them. Gums are healthy, teeth are white, and from what I can tell, no visible cavities.

He covers his mouth with his hand. "Sorry. My breath must be terrible."

"No, no, that doesn't bother me. I'm a dentist, and I was admiring your teeth. You take care of them."

"I'm afraid I can't take credit for that. I'm not prone to human diseases, so I don't get cavities or gingivitis. Unfortunately, bad breath is still common." He smirks. "A dentist? No wonder you have the most beautiful smile I have ever seen, in all my years."

I bite my lip, twisting a piece of hair around my finger. He is a smooth talker. Charm oozes from him without effort. It's getting harder to fight him. I don't even find myself afraid of him anymore. Wary, yes, but afraid? No.

He won't hurt me. I don't know *how* I know that. I just... feel it.

"Can I make you some coffee?" The bed dips as he stands, the mattress squeaking from the weight change. "I'd like to talk to you, get to know you if that's alright."

"I'd like that. Do you have cream? I like a lot of cream in my coffee."

"I can do that for you, Darlin'." He stretches his arms over his head, my eyes falling to his torso. His body becomes leaner in that moment, his sweatpants falling enough to show the beginning of his dark brown bush. The V is carved on his hips, giving me a paved pathway to his cock.

I want to lick the ridges of his hips, kiss my way down, and suck him down my throat.

His cock presses against the thin material of his grey sweat-pants, leaving nothing to the imagination. He is long, the shaft pressing against his thigh, and the crown outlined. I toy with the blanket to keep my hands busy. I'm one more 'Darlin' away from losing my shit and curling my fingers in his waistband to yank his pants to his knees.

He growls, his hands falling to the bed. Kentucky's eyes burn crimson. His nostrils flare. He tilts his head, those dangerous eyes sliding up and down my body.

"While I love you looking at me like that, I want to remind you that I smell everything. Your fear, nervousness, uncertainty..." He inhales again. "Lust."

I cover my body with the blanket as if I've been caught naked.

"I know you don't want that right now." He runs his index finger across my jaw, humming in appreciation. "But I need you to know, that's the best fucking scent I've ever had the pleasure of pulling into my lungs." He lifts my chin with the same finger, the slight scratch of the callous causing me to swallow. "You are a temptation I never knew I needed," he whispers, brushing his thumb over my lips. "You dare my control, Dru." He leans in, his lips mere inches away from mine, causing me to hold my breath.

With a snarl, he is gone in the next blink. The small breeze he creates when he rushes out of the room cools my heated cheeks. I hear him tinkering in the kitchen to make the coffee, leaving me with uneven breath and messy, tangled thoughts of us rolling in these sheets.

I use the time he is in the kitchen to go to the bathroom. The walls are painted dark green with crown molding. A vintage white claw-foot tub sits in the corner by the window, where the view of the pasture is. The floors are warm under my feet, extinguishing the slight chill in my body. A lamp sitting in the corner is the only light source. Flicking the switch, a warm glow is gentle on my eyes as I use the restroom, brush my teeth with a spare toothbrush I found in the cabinet, and wash my face with cold water to help wake me up.

A knock at the door makes me jump, grabbing the sides of the vanity. I can't remember the last time I was scared by the simplest noises.

"Sorry, I didn't mean to startle you. Coffee is ready, and I'm fixing breakfast if you want to join me."

I swing the door open, this time startling him. I grin. "Sorry, I didn't mean to scare you."

"Smartass. Come on. I could hear your belly rumbling from the kitchen. You must be starving."

"I could eat a horse—" I slap my hand over my mouth, horrified. "Oh my god, I didn't mean an actual horse. It was just a figure of speech."

"You'd better hope Romeo didn't hear you."

I stop dead in my tracks in the middle of the doorway. "Are you serious?"

"He has vampire abilities too. I'm sure he heard you."

Panic grips me again. I catch myself on the wall, my head becoming dizzy with violent images of his damn horse running me over, or worse, eating me.

"Hey, whoa, Darlin', look at me." Kentucky's touch brings me back to reality, away from the mess of my mind, and I'm left staring into his chestnut-colored eyes, the vampire red vanished from his irises.

Why do I miss looking at them already?

"I was joking. I'm sorry. It was too soon to make a joke like that. He isn't going to hurt you. He isn't paying attention to you anyway. He is hunting in the woods right now." Kentucky's hand finds my lower back, the gentle guide easing me down the hallway. "I'm sorry to scare you like that. Forgive me?"

"Only if you tell me what he is hunting," I murmur.

"Squirrels, rabbits, deer, small bears, animals like that. He doesn't eat humans. That I promise."

Kentucky's answer settles the worry I had because if I lived through all this and ended up dying by a damn vampire horse, I'd be pissed.

"That's a relief."

He grins. "Forgive me now?"

I wave him away, pretending not to notice the first-place ribbons on the wall for barrel racing. "Don't worry about it. I'm still getting used to a horse being a vampire. He scares me."

"He's nothing but a mush, believe me." The baritone of his voice is so soothing, calming my racing heart.

The fragrant smell of bacon has my mouth watering when we enter the kitchen. This is the room that is lived in the most. He has a top-of-the-line antique stove that is royal blue with gold knobs. Hashbrowns are sizzling in the pan, the steam rising high above the skillet.

Kentucky pulls out a high, leather-cushioned barstool from under the kitchen island. "Come on." He pats the seat. "Let me take care of you, Darlin'."

Take care of me? I can't remember the last time someone took the time to be so thoughtful. Why does Kentucky care? Why does it matter to him if he feeds me or is kind to me? Why won't he hurt me like the other vampire?

I have endless questions, and I hope he will answer them.

I sit down in the chair, and he pushes me closer to the countertop.

"Your kitchen is gorgeous, Kentucky." I run my hands over the wooden countertop, noticing more hand-carved details. Wild horses are running through a field with long grass under the night sky. There is a thick, clear coat of epoxy to protect it. "Did you carve all this? The door to the bedroom, the coffee table, and now this countertop? They are beautiful."

"I did." He throws me a confident smirk over his shoulder. "Thank you for noticing. I like to do it in my downtime. I've been woodworking for more years than I can count. I don't keep track of time."

"Makes sense given how long you have lived. These carvings are so impressive. You could sell these. You could open up a shop in town or something."

He slides me a mug steaming with delicious coffee. On the side it reads, 'I Love Dead Man's Ranch.' I giggle, wrapping my hands around the cup. "The big bad vampire has merch?" Sipping my coffee, I moan at how perfect the coffee-to-creamer ratio is. It is sweet, meaning there is more creamer than coffee. "It's perfect."

His eyes are red, and he spins around, hiding himself, hunching over the sink. The muscles in his back become tense, popping the veins in his arms from how hard he must be gripping the edge of the counter.

"You can't be making noises like that, Darlin'. I'm already on edge. You smell so good, and controlling myself is...difficult."

I sip my coffee, a twinge of guilt eating away at my empty stomach. Just a twinge because I find I actually like knowing I drive him so crazy. "I'm sorry, Kentucky. I didn't know."

"Why would you? It's one of the things I want to talk about. And don't ever apologize. I'm not sorry for wanting you."

I sit there, debating if that's an invasion of privacy. I'm not able to hide anything from him. He can smell it. No secrets are safe, but the better question is, do I want to keep secrets from him?

He grips the skillet handle, his skin sizzling from the heat, to flip the hashbrowns.

"Kentucky!" I scream, spilling my coffee all over the counter.

He lifts his hand in the air, and the ugly, burnt, bleeding palm begins to heal. I watch in awe, the flesh stitching back together, his blood reversing into his body, and the ruined skin is brand new.

"Oh my god." I'm dumbfounded. I've never seen anything like that in my entire life. "That's amazing! That's...wait...you could probably cure cancer—"

"—No," he cuts me off before I can finish my sentence.

"Okay." The excitement is gone just as quickly as it arrived. "I'm sorry. I didn't know. I didn't mean to pry."

He sighs, turning off the stove, then snagging a towel to clean up my spilled coffee.

"Apologies, Dru. Please, forgive me for snapping like that. I had the same thought once. A very long time ago. I thought I could help the world, cure kids with cancer, anything, every-thing, I was fine with donating a drop of blood if it meant a child could live."

Swoon. Don't fall in love with him. Don't fall in love with him.

Who am I kidding? I'm halfway there.

"My friend Lorcan, he is a Void—"

I choke on my coffee. "A what?"

Kentucky plates the food for me, piling it with bacon, hashbrowns, and fluffy pancakes. "Apologies, again, Miss Whitley," he drawls with another charming crooked grin. "A Void. It's best to think of him as a grim reaper. He works for Death."

I bite into a crispy piece of bacon and almost moan out loud again. "Death? Like The Four Horsemen?"

His brows raise as he grins in surprise. "You know your lore."

"I wouldn't call it lore since it is real."

"Good point." He shakes a piece of bacon at me in place of his finger. "He reaped my maker, and he was kind enough to return to me, to help me, guide me, and give me the basic information to survive. I asked him not to tell me everything about vampires. I only wanted to live the rest of my life in peace, but then it hit me, my ability to heal. I figured if I'm a vampire, I might as well do some good. Lorcan was very quick to shut that down, and I can't say I blame him. Vampire hunters exist. Humans don't really accept anything or anyone different than them. He reminded me that I could end up in a facility to be tested on if I got caught giving my blood to anyone. It's too dangerous."

I scoop hashbrowns into my mouth, wanting to moan again, but I can't help it. I love food. It's been ages since I've had a real breakfast. I usually grab a granola bar on the way to work, filling up on dusty oats and coffee.

Kentucky removes the warmed maple syrup from the microwave when it beeps. "Tell me when," he warns me, pouring the sweet maple over my pancakes.

He keeps going.

And going.

Until it begins to pool under the stack of pancakes.

"I can't believe you don't have any cavities. Look at all that sugar!" He laughs, a sound I'm coming to like very much.

"When!" I finally inform, lathering my bacon in the syrup, drenching the bottom of the plate. "And I take care of my teeth just so I can enjoy life's simple pleasures. Have you never had bacon and syrup?"

"I haven't."

"You have to! How could you have lived all these years and not have something as simple as bacon and syrup? That's a crime."

"Well, I can't go getting thrown in jail for something that's fixable." He crosses his arms on the counter, leans forward, and opens his mouth.

My hand trembles with nerves as I dip a piece of bacon into the maple syrup, swirling it around so the crispy piece is drench in the sugary goodness. Placing a hand under so it doesn't drip, Kentucky and I lock eyes as I feed him.

He chews, his lips shining with bacon grease and syrup. All I want to do is lick the plump clouds clean, wondering if the syrup would taste better coming off his lips.

I ogle his mouth, the familiar fever overtaking my body again with pure want and need.

His nostrils flare again, reminding me that he can smell any differences in my scent. Kentucky leans in again, his eyes tinting with that vampiric hue, and his gaze falls to my lips.

"You have no idea how bad I want to kiss you, Darlin'. You have created havoc in my soul, something I thought was dead for a very long time."

I gulp, licking my lips to wet them. "You—you want to kiss me?" I stammer, my nerves getting the best of me.

"I do," he groans. "I really do." His thumb tugs on my bottom lip, and the taste of his flesh mixed with syrup explodes across my tongue. "I want to kiss you until you forget how to breathe. I want to kiss you until your lips are swollen from how much I want you. And when I do kiss you, and I mean when, *not if*, I'm going to steal the breath from your lungs so the only air you need is mine. We will breathe each other in, get lost in time, memorize each other's lips, and the way we move. They will be long, slow, and deep. I'm going to take my time imprinting my lips onto yours. I know one kiss from you will revive my humanity—something that has been numb for a number of years."

Like a magnet, I'm leaning forward to start the long days of kissing him.

His fingers stop me, pressing against my lips. "Not yet. As

much as I hate myself for saying that, not yet. There's still a hint of fear you feel, and there's so much you need to know before you go offering your kiss to me like that."

"You don't want to kiss me now?"

Faster than the speed of light, he is by my side, wrapping a hand around my throat to lift me closer to his mouth. My body responds, and I can't hide the groan. I can't hide the want of being handled this way. I know he can smell the lust pouring off me in waves.

"I don't want to kiss you, Dru. I *need* to." His tongue flicks across his bottom lip, those bright, flaming coals staring at my mouth. "It's all I think about since meeting you. It consumes me—you consume me." He lets me go, leaving me gasping for air. "Give me four days, Dru. Before you make any decision about going home, give me four days for you to fall in love with me, and then I'll tell you everything. Meaning no calls to your friend or work. I know that's bad, but I need the four days."

"That's it? I get no other information?"

He shakes his head. "No, Ma'am. That's all I can offer at the moment."

Four days?

That doesn't seem so bad. I've already been gone for a few days. What's a few more? The thought of leaving fills me with dread. I'm not ready to leave. Some type of force is keeping me here, and I plan on figuring out what it is.

Since I apparently have no survival instincts, I hold out my hand for a vampire to take. "Deal."

With a gentle caress, he wraps his hand around my fingers and kisses the top of my knuckles again.

Did I just make a deal with the Devil?

CHAPTER ELEVEN

KENTUCKY

"Just like that?"

Dru cuts a pancake that is soggy with syrup, basically slurping it into her mouth. "Just like what?" She washes her giant mouthful of food down with a sip of coffee.

I can't help but be mesmerized by how she eats. She isn't afraid of the mess she's making. Syrup is on the countertop, on her cheeks and chin, and bacon crumbles are sticking to her. It's adorable. I've always loved it when a woman has an appetite.

"I expected you to fight me on leaving. I would have understood too. You just agreed to stay with a stranger. I'm surprised. Unless you plan to stake me in my sleep, then I'd very much prefer if we talk out any issues you might be worried about."

She snorts, a piece of hashbrown flying from her mouth, and it lands on my chin.

Dru slaps a hand over her mouth, her eyes so wide and unmoving. "Oh my god. I'm so sorry. I'm just a mess right now! I can't believe I did that."

I chuckle, plucking the piece of potato from my chin, then

popping it into my mouth. I lick my finger, wanting to show her I will happily eat her food, whether it's on a plate or not. "Still tastes good too."

"Kentucky," my name, shy and suggestive, falling from her sweet, syrup-coated lips.

"Don't bother me none, Darlin'." I curl my fingers around the handle of my mug. "I love a woman with an appetite."

She wipes her mouth with a napkin. "I was hungrier than I thought and forgot where I was for a second." She wipes the corners of her lips, placing the napkin on her lap. "And to answer your question, I don't know why I'm not fighting you about leaving. I just know I can't. Not yet. I would like to check in with my friend Carmen, though. I can tell her not to worry."

"She won't believe you. She will think you're being held hostage."

She lifts her fingers up and presses them together until they almost touch. "I am a little bit. Just a little, though."

We fall into a comfortable silence while we finish our food, smiling and taking quick glances at each other when we think the other isn't looking. My mind begins to drift to the plans I had of dying, a part of my soul still torn on the decision that needs to be made.

I'm unsure if I can damn Dru to forever since forever is an awfully long time to live. It might not be a big ask for most, I know. Some humans would kill to have this opportunity, to live for all eternity and build wealth so they can have anything and everything the world has to offer.

Humans, and I'm allowed to say this since I used to be one, have become greedy in nature. Nothing is enough. They always want more, and sometimes, they will even kill to get it. Everyone thinks money is what makes the world go round. In my opinion, that couldn't be further from the truth.

It's what is right in front of me that keeps my world spinning. I've been a poor man and I've been a wealthy man, but I've never been as rich as this.

"My name is Kentucky. I love chasing sunsets and love guns. Pew. Pew."

I groan, hanging my head in defeat. I'll never have a moment of peace when it comes to Lorcan.

"I do not sound like that, Lorcan."

"Hate to break it to you, bucko, but you do sound like that. Pew. Pew. I'm dangerous and have a big horse. Pew. Pew."

I glance up to see him in the exact same cowboy hat I own on top of his skull, cowboy boots with the spurs, and a gun holster around his waist. Luckily, and I mean that with all my heart, he has a fake gun in his hand. I can't imagine what Lorcan would do with a real one.

Dru is dumbfounded, staring at Lorcan as if she is seeing a ghost. I suppose, in a way, he is, since he comes and goes as he pleases.

"You must be Dru." Lorcan hooks his fingers in the holster, stomping his boots hard on the ground so the spurs create noise. "Nice to meet you, pretty lady." He pinches the brim of the hat, giving her a head tilt.

I'm the only one allowed to give her a head tilt.

Sneering, I'm in between them, blocking her from him. "Don't even think about flirting with my m—her," I correct myself, not wanting to spill the secret too soon.

I know lying isn't good to do, especially so early on, but is it so bad that I want her to love me first before she feels like she has no choice because she is my fated mate?

She deserves a choice, and if she'd rather die than be with me, I'll respect that and die beside her.

"Meow, kitten. Claws are out." Lorcan scratches the air and hisses. "Okay, okay, sheesh. Relax, will you? I'm only poking fun." He slings the hat across the room, hooking it on the coat rack.

Impressive.

"I've heard a lot about you, Dru. I'm Lorcan." He holds out his hand in greeting.

I stand there, crossing my arms over my chest with an eyebrow lifted.

"Ugh, seriously? She can't even shake my hand? You're one of those types of…"

I pinch my mouth together, my jaw curt and tense as I stare at him.

"Vampires…?" He ends up sounding like he's asking a damn question. As long as he doesn't spill my secret, we will be good. Lorcan has a big mouth, one that vomits words when he isn't supposed to.

"Kentucky, I'll be okay. You said this is Lorcan, right? The Void?" Dru asks, peeping around me. "I'll be okay if he is as nice as you say."

He *can* be nice.

When he wants to be.

"Aw, he said I was nice? That's so sweet." He grins, holding his hands together over his heart, and if he had eyelashes, I know he would be batting them at me.

Begrudgingly, I step aside to let them meet. I suppose it was only a matter of time, considering he is my only friend.

Dru plasters a big smile on her face, shaking his outstretched hand. I can smell how nervous she is. She pushes through the unknown, willing to meet a paranormal she knows nothing about.

I love her courage.

"Your hand is bone," Dru points out, staring at it like a kid glaring at a stranger.

"I do have another form that is nicer to look at. I prefer this one, though."

"Do you want a plate? We were just going to talk about

vampire stuff. Kentucky was going to answer any questions I have."

Lorcan doubles over with laughter, wiping away a fake tear since he can't cry. "He was going to answer your questions? He was?" He jabs his thumb at me. "It's a good thing I make myself at home. He doesn't know anything about vampires. He couldn't tell you anything. Oh, that's funny. Oh my god. My cheeks hurt."

"You don't have cheeks," I grumble, flicking his cheekbone.

"Ow." He rubs the spot I intentionally annoyed. "And if I did have cheeks, that would have actually hurt, thank you very much."

Dissipating into smoke, he emerges on the couch with his legs crossed. "How can I help ease your curious mind, Dru?"

"You're too comfortable here." I pick up my coffee, checking the glowing time on the stove. I need to leave soon to finish the chores on the ranch. "I only have a few minutes before I need to go."

Dru takes Lorcan in stride, practically skipping from the kitchen to the living room to sit next to him.

I don't like that.

"Are you from Hell? What's it like? Is Lucifer, you know, real? And if he is, is he mean? And—"

"—I thought you had questions about vampires?" Lorcan interrupts her excited curiosity.

"Excuse you. You owe the lady an apology for cutting her off like that, Lorcan. She's been very calm and collected about the paranormal world so far, minus being kidnapped by shifters and two different vampires. Cut her some damn slack before I have one of my barn kittens scratch your skull." I take the open spot next to Dru, setting my mug on my knee while keeping a firm grip on the handle.

I can already tell my coffee is cold. "Lorcan." I hand him the mug.

"I swear, sometimes I feel so used." He touches the mug, warming it in an instant.

Steam billows from the top just how I like. Bringing it to my mouth, I sip. "Ah, thank you, buddy. See? Such a good friend."

"You're welcome." He turns to Dru. "I'm sorry for being so rude and cutting you off. Your interest in me took me by surprise. Hell is real, so is Luci, but he hates to be called that, so don't do it. He isn't anything like humans have turned him into. He's a cool dude. I'm created by Death, the number one grim reaper, and we are his junior reapers, I guess? I'm trying to figure out how to explain it to a human—no offense or anything." He winces. "Can we change the subject? I hate talking about myself."

"I never would have guessed that," I mutter into the mug, earning myself an elbow jab from Dru.

In a move I haven't done since I was a teenager, I stretch my arm to the ceiling and drop it across the back of the couch. When Dru doesn't catch on, I slide down, draping my arm across her shoulders.

She nestles against me, getting comfortable by pressing her back against the nook of my shoulder and chest.

Is this what peace is? I glance up at Daphne, noticing for the first time that the glass of her picture frame is cracked. I wait for rage, for resentment, or even guilt. With my fated mate so close, I don't feel any of those emotions.

Daphne was another time, another life, and I know this is exactly what she wanted for me. She is, after all, the reason I lived long enough to meet Dru. She made sure I never missed an opportunity to find happiness.

"Kentucky," Dru asks. "Why do you do all the ranch work alone? And why don't you do your zippy blurry thing to get it done faster?" She moves her hands as fast as she can to show what she means by 'zippy blurry thing'.

"Well, the more energy I use, the hungrier I become. Plus, I've always liked honest work. That's what life is all about. I enjoy what I do. There's no reason to get it done quicker."

"Why can you go out in the sun without burning?" She's fast with her next question, staring at me with those big, curious hazel eyes.

"He doesn't know this one," Lorcan inserts. "Vampires can walk in the sun. The fact that they can't is a myth, except when a vampire gets bitten by a werewolf. Then, that vampire is cursed to a coma until their beloved finds them. If they awaken, they become creatures of the night, and if they step into the sun, they will burn. I know a coven like that. The Master is waiting for his coven witch, who is also his beloved, to find a spell to reverse it. The spell is in the hands of an evil warlock though. It's a big, long story for another time."

"Wow, that is so terrible." Dru places her hand on her heart. "I can't imagine how awful that is. I would hate not to feel the sun."

"Me too. Watching the sunset and sunrise is the best part of the day," I add a fact about myself, hoping she likes what she hears.

She smiles at me, and that happiness proves I will do anything to have her look at me like that.

"Garlic?" she questions.

"Nope. I love it. I put it on almost everything," I answer.

"Holy water?"

"No," Lorcan answers, conjuring a cup of tea in his hand and stirring it by rotating a finger above the rim. "Demons hate it though."

"Silver? Crosses?" She tries again, becoming more and more excited with each question she thinks of.

"Silver burns like a hot iron poker searing your skin. It's

the most painful." My thoughts fall to the silver locket hanging from Daphne's picture frame, remembering how the silver felt the other morning before I got a whiff of Dru's blood. "And crosses don't do anything."

"So I've probably walked by vampires and didn't even know?" Her voice becomes higher with every word of that question, her anxiety sneaking into her system again.

I kiss the top of her head, skimming my hand up and down her arm. The fumes of uncertainty fade. Happiness replaces the foul smell.

"Oh, definitely." Lorcan sips his tea, the liquid dripping onto the hardwood floor after splashing through his empty insides. "Vampires, werewolves, angels, demons, hellhounds, phoenix, elves, dragons—"

"—Okay, so everything I can imagine is what you're saying."

Her heart rate increases, the sugar in her blood sweetening the air. I bury my nose in her neck, inhaling the decadent aroma. My fangs breach with the need for her to become my prey.

"Pretty much." Lorcan shrugs a shoulder as if he didn't uproot everything in her life. "But most of us are just trying to make the best out of life and won't bother you. Sure, we have some bad eggs, but so do humans."

"Good point. I mean, no one ever bothered me until now."

"And I want to know everything about the vampire who broke your trust and hurt you. I promise, I'll find him." I bend down, my lips brushing the top of her forehead.

A spice similar to cinnamon adds to the sweetness in her blood. The sudden wave of heat calls to my true nature, wanting nothing more than to answer her body's call.

The mating heat. That is what this has to be building between us. It's too soon. It isn't right. It isn't fair to her to have to be driven to want me like this. Fate is an external force, pushing two mates together. Paranormals are used to that; they crave it, but humans? They would find their choice to be taken.

And I'm all too familiar with that.

We don't have much time before we both give in. I'm already on edge. Last night in the barn eased the agony of not being inside her. I know Dru had the same experience. I saw her watching me from the house, peeping through the telescope. It urged the fury of desire I felt for her.

I answered her call.

I hope I gave her a performance she will remember forever. I know I will be taking the memory of her finger fucking herself with me every damn step I take. I don't know if there will be a day when I don't think about her pushing her fingers in and out of that sweet cunt that I'm so desperate to taste.

"You said silver hurts you, right?" Dru tilts her head back, directing the question right at me.

I nod, gulping my coffee. "Yes, ma'am."

"Why do you keep that silver necklace, then? Is it because of the woman in the picture frame?"

I wince, not from the question, but from the hurt pouring from Dru. She's doing an amazing job at hiding how much it must devastate her knowing I was with another.

There is a twinge of guilt for knowing I loved another woman. I have no doubt I would have died long ago if it weren't for Daphne. She kept me going for this, my fated mate, wanting me to find that everlasting love I could only have for who Fate chose for me.

How could I ever regret a love so selfless?

"I'm going to take that as my cue to go. I'm just going to..." Lorcan stands from the couch, hooking his thumbs in the holster of his fake gun. "Pew. Pew, partner." An awkward cackle comes from him. "Pew...okay, I'm going to go because this is out of my"—he waves his hands in the air in big wind-mill circles—"wheelhouse." He snaps. "Yes, it is out of my wheelhouse, above my pay grade. All that jazz. Mmmkay? Great. Also, Kentucky, I signed you up for the local rodeo again. Please don't be mad at me. Lovely meeting you, Dru. Okay, byeeeee."

With a snap of his fingers, he is gone again. He didn't bother to clean up his damn tea on the floor though. He never does.

"You deserve to know about her. I'll tell you everything I know about Ms. Daphne Reynolds."

I didn't think it would be so hard, telling the woman I'm destined to and love, about a woman who loved me so much, she saved me for someone else.

A soft patter of rain kisses the windows, providing me with a soft beat to tell the story of a life I never thought I'd ever have to relive.

DEAD MAN'S RANCH

CHAPTER
Twelve
DRUSCILLA

Kentucky walks in front of the wood-burning fireplace, tossing a few logs in that he keeps to the side. After igniting some kindling and tossing it on top of the chopped wood, he straightens. A baritone thrum sounds from him, adding to the rhythm of the rain against the windows.

I love this weather. It's my favorite kind. Most find rain to be depressing, but not me. I love the serene quiet it brings. The peace one feels during weather like this is different. It's like nothing else exists in the world. There's no fear, no harm, no violence—just rain calming your mind.

Kentucky plucks the necklace from the frame, his flesh burning immediately. The smoke drifts and sways. He doesn't flinch.

"Does it not hurt?" I don't want him to be in pain to prove anything to me. "Put it down, Kentucky. Don't hurt yourself."

"Don't worry, Darlin'. It doesn't hurt. Not anymore. I'm used to it."

My heart cracks a little knowing that piece of information. "So you've done this a lot then?"

"Every morning for many, many years."

"You still love her, then? You're in love with her?" A lump of sadness parks itself in my throat and stomach. I figured any feelings that were growing for Kentucky would be useless. Kentucky has lived so many lives and has probably loved triple the amount of women. "Where is she? Does she know I'm here? I'm not trying to—"

"—No. No. Nothing like that. I would never do that to anyone. I pride myself on being a good man, an honorable one. You don't have to worry about that with me." He comes over, placing the picture on the coffee table, and hands me the necklace. Opening the locket, he shows me the pictures hidden in the two ovals.

"There's something you need to know about me before I get into this story. I never wanted to be a vampire. I never wanted to live an extended life. I'm a traditionalist in that sense, I suppose. You are born, you live, you work, you try to do right, you admit your wrongs, and when you die, hopefully you die with beauty and no regrets. I was happy with that mindset. All I wanted to do was be a cowboy, have a wife, maybe a few kids, and just..." he blows out a big breath. "... I don't know. Be happy until Death finally came for me."

I scoot my legs under me, turning my body towards Kentucky. "I don't understand. You said Lorcan took your maker to Purgatory? What happened? Did you not like your maker? And I'm assuming your maker means this person turned you into a vampire? 'Made you' in a way?"

Kentucky nods with a forced smile. "I met my maker, Audrey—"

"Audrey? Not Daphne?" I point to the frame, showing the woman I thought we were talking about.

"In order to get to the story of Daphne, I have to tell you about Audrey. I'm bad with dates, intentionally. I don't pay attention to time. Time means nothing to me. Sometime in the 1800s, I met Audrey, and she was a breath of fresh air at that time when she came to town. I had never met a woman like her. She was so carefree, so wild in comparison to me, so full of life, that I really thought I had found the love of my life."

His hand lands on my knee, giving it a good squeeze. "I'm not saying this to hurt you."

I forgot he can smell what I'm feeling. "Don't worry about my emotions. I know you have had lives and loves. Plus, I'm not anything to you. You don't owe me an explanation."

His eyes flash red as anger stitches across his face. "Don't ever say that. Don't ever say you aren't anything to me when you...you're everything."

We stare at one another as I wait for him to spill the secret he hasn't been telling me. I know it has to do with him needing the four days he asked for. I don't know why, but I will figure it out.

Curiosity always reveals the truth, which is why I will never stop being curious.

He clears his throat, covering his mouth with his fist. "Well, one night, Audrey and I started talking about the future. She started talking about a thousand years together. It confused me. I thought she was joking around at first."

I scoot closer to him, taking his hand in mine in hopes it brings him a small amount of peace to get through what he has to tell me.

"She revealed herself to me—her vampire nature—that is."

"I gathered," I tease, knocking him in the shoulder with my own.

"I told her I didn't want a thousand years. I wanted my human life; anything extra wasn't natural. I valued my humanity, and, in many ways, I still do. At least, I do my best to hold on to the amount I have left. She didn't like that answer. She refused to be without me."

"A thousand years? I thought vampires were immortal?"

Kentucky shakes his head, confusing me even more. "No, we naturally live longer. Audrey said unmated vampires live two hundred years. Vampires who choose to mate with someone they love can live for a thousand years, and then there are vampires who meet their fated mates. They live forever. They are the ones with immortality."

"Wow." I'm awestruck, speechless, and confused. "Wait. How old are you?"

"I'm not sure? I think I have another twenty years before I die. Anyway, she thought I was weak for having such human thoughts. She changed me. In order to be changed, I had to die with her blood in my system, and at the same time, I staked her."

"That must have been terrible for you. To be something you never wanted to be."

"It was. I readjusted my way of thinking. I decided to be alone until I died. One day, years later, I went to the feed store, and I met Daphne. I had mystified everyone in town into not thinking about my age so I could stay here. This is my home, and I wasn't going to get pushed out because of who I was now. I had never met her before. She was new to town and Hank's—the owner of the feed store—step-granddaughter. It was why I had never seen her before. He was going to train her to take over since he was aging. I fell in love with her in the best way I could. Even though she wasn't my fated mate, I loved her anyway."

"I like that you weren't alone. You're too good a man to be living a life by yourself. What was she like? Why didn't she get turned? And if you can have a mate for a thousand years, why not do that so you could be together?" Even speaking those words sends a searing hot blade through my heart. The idea of him with another woman is almost painful enough to send me to my knees.

"She didn't want to live that long. I respected her decision. It wasn't easy, but we made it work. I never bit her. She always gave me a few drops of her blood in my coffee, or I'd have blood bags, but I never fed from her. I wanted to save my bite for my mate, if I ever met her, and Daphne was okay with that. Plus, biting her would have mated us, and I wouldn't lose control to go against her wishes like that. She lived a long, happy life. She's buried by the tree right there, where all those roses are. Those were her favorite flowers. I was there with her to the very end. I held her wrinkled, aged hand, listened to her heartbeat slow, and she died with a smile on her face. It was one of the hardest moments I've ever experienced. She always said I was here for a reason because I was so kind, but I couldn't disagree more." He stops speaking, eyeing me as if he wants to say more.

"I'm so sorry, Kentucky. She sounded like a very good woman. I'm so sorry. I'm happy you found a person to spend a part of your life with. That is beautiful. You created memories in a time when you thought you wouldn't." I climb into his lap, wrapping my arms around his neck, and bury my face into his shoulder. "I can't imagine how hard that must have been." I lean away, needing to see his handsome face. "And now what? You're waiting to die?" There isn't a part of me that can understand all the heartbreak and betrayal he has experienced.

So many years of being alone, being denied the life he dreamed about, losing what he has loved over and over again. The agony of that must be soul-numbing.

"Daphne kept me alive in hopes I'd find my fated mate; without that, death seems like the next peaceful step. Right out in the pasture, under the sunset, so I can see the colors in the sky one last time. I'd see all the stars, get lost in their beauty, and then, in one last exhale, I'll fade to dust, allowing the wind to take me."

"There's nothing that could change your mind?" I sniffle, hiding my face in his shoulder so he doesn't see me cry.

He grips the back of my neck, forcing me to look at his handsome face again. "Hey, hey, hey, none of that. Don't be sad for me. Don't cry for me. I don't deserve your tears, Darlin'. I'm not worth the energy spent. I've lived for so long, I've made my peace with death." His thumb brushes over the apple of my cheek, erasing the tears meant for him.

"There has to be something to get you to stay. What if you met a human who loved you and was okay with mating? And you could live for a thousand years?"

The outer rims of his irises flare in response to my question, and I find myself completely hypnotized by the creature that lurks within his skin.

"I couldn't do that to anyone. I couldn't take someone's will like that and force a thousand years on that person. It isn't right."

"What if they wanted to?" Another warm tear breaks from my lash line, falling onto his arm.

"The only woman I could live like that for is my fated mate."

"And if you found her?" I dare to ask, my heart thumping so loudly and hard, there is no way he can't hear the rush of blood pouring through my veins.

"She'd have to be okay with forever, but forever is a very long time. Everyone she loves and knows will die. Everything in the world will change a million times. People will change. The climate. Paranormals will most likely outlive the human species. It might be a lonely existence."

"Maybe it will be scary, but it might also be absolutely beautiful." My hands frame his square jaw, his skin softer than I thought it would be. He feels so human.

Becoming brave, or stupid, considering he could drain me of blood before I could scream, my fingers drift through his pitch black beard, which is also a lot softer than I thought it would be.

"What are you smiling about?" he teases, running his palm up my nape, his fingers massaging my scalp.

"You. You surprise me. You feel so human. Your skin, your hair, I know that's such a silly thing to say. I expected your hair to be harsh or your skin to be rock solid."

"That's not silly. My skin does have a much stronger barrier than yours, but the beard? That's just the beard kit I have in my restroom. Can't even blame it on the vampire genes."

That crooked smile returns, causing my stomach to flip.

"You'd be open to loving someone again?"

He circles his arms around me, a slight purr coming from his chest. "Depends on who that someone is."

I get lost in how he looks at me. I have never had a man drink me in like this. He takes his time as his eyes wander down, then up, fixating on my lips.

Every breath becomes heavier, the slight scent of syrup sweetening the small amount of space between us. The rough hold he has on me proves he is fighting control too. Kentucky's fingers dig into my back while mine claw into his firm shoulders. I need him to keep me grounded, to keep me in place, or I might wake up and be disappointed that this was all a dream.

"Kiss me to put me out of my misery." The words slip out of my mouth before I can stop myself. "Or let me go because I don't know if I can survive four days of this." My hand drops to his bare chest, appreciating how his shoulders rise with a deep breath from my touch.

A second passes without him taking me up on my offer.

He is deep in thought, considering how furrowed his brows are.

Taking that as a hint, I slide off his lap and regret taking that huge leap. I thought we had a spark all this time. Did I misread his kindness for me?

It's time for me to go home, not create a new one with a man I don't know.

Maybe his heart is still taken by a ghost.

Chapter Thirteen

KENTUCKY

I snag her wrist before she can get too far away from me, tugging her back into my lap where she belongs. I only needed a moment to wrap my head around what she said.

She wants me to kiss her, and what kind of man would I be if I didn't deliver?

Dru inhales a sharp breath; those hazel eyes I seem to get lost in are locked on me, giving me her complete attention.

I'm becoming a greedy man.

I don't only want her attention.

I want her devotion just as I am devoted to her.

"We shouldn't." I ghost my lips across her jaw, tempting myself with her scent.

I grip her hips, fighting for my life to regain an ounce of control. She's too tempting, too beautiful, too out-of-my-league, and yet somehow Fate thought I deserved her.

"Why not?" The question is a breathless whisper as she tilts her head back, giving me access to the silk canvas of her throat.

I love the depth of her skin and the glow it naturally has against my pale, leather-like flesh that's ruined from the sun.

Even with my healing abilities, some wrinkles and calluses will never fade.

She makes me look a whole lot prettier than I really am just by being next to me.

I'm enamored by her perfection, and my fangs ache to have a small taste. I bet her blood would be the sweetest nectar. I'm ready to be drunk on my fated mate, and what leaves me stunned is, she might be experiencing the same.

"Because there's still so much more you don't know." I slip a finger under the collar of her shirt, exposing her collarbone. "You're so soft." It's impossible to hide my awe, how I'm inevitably enamored by her.

While she is inevitably doomed by me.

I glide my finger across the ridge, my mouth dying for a taste of her skin, her sweat, her blood, the fatigued perfume lingering on her—I want it all.

"As much as I love to see you in my clothes, Ms. Whitley, I do believe it is time for us to get you some proper amenities," I drawl, slipping her shirt up to expose her taut stomach.

She inhales a sharp breath, her muscles trembling under my touch. "That—that would be nice, Mr. Jones."

My hands glide up her back, my fingertips caressing the divot of her spine. "I should take better care of you. I've been selfish by keeping you at arm's length, but I promise, I was doing it for your own good."

"Don't then." She lifts her arms, signaling me to take her shirt off.

I've never moved so fast. I tug my shirt free from her, exposing her body at last.

It's my turn to stop breathing. It's my turn to devour and appreciate. Every time I exhale, a growl speaks for me. I'm unable to stop. I have no control over what she creates inside me.

"Kentucky?"

There's a tremble of uncertainty in her voice. I realize I've been staring for far too long, creating—what was a heated moment—into one where she second-guesses herself. She lifts her arms to cover her breasts, and I snag her wrists, pinning them to her sides.

"Darlin', don't you dare cover yourself. You don't ever have to do that with me."

"You weren't saying anything and I—"

"Because I'm stunned. Because I'm speechless. Because I finally see what I've been dreaming about since I laid eyes on you. You're prettier than any sky, any sunset, any star, I have ever fucking seen," I marvel, drifting my hands up her sides. "You make me want to get carried away."

Dru leans forward, grinning from ear to ear, and wraps her arms around my shoulders. "Maybe that's exactly what we need to do, then."

I can't hide what she does to me. She has me losing control of how well I'm able to will myself to be good, to not give in to the violent nature. If I wanted, I could take her now, bite and claim her, seal the fated mate bond, and force her to be with me forever.

That's what I want. More than fucking anything, that's what I need.

But—and there always is a but—that would take away her choice. Her will. Her decision.

I couldn't bear the regret of her hating me for that. She might not understand it now, but she will. Just a few more days of us getting to know one another, and we can give in—if she chooses to stay.

Not wanting to overthink for another minute when I have a beautiful woman half-naked on my lap, I allow my hands to wander. The simple touch has her nervous exhales ghosting over my lips, tempting me to take a kiss.

I've never wanted to take my time like this before. I want

to educate myself on every curve, every inch, every mark, and freckle she has on her body. I need to know which part she loves touched. The one that will force her to arch her back and moan my name.

There's so much I need to know, and while I have plenty of time, Dru doesn't. I don't want us to worry about the clock ticking, her aging, or seconds being missed while I ravage her in a very vampiric, animalistic way. A side of myself I have never given in to.

I cup her breasts, the softness of them gives under my ministrations as I knead, my thumb brushing over her nipple. Her fingernails dig into my shoulder, and I cut my eyes away from her body to her face.

She's watching my hands, her bottom lip caught between her teeth, and I can smell how much she wants this.

Wants me.

"Kiss me," she pleads, inches away from my mouth. "I need you to kiss me." Her touch becomes needier, one palm against my cheek while her other palms the back of my head.

And. I. Break.

I love being touched like that.

Using my speed, I press my lips against hers just when she is about to beg me to kiss her again. I've already waited too long. Enough is enough.

My arms wrap around her, bringing her in closer, needing her skin against mine. When she gives in, she tightens her hold around me, sinking into the embrace.

The warmth between us builds into a blaze, not just physically, but internally. The mating heat that Lorcan warned me about is burning in my blood, my nature urging me to claim what is mine.

I growl down her throat, reeling in that desperation of binding her to me. Our tongues twist together, deepening the kiss. Her fingers slip through my hair, gripping my scalp as the passion becomes too much to fight.

Her moan slips down my throat like warm whiskey, no burn—just heat.

Those lips of hers fill me with power, invigorating me with life I forgot I had inside me.

Our kiss turns into something more, needy and desperate. She begins to rock against my hard cock, seeking friction.

"Kentucky, I need you." She continues to kiss me in between words. "I can't do this. I can't burn like this. You're all over me, surrounding me, it's as if you're eating me from the inside out. Please, I can't take this. I don't understand why this is happening."

And that's exactly why I can't go further, not like this. Not without her knowing everything. Just a few more days.

"Please," she continues to rock, bringing me closer to orgasm with every fucking move she makes against me.

I can feel how warm and wet she is for me through our clothes. I can smell it. Ripping my mouth away from hers, my fangs lengthen on their own accord. My nails turn to long black claws, my vision fading from an array of colors to a strict, unforgiving red.

I'm a second away from doing something both of us will regret for the rest of our lives. She feels so fucking good.

I can't. I can't.

Speeding away before she can fight me on it, I leave her on the couch, gripping the mantle so hard, it breaks in half.

"Kentucky?"

The way she asks for me almost sends me to my knees.

"Kentucky? What's wrong? Did I do something?"

Her breathlessness is adding fuel to the fire.

"I need..." I gasp, grinding my nails in the wooden mantle I carved. "I need a moment. You're making me lose control."

"That's good, right? You're making me completely lose myself. Come here. Come back."

"I can't." I shake my head, saliva pooling in my mouth at the thought of her blood swarming my tongue.

"Let me see you." Her hand touches my back, and the simple knowledge of having her hands on me has me spinning around, grabbing her shoulders, and speeding us to the nearest wall.

"Do you see me?" I roar, lifting her leg over my hip to keep her close. "I'm losing my mind," I basically whimper. I look away, ashamed, because she deserves better. I close my eyes, wishing I couldn't be a danger to her.

"Don't hide from me." She lifts my chin with her finger. "Let me see you. All of you."

I snap my eyes open, allowing her to see me in full vampire form. She traces my jaw, my lips, lifting them up to see my fangs. She strokes the left cuspid, and my knees turn weak as I groan out loud.

She grins. "You like that, don't you?"

I nod. "I've never had anyone touch them before."

"Ever?"

"I couldn't risk it." I watch as she brings each claw of mine to her lips, kissing each one separately.

That's when I realize there is no fear in the air. She's not afraid of me.

"You're beautiful, Kentucky. I know you won't hurt me. Kiss me just like this. Kiss me as yourself. There's no other I want like I want you." She uses her touch again, caressing my face as if I'm a rare object she adores.

I melt.

Every muscle in my body, besides one, relaxes, and completely gives into her musings when it comes to me.

"I will not bite you, not yet, not until you understand everything. Not even if you beg for it."

She yanks my head back by my hair. "Now, kiss me again before I go mad."

"Yes, Ma'am," I purr, slamming my mouth onto hers.

It's rude to keep a lady waiting.

Our teeth clank together, the kiss turning into an uncontrollable frenzy. My fingers dig into the voluptuous thickness of her ass, using her body to rock against my hard, leaking cock.

"Fuck," I growl, ripping my mouth away from hers. I knee her thighs apart, gently wrapping a hand around the side of her neck while my thumb presses against her lips.

Kissing my way down her chest, I deviate, sucking a pebbled nipple into my mouth. I flick it with my tongue, toying with the sensitive bead with my teeth.

She keens, the sounds are music to my ears with every melody that I seem to pull from her. I keep her pinned against the window by her throat, adorning one breast before moving my way to the other.

I can't leave any part of her flesh without my touch. I need my scent all over her. I need every male to know she belongs to me when she steps outside. There will be no question if she has a mate—even if we won't be fully mated.

My tongue becomes needy, the tip scaling down her stomach, and my taste buds brighten from the taste of her. I fall to my knees when I can't bend down further. She runs her fingers through my hair as I stare up at her from the floor.

Oh, I do like this position.

On my knees, worshipping my goddess. It doesn't get more heavenly than that.

I tug my sweatpants from her, tossing them to the side, and my mouth waters when I reveal the trimmed reddish tuft of hair settled on her pussy.

"I need to taste you." I lift her left leg onto my shoulder, kissing the small horseshoe tattoo on her ankle. I smirk, knowing she had no idea how fitting this tattoo would be when she got it.

"To bring me luck," she manages to say through broken moans.

I place a kiss on her calf. "I think you're about to get very lucky, Darlin'." Every time my lips meet her skin, she inhales, her fingernails digging into my scalp as she tries to find some sort of control over her body.

My long claws dig into the sensitive flesh of her thighs, leaving pinpoint indentations. They are temporary marks, and they appease my need to claim.

For now.

Eventually, she will have a scarred mark on her neck. A scar that will hold my scent for all eternity.

I bury my face between her thighs, inhaling her scent until my lungs memorize her.

"Fuck," I growl against her. "You smell delicious."

"Kentucky." The shy quality of my name falling from her lips has my cock flexing in my sweatpants.

I ease my tongue through her velvet lips, teasing her clit in a circular motion.

"Kentucky! Oh! Oh! Yes, please don't stop. Don't stop," she pleads, pushing her hips against my face for more attention.

"You'll have to stake me to get me to stop, Darlin'." There's an additional spice hanging in the air, one that tempts my need for blood and causes a throb to fill my fangs.

Grabbing her hips, I move her closer against my mouth, burying my tongue into her tight pussy.

And that's when I taste it.

Blood.

She has no clue she's just started her courses, and I don't want to mortify her, but for me, this couldn't have come at a better time. I don't have to bite her. I can drink from her just like this. While it isn't the same as the blood that pumps through her veins, it will do in a pinch and satisfy the urge I have to sink my fangs into her femoral artery.

My claws skim down the back of her thighs as I feast, plunging my tongue in and out. My nose is against her clit, and with every motion of my head, it rubs against the mass of nerves.

My name is a moan coming from her, "Kentucky. Oh, fuck. You feel so good. More. Faster. I'm close."

My left hand glides up her body, cupping her breast while the other dips between her thighs, and rubs her clit with more pressure.

She smacks the glass behind her, continuing to rock herself against my tongue. I hum as a small amount of blood floods my mouth. I drink it down with greed, finally getting a taste of what is to come.

She invigorates me.

Is this what it's like? Why would I want death over my fated mate's taste? She is satisfying a hunger I never knew I had, empowering me with blood that was made specifically for me.

Her cries become louder, quicker, and the harsh scratch of her nails on my shoulder tells me she is close. I free my cock from the constraints of my sweatpants, wrapping a hand around myself for relief.

"Oh, god. Kentucky! I'm going...you're going to make me...I'm—" She tosses her head back, shouting to the ceiling with pleasure. I eat her through her orgasm, prolonging the pleasure sparking through her body.

I kiss her clit, and Dru doubles over from the sensitivity. Pulling away, I don't bother to wipe my mouth. I want her to see how I don't care about her courses; if anything, I fucking love it.

And I'll want to do this every day during the duration of her monthly cycle.

Her eyes manage to open at last, glazed from the high of her orgasm.

"Is that? Is that my—" She covers her mouth with her hand as she sinks to the floor, climbing onto my lap. The tip of my cock edges against her drenched entrance, taunting me to take her right here on the floor. Her thumb wipes the corners of my mouth. "Did you bite me or is that—"

"I didn't bite you," A guttural snarl vibrates the space between us. "Don't be embarrassed, Darlin'. I fucking love how you taste. I'll happily do it again, and again, and again."

Much to my surprise, she slants her mouth onto mine, kissing me to the point where I know she can taste herself. Not wanting to break the spell between us, I wrap my arms around her and, with swiftness, take us to my bedroom.

The bedroom is a solarium. The walls and ceilings are made of thick, impenetrable glass. I like to lie in bed and look up at the night sky, the stars right above me, or when it rains, I can witness thunder and lightning battle for dominance.

I toss her on the bed, wanting her blood to stain my sheets so they smell of her.

"But I'm going to make a mess on your bed—"

"—I fucking hope so." I sling my pants off, standing by the bed naked in front of a woman for the first time in many, many years.

A sliver of insecurity rattles me, wondering if she's happy with what she sees.

Her gaze is slow as she takes all of me in. A fresh wave of blood leaks from her when her eyes fall onto my cock, and a new cloud of lust fills my bedroom.

"You are perfect," she breathes, followed by an audible gulp. "I need to tell you something. And I'd understand if you want to stop, but I don't. I just think it's fair you know before we move on."

I crawl up her body, peppering kisses on every body part I pass before I hover over her face. "What is it, Darlin'?" I lean down, pressing a kiss to her cheek.

"I'm a virgin," she whispers into my ear.

The words sink into me, wrapping around the primal instincts of her belonging to me. She's mine and will only be mine. No other has had her.

Only me.

And it makes me lose control.

DEAD MAN'S RANCH

Chapter Fourteen

DRUSCILLA

He trembles beneath my touch.

"Kentucky?" I drift my fingers down his back. "Are you mad?" I can't tell by his reaction. He hasn't said a word.

His growls fill my ear. Every breath that escapes him sounds like it's coming from a wild animal waiting to tear apart their prey. I can't decide if that is good or bad, considering our situation right now.

"Kentucky?"

He licks the side of my neck, his fangs sharp as they skim across the vein. I submit to him in return, wanting him to feed, wanting to feel what it is like to be properly bitten by a vampire.

Goosebumps arise on my skin from the back and forth of the sharp points threatening to break the barrier shielding my vein. Still, I'm not afraid. I trust him.

He thrusts my legs apart, settling between them without saying a word. Kentucky continues to bury his face in my neck, sucking a chunk of flesh into his mouth.

My hip becomes the leverage he needs to hold on to. His claws threaten to puncture my skin as they sink into my flesh.

The slight pain causes me to arch my back. I want more of his wild abandon. I want more of him losing control.

He finally speaks when the head of his cock slips into my entrance. "Dru." My name is a shaken attempt from him to speak. "So fucking wet for me," he praises, sliding a hand down my thigh.

He lifts from me, his eyes brighter than I've ever seen them. "You are all mine, Beloved." He pushes forward, stealing my ability to string a thought together.

I clutch the bedsheets in my fists, arching my back as I work through the small amount of pain. His eyes roll to the back of his head when he inhales, then his tongue licks one fang before he lazily drops his gaze to where we are locked together.

"I love it when you bleed for me."

He slides out, only to slam back in, unforgiving and relentless, as if he has been waiting to take me.

"You waited all this time to give yourself to a vampire?" He wraps a hand around my throat, his fangs nipping at my chin. "Why is that, Darlin'?"

"I—I—" My answer turns into a moan.

"What is that?" He squeezes my throat a bit harder. I can still breathe, but I crave the pressure from his grip on either side of my neck. "I couldn't hear you with my cock nine inches deep."

"—I don't know," I call out, clawing at his shoulder as hard as I can. It doesn't matter if I make him bleed.

He will heal.

"Yes, you do." He flicks his tongue across my chin, outlining my mouth before he dives between my lips, kissing me with harsh bursts. "Tell me." He thrusts faster, our skin slapping together as he picks up speed.

"Kentucky," I moan, unable to keep up with his demands as he pounds into me.

My throat becomes a podium for his hands.

"I said to tell me, Dru. Or I won't let you come. I'll use you. I'll fill this pretty cunt up with all my come, leaving you needy and throbbing."

"You wouldn't!" I cry as his pace increases again, burying himself as deep as he can inside me.

Two fingers slip into my mouth, hitting the back of my throat, which causes me to gag.

"I have lived for a very long time. If you think I can't use you, you are mistaken. Now, tell me before I get my lasso out, bind your wrists and ankles to the bed, and let you lie here day in and day out while I use you over and over again."

I groan, loving the idea of that.

He brings his lips to my ear, and a dark chuckle has me holding my breath. "Tsk, tsk, Darlin'. You aren't supposed to love that idea, but I smell how much you do." He lifts my leg to his shoulder, somehow allowing him to sink further inside me.

His fangs tease down my neck and up again. "Maybe that's an idea we can try later." Kentucky nibbles my earlobe, the slight sting of the dangerous points makes me wetter. "Mmmmm," he growls, licking the side of my throat again. "You have no idea how badly I want to drink from you, Darlin'." His fingers trace what I assume is my vein. The rough pads of his fingertips spark lustful chaos in my blood. "I bet you'd taste so good. I've imagined what you could taste like. I bet you'd be warm with a hint of cinnamon and smoke—the best kind of whiskey a man like me could ever crave." He flattens his tongue again, licking a path from my collarbone to my jaw. "I know you would always sate my need."

"Always. Whenever you need me." I kiss his shoulder, neck, and jaw before I take his lips, needing to feel more of him. One hand drifts down the strong plains of his back, gripping a firm cheek in my hand. The muscle flexes with every hard thrust he gives me.

With a snarl, he flips me over, placing his hand between my shoulder blades to keep me pinned against the bed. He fists my hair, craning my head back. I'm not sure what it is about this position, but he hits a spot that feels too good. I can't stay quiet. I cry out with every drive of his cock to the hilt, giving me every inch.

"I love how much I stretch you. I wish you could see what I do, my fat cock stretching this virgin cunt. You're going to be so sore tomorrow, and I'm going to love every single second of your discomfort." He slaps my ass with his palm, a warm sting blooming across my cheek.

He slaps me again.

And again.

Until the stings morph to pleasure, my orgasm bursts through my body.

"Fuck," he growls. "You're *gripping* me, Darlin', and making an absolute mess. So fucking perfect." He leaves me empty, falling to his stomach, clutches my hips hard enough to leave bruises, and yanks me to his mouth.

His tongue is *there* again. The soft glide warm and wet, against my abused entrance. He moans in delight, delving his tongue as far as possible, gathering a mixture of my orgasm and blood. He drinks it down as if he is a man dying of thirst.

Kentucky pinches my clit, rolling it with the perfect amount of pressure to ignite yet another orgasm. My thighs shake from too much pleasure, yet I still feel like I haven't gotten enough.

My body is on fire for more. Not just more sex. I want him to bite me. I *need* him to bite me. My soul is calling for him to give me everything he can.

He mouths my neck again, placing a kiss before flipping us into a new position.

This time I'm on top.

I stare down into red, fiery eyes and sharp fangs. His hands are on my hips, the black claws sinking into my flesh so hard, beads of blood roll down my leg. Kentucky swipes the blood free, rubbing it onto his fangs.

"What's wrong, Darlin'? I scent your unease."

"I...I don't know what to do." My cheeks become hot with the admission.

"Let me guide you, Beloved." He applies more pressure, moving forward and back. I gasp, my clit rubbing against him while his cock sinks into me. "You belong up there, Dru. You look so fucking beautiful. A fucking goddess. I could praise you every day, and it wouldn't be enough."

The way he talks to me gives me the confidence to move against him, to use him, to bring myself to another orgasm. I gain speed, fucking him harder with every rock of my hips.

"Kentucky." I lick my lips, panting as I ride him, chasing the orgasm that is lingering so close. "You're so big. Oh, god, you feel so good." I pinch my nipples, giving them a rough tug.

"You never told me," he snarls, wrapping his arms around me.

He sits up, kissing the middle of my chest. "Why wait all this time for me?"

"No one else ever made sense."

"And I do?"

I push his hair out of his handsome face, locking onto his crimson gaze. "Nothing has ever made more sense than you."

His fangs gleam against the sunlight pouring through the windows. The rays warm my shoulders, but that's not what is causing me to sweat. It's the man beneath me.

"You are stunning on top of me. Don't fucking stop, Dru," he seethes through clenched fangs. "Don't stop."

"I'm going to come. I can't wait. I can't…" I breathe in, doing my best to hold in my orgasm. "I…"

"That's okay, Darlin'. Come all over my cock. Show me how good you feel because of me."

I toss my head back, crying out to the afternoon sky peering down on me, clenching around him again.

He moves so fast, he becomes a distortion, pinning me on my back. My head hangs over the bed, and he moves in a blur, fucking me so hard and fast that I can't see him, another orgasm shaking the bones in my body from how many times he has pleasured me.

A monstrous roar vibrates through the room as he fills me, his orgasm long, filling me so much, his come begins to drip from me.

Only this time, his growls are deeper, uncontrollable, and carnal. He scurries away from me, falls off the bed, and catches himself on the glass wall. His shoulders rise and fall in harsh motions, his fangs shadows against the light.

"Kentucky?" I crawl across the bed to get to him. "What's wrong?"

"Don't!" he yells at me, his voice not his own, but riddled with the part of him who is a monster. "Don't come any closer."

"Is it something I did?" I gather the blankets, covering myself. "Was…I that bad?"

He cuts his pain-ridden eyes on me. "What? No. You're fucking amazing. The best fucking feeling I've ever had in my entire life. I"—he rolls his head over his shoulders, and those claws rake down the window, leaving five long grooves—"I want to bite you so bad. It hurts. It physically pains me."

"Kentucky, if you need to feed, take it." I hold out my wrist for him. "It's here. I'm right here."

"No, it's more than that, Dru. It's so much more. I can't.

Not yet." He falls to his knees, a long string of saliva dripping from his mouth onto the floor. "My god, I can smell your blood pumping in your veins. I can hear it."

He doubles over, and I'm off the bed to help him, but he holds out his arm to stop me again. "Don't," he warns, desperation shining in his rubies.

His sights lock onto the space between my legs, a rush of come mixed with blood drips down my leg, and he snarls, launching himself at me.

Kentucky throws me on the bed, blurs to the furthest end of the room, and bites into his own arm, shouting into the wound with frustration. It's somehow enough to calm him. He slides down the wall until he is sitting on the floor. Blood drips from his arm, but he doesn't remove his fangs.

His face seems pale. Dark circles appear under his eyes. His arm falls to his side, and dark red drips from his mouth. "I'll never take away your choice," he murmurs. "Never."

Kentucky's eyes roll to the back of his head, his body slumping over.

"Kentucky?" I whisper his name with fear. "Kentucky!" I shout, jumping from the bed to rush to his side. I grab his shoulders, shaking him in hopes he will wake up.

He doesn't move.

His arm is slower to heal. The wound still oozes blood, a small pool collecting on the floor beneath him.

"What do I do? What do I do?" I chant, leaning down to check to see if he is still breathing, pressing two fingers against his neck.

I don't feel anything.

"Oh my god. Kentucky!" My eyes fill with tears and panic, not knowing what to do in this situation. I place my hand under his nose, exhaling a huge breath of relief when hot air brushes by.

Why can't I feel a heartbeat, then?

"Um. Okay, it's okay. He is alive. Barely, but alive. What do I do? Think, Druscilla, think." I have always spoken my issues out loud. It makes it easier to think of solutions when I can hear what the problem is. "He is unconscious. You have no idea what from. He is pale. He isn't healing as fast. Clearly, he is sick. Maybe vampires get the flu? No, that doesn't make sense either. He said he can't get human diseases. Unless it is the vampire flu." I roll my eyes at how stupid that sounds. "I bet that doesn't even exist."

I try shaking him awake again, but it doesn't work. He still lies there unconscious, barely breathing, with a heart rate of three. I don't know how that is possible.

Nearly tripping over myself when I run to the bed, I snag a few pillows, the comforter, and an extra blanket that is folded at the bottom. I place a pillow behind his head, shove the others under his legs to elevate them, cover him with the comforter, and rush to the bathroom to clean up a little.

I wish I could appreciate how beautiful the bathroom is. There's a huge walk-in shower to the left, made with wood paneling. According to the screen on the wall, it also doubles as a sauna. To the right is another claw-foot tub, and the vanity has two sinks with antique mirrors hanging over each of them.

His closet is directly to the left when you enter the bathroom, big enough for four people. Half of it is unused while the other half has his jeans, shirts, and hats. There are a few drawers that I rummage through. I'm relieved when I find a pair of underwear, and I steal another Dead Man's Ranch shirt off the hanger.

I don't get dressed just yet. I need to clean up.

I roll up toilet paper and stuff it between my legs as a makeshift pad, hoping I can get the products I need soon.

When I'm done, I wash my hands and splash some cold water on my face, staring at myself in the mirror. I'm brainstorming. Maybe Kentucky is resting, and I'm overthinking. I tend to do that when I have no idea what is going on.

Patting my face with a fluffy towel, I scurry into the bedroom and sit by Kentucky's side. I take his hand in mine, leaning my head against his shoulder, waiting.

What if all I end up doing is waiting?

I lift his arm over the blanket, staring at the wound where he bit himself. Why would he do that? That doesn't make any sense when I offered him my wrist. The wound isn't bleeding anymore, which means he is healing.

"What aren't you telling me?" I ask him, despite the fact that he can't answer. "Would Lorcan know?" I bet he would. How do I summon him? Is it like "Bloody Mary" where I say his name three times while looking in the mirror with all the lights off?

"Um, Lorcan! Lorcan!" I decide to try, shouting his name into the quiet room. "Lorcan, it is an emergency!"

"You rang," he sings, appearing in the darkest corner of the room.

"Lorcan, I need you to help me." I tuck the blanket under Kentucky's legs, so he stays covered. "Something is wrong with Kentucky."

Lorcan turns to smoke, drifting closer to us. His torn black cloak drags across the floor. Kneeling, he presses his hand to Kentucky's forehead, his lips pinching together.

"Well, he isn't in rodeo shape. The damn thing is Friday. I lose money every year betting on him."

"Lorcan!" I point to Kentucky. "Do you think I give a shit about a rodeo when he seems to be barely breathing? Also, his heart rate is very low. It's three beats a minute."

He waves his bony fingers through the air. "That's normal

for a vampire. Fun fact, every vampire has a different heart-beat." He sighs, pressing his fingers to his temples as if it could actually relieve his headache. "I can't tell you what's wrong because I'd be going against Kentucky."

With a sneer, I grab him by his cloak and slam him against the wall. "Listen, Bone Boy, I don't know what fucking games you two are playing, but I'm sick of it. You're going to tell me what is wrong right now, or I swear, I will start breaking your bones one by one in order for you to tell me what the hell is going on. How can I save him? Why isn't he healing?"

"Okay, retract the claws. I'll help, but you have to promise you don't know anything when he wakes up."

"Fine. What is going on? Please, Lorcan. I...I care about him more than I understand."

"I told him to tell you. I told him. He is so damn stubborn, but he wanted you to have the choice, Dru. Choice is very important to him. If I do this, I'm taking that away."

"If you don't tell me, can he die?"

"Can you let me go? You're oddly strong for a human."

I narrow my gaze at him, debating if letting him go is the right thing to do. He seems to respond best to attitude.

"Right. I thought I did already. Sorry." I let him go, and he straightens his robe, brushing out the wrinkles even though he clearly needs a new one with how torn and ragged it is.

"Before I talk about him, I need to know how you are doing? How are you feeling? Outside of this moment, you need to tell me everything," he says, bending down to examine Kentucky's arm. "He bit himself?"

Tears fill my eyes. "Yes. I offered my wrist to him. He was struggling so bad, Lorcan. He flew from the bed, yelled at me to stay back, and then I offered him my wrist for him to drink, but he bit himself. I tried shaking him awake. He's out cold."

"And how do you feel? Not the panic, I mean, how do you feel around him in general? I need to know how far this has gone. I see you gave in to the heat," he says, pointing to the bed.

I choke on a cough, twisting one of my curls around my finger. "We have been fighting it for the last few days. I don't know what happened. I feel this need to be close to him at all times, my body is always hot like I have a fever, and when I'm around him, I fall more in love with him. The thought of being away from him kills me. I don't want to go home if it means leaving him. This feels like my home now, and I don't understand. We fell into bed, and it was...amazing. It felt right. It felt natural. I don't know why he wouldn't take my blood. Is something wrong with me? Will my blood hurt him or something? I'm type AB negative. Does he not like that? Does he prefer another? I can try to go get him some. I'll break into a blood bank."

Lorcan smiles at me, wiping away my tears with a rough bone. "No, Dru. Someone else's blood won't work." He groans in frustration. "This isn't how this is supposed to go."

"Lorcan! Just tell me!" I sit down next to Kentucky, taking his hand in mine. "Please."

Lorcan sits down too, joining me on the floor next to Kentucky. "He can't take any other blood but yours, which is why he bit himself. If he bites you, it seals the bond between you. Forever. He is like this because he needs your blood. Have you felt desperate? Achey? Or feeling like you will die if he doesn't bite you?"

I nod, bringing Kentucky's hand to my lips, kissing his palm. "Yes. All those things."

"You're his fated mate, Dru. It's why all this is happening. The heat you're feeling? It's called a mating heat, and it won't get better until you seal the bond. The fever will get worse, you'll become more desperate for his bite, and he will drive himself out of his mind until he bites you. You're already half-bonded by the smell of it," he clears his throat. "Since you know...” He juts his head toward the bed. “I’m assuming you didn’t wear protection.”

I look away, still feeling the warmth of him between my legs. “No, we didn’t.”

“If he bites you, that’s it. You’ll live forever. He will live forever, and that’s another thing he has been struggling with. For as long as I have known him, he has only wanted to die. Meeting his fated mate is the last thing he wanted, until he got to know you, Dru. He told me he wanted the choice to be yours, but know this, if you say no, you will die too. Fated mates can’t live without each other. He didn’t bite you because that would be taking away your will, and with how he was turned, choice is too important to him. He would rather suffer than trap you like he was trapped. It’s a big decision.”

“It’s not,” I admit, holding Kentucky’s hand to my heart. “I want forever with him. I want to be his mate. I want him. Not because of Fate, but because of who he is as a man. I can’t believe he would bite himself to save me from being tied to him. Why wouldn’t he tell me any of this? I deserved to know.”

“He wanted you to love him without knowing you’re his fated mate. He didn’t want you to feel like Fate was forcing your decision. The most important thing to Kentucky is your right to choose. If you’d rather have a life with him, great; if you’d rather die than live forever, he would understand. He has been preparing for death for a very long time. You were not expected. You’ve changed him. In a good way. He seems more...alive than I have ever known him to be.”

“Even with Daphne?”

“Kentucky doesn’t know this, but Daphne was a Dimseer. Kind of like a psychic, but she had the ability to see into every dimension, past, present, and future, in all worlds. When she met Kentucky, she saw every path his life could lead, with all the different choices he would make, leading him to the same end—death. Until she saw you. She loved him, of course, but she kept Kentucky alive to meet you. Dimseers are so special. They are protectors, in a way. Kentucky's heart was protected with her, for you, Dru. It's also why she died like she did."

"Of old age? Kentucky said she was in her seventies when she passed."

"Dimseers live extra-long lives. Their normal lifespan is one hundred and fifty years. When they find someone to love, they sacrifice their ability to see into the dimensions, which also cuts their lifespan in half."

"She sacrificed her life for us?"

"Yes, because in all the lives she saw with Kentucky, you were the only one who could truly save the man she loved. She knew they weren't fated. She knew the role she had to play. Kentucky loved her in the best way he could, but she knew the only woman he could ever dedicate himself to was his fated mate. He never fed from her. They both agreed *that* would need to be saved for his mate, if he were to ever find her. *You.*" Lorcan boops my nose to make his point.

I clutch onto Kentucky's hand harder, wishing I could hug Daphne for everything she sacrificed to bring Kentucky to me. She kept him alive when he ached for death. All so we could have forever together. I don't think I've ever known anyone who would do such a selfless deed.

"Makes sense why I trusted him so fast. We are meant for each other, then?"

Lorcan grins. "Yes. Your souls are bound. You were both created with the other in mind. It's unfortunate how he was turned, but the moment he was, Fate knew who his mate needed to be. Kentucky needed a strong, kind, curious woman. One who didn't shy away from the truth, no matter how hard it was to accept, because he still struggles with who he is, Dru. You don't. You know who you are, through and through. He doesn't take being a vampire in stride. He hates that part of himself."

"I love that part of him," I state, caressing the side of Kentucky's face. "I love him."

"If you accept him, all of him, then eternity will be a very happy experience for both of you."

"I have to act like I don't know all of this? That I don't want him to finish claiming me? I don't know if I can."

"Dru, I can't emphasize this enough. If he feels that in any way your choice was taken away to make your own decision, he might not believe you want him. He will think you were swayed. Why do you think he asked for four days? He thought he had more time before he needed your blood, but I'm not sure if he will make it another two days without it. You seem to be doing alright. Every human is different. You could be fine now, and in an hour, you could be curled in on yourself crying."

"I did that last night," I grumble. "When I thought he still loved Daphne." I can't believe I admitted that out loud.

"He will always love her, but not in the way he was meant to love you." Lorcan places his hand on top of mine. "The mating heat will get worse too, until he bites you. Prepare yourself for that."

"Will I be a vampire too? Also, another question, having my blood won't seal the bond? Just the bite?"

"No, not unless you want to be? You will live as a human forever, and you won't age. And to answer, yes, it is the bite that seals the bond. Don't get me wrong, the blood takes you a step closer, but the bite is key."

Okay, that's good. We have more time then, like Kentucky wants. "And if I wanted to be? Would he still be able to feed from me? I don't like the thought of him feeding from anyone else."

"You would feed off each other. That wouldn't change.

Are you seriously thinking about asking him to do that? I don't know if that's a line he will cross, Dru. At least, not right now."

"I want to be able to keep up with him. I want to experience what he does. There's no rush, obviously. Being with him doesn't scare me. None of this scares me."

"You're a weird human."

"I don't mind that one bit." I run my fingers through Kentucky's hair, wishing he would open his eyes. "I only have my best friend Carmen waiting for me at home. I have my job, but I think I'll be able to be a dentist here too. I don't have to give that part of myself up, do I?"

"No. You can do whatever you want. You're seriously okay with all of this? You're going to freak out later, aren't you? The facts haven't hit you yet, right? You're going to panic and run away or something."

"I'm logical, Lorcan. I wanted all the facts so I can determine what I want. I was confused before. I didn't understand why I felt the way I felt. It all makes sense now. I wish he would have told me the truth." I continue to stroke Kentucky's hair, missing him even though he is asleep. "My choice is him, and it's been him since the moment I saw him. He's my choice, Lorcan."

"You're a good human, Dru. Not many would take this in stride, especially after everything you have been through."

"It led me here. How can I be mad about that?"

"An odd human yet a good one." Lorcan stands. "Do you need anything else?"

"Actually, yes, and I'm not sure how you're going to feel about it. I need clothes, underwear, a bra, and feminine products. I would ask Kentucky, but..." I point to him, showing that can't happen.

"I can do that." A notepad and a pen appear in his hand.

"I need your sizes for everything. Also, do you like a variety pack of the tampons?"

"You don't mind? Seriously?"

"I've been alive for a very long time. This does not bother me. Plus, it's the least I can do for the woman who is taking care of my friend."

"Thank you. I appreciate it. I don't want to leave him to go to town. I could use his old truck or...take Romeo. Not that I know how to ride a horse. It can't be that hard. I bet I could figure it out. If I left, I'm worried Kentucky would wake up alone, thinking I left him."

"I hope when I meet my fated mate, she's as open-minded as you are when it comes to the paranormal world."

I launch myself at Lorcan, giving him a big, tight hug. "And I can't wait to meet her."

"You and me both. Okay, I'll be back soon. If you want him to wake up without a headache, give him your blood, but don't let him feed from your wrist. He'll bite you. He needs to do that when he is in the right frame of mind, or he will never forgive himself." He hands me the notepad and pen. "Now, write down your sizes so I can go shopping."

"Do you need cash?"

"I'm a grim reaper. No, I don't need cash."

"Then how will you—oh." It dawns on me how he will get all the items. If it were any other day, I would argue about how stealing is wrong.

"There it is! Okay, tootles!" He snatches the notepad from me after I get done writing, then vanishes into thin air.

I kiss Kentucky's cheek. "You're going to be okay. I'll make sure of it. Don't hide anything from me anymore, okay? I want this. I want you." I press a kiss against his lips before easing his head onto the pillow.

I know how to get him my blood without issue. I'll do what Daphne did.

One coffee coming up.

I dash to the kitchen, preparing the coffee pot, and allow it to brew. Grabbing a mug from the cabinet, I take a knife and press the sharp end against my finger. A bead of red comes to the surface, and I squeeze it, allowing the blood to drip into the coffee cup. I don't stop applying pressure until the bottom of the mug is completely covered and can't be seen through the blood.

Sucking my finger into my mouth to stop the bleeding, the coffee pot beeps to signal it's done. Pouring the hot liquid into the cup, the blood mixes in well, giving the black coffee a reddish tint.

I do my best not to spill it too much. With every step, the coffee sloshes over the rim, leaving a trail behind me as I swiftly walk to the bedroom.

"Okay, My Sweet Cowboy, it's time to drink up." I tilt his head back, open his mouth, and tilt the cup.

Almost instantly, he begins to heal.

The wound on his arm fades. Next, his eyes flutter open, still bright red with hunger. Groaning, he takes the mug from me and gulps the coffee down, uncaring how hot it is.

I suppose it doesn't matter since he heals so fast.

His eyes fade to gorgeous brown as he stares at me. "You put your blood in my coffee," he rasps, trying to sit up, but he doesn't have enough strength yet.

"Relax. It's okay. I'm here. No need for you to get up. And of course, I did. You needed blood, Kentucky. Be honest with me and I'll always give you everything I can."

He presses his forehead against mine. "Thank you, Darlin'. Thank you."

"Always, My Sweet Cowboy. Do you need more?"

He shakes his head. "No, I feel it working. Your blood tastes better than anything I've ever had. I'll want more eventually," he smirks through his exhaustion.

"You can have as much as you want. My veins are your veins. You scared the hell out of me."

"I'm back!" Lorcan drops a ton of bags on the floor. "I stole all of this, by the way. They said I was going to Hell but zing! I have an unlimited pass. Joke's on them."

I giggle, laying my head on Kentucky's chest, and try to hide how happy I am that Kentucky is mine.

CHAPTER FIFTEEN
KENTUCKY

I open my eyes to the faintest amount of stars still clinging to the light purple of the sky as the sun creeps above the trees. The sun never lasts too long here. Eventually, the clouds will roll to cover us. That's what I love so much about lying here at night, staring up into the stars.

The clouds always part in order for me to enjoy the galaxy. Every now and then, a shooting star will pierce the darkness, and I make a wish. I used to wish for death, but with my mate next to me, her head on my chest, she deserves a lot more than a man who is waiting to die.

She's too full of life not to live an existence full of excitement. I vow to give her the best eternity she could ever wish upon a star for.

"You're awake," she mumbles against my chest, still sleepy and adorable.

"It's early, Darlin'. Go back to sleep. I'll make us some coffee, and we can shower to get ready for the day."

She grumbles, burying her face in the pillow. "Too early. It's still dark." She peeks one eye open at the ceiling. "It's still dark-ish."

I chuckle, leaning down to press a kiss to her forehead. "Go back to sleep. There's no reason for you to get up. Rest. I have to get started with the chores."

She opens one eye again, that hazel eye riddled with the need to sleep. "Chores? So early?"

"Every day." I tug one of her curls before dragging my finger down the side of her cheek. "You deserve to stay in bed all day. You should never have to lift a finger. I'll do all the liftin'."

A sleepy smile spreads across her face. "You're making ranch living sound really good. If you don't stop, you'll never get rid of me."

I become serious, emotion lodging in my throat. "Good. Getting rid of you is out of the question. Don't even think like that."

And I've tasted her blood. I don't know if she knows that means it makes us even closer to being a mated pair, for all eternity. A part of me doesn't want her to know. I'm too afraid she will run away.

I remember talking to Lorcan about fated mates years ago, and he kept trying to convince me not to look forward to death so much. But I couldn't help yearning for death when life hadn't been kind to me.

Truly, I thought if I ever met my fated mate, she wouldn't be enough to convince me to live. My mind was made up. If I could have walked into the sun ages ago to turn to ash, I would have.

Now, Dru is here.

And life doesn't seem so cruel anymore. Don't get me wrong, when the dark thoughts grip me, I spiral. There is a part of me that thinks death would be better for both of us than to be cursed to outlive a planet.

Then, I stare at the beauty who is lying in my bed. She's so selfless and caring, and I know that there isn't anyone else I would want to search the night sky with.

Life doesn't seem like a burden anymore.

The real question is if Dru will feel the same.

She yawns, staring up at me with sleepy eyes. "What do you do so early?"

"Well, I have to feed everyone. I need to check the fence line to make sure nothing needs fixin'. There's fresh hay, and I need to put new shoes on Romeo."

"Shoes? He wears shoes?"

She's so cute when she's confused.

"Horseshoes."

"Ohhhh." It dawns on her. "And you have to do all that today? By yourself? Why don't you have any ranch hands?"

I bend down, kissing her bare shoulder. "Because being alone was easier. I didn't have to worry about people if I died."

The sleep hanging on to her disappears, and she sits up, her eyes round as the moon. "You really wanted to die?"

A spike of annoyance has me clenching my teeth together. "I see Lorcan is telling business that ain't his to tell."

"He was only trying to help me yesterday when you were unconscious. Don't be mad at him. He helped me."

"My feelings about life are complicated, but with you here, it isn't so bad at all. Go back to sleep, Darlin'. You don't deserve to be up before the birds." I kiss her forehead, and the moment my lips touch her skin, the same fever that broke me last night begins to sizzle within my veins.

I growl, closing my eyes to fight the urges. Now that I know what her blood tastes like, my fangs ache to sink into her neck. I want to claim her to ease this ache inside my bones, my teeth, my skin. There isn't a spot on my body that doesn't hurt from needing to be bonded to her.

Only a few more days before the truth can be set free, and she can decide what she wants out of this life.

"You're sure you don't need help? I can learn. I want to learn. Lorcan got me so many clothes, and now I have boots!"

"Darlin'—" I eye said boots across the room. "They're pink. With sparkles. I'm not sure if he got you the right kind of boot."

She sticks out her bottom lip. "I like them though."

Unable to help myself, I tug her lip with my thumb, growling as I imagine her mouth around my cock. Hmmmm, I bet she would feel so fucking good.

"Well, if you like'em, then I suppose that's all that matters. Ain't that right?" I grip her chin between my index finger and thumb, drunk on the thought of these lips wrapping around me. I haven't been able to think about anything else.

"Your eyes are red, Cowboy." The stale air is replaced with the sweet and spicy scent of her arousal. "Is there something you're wanting before you start your busy day?" She sits up, allowing the blanket to fall from her body.

I'm fixated on her. Up and down, I take her in.

I can't believe this woman is mine.

Her finger glides down my chest. If it were possible, flames would dance in the path of her touch. She swirls her fingertip, teasing me as she gets lower, only to deviate when she gets right where I want her to be.

A low growl reverberates in the chamber of my throat when she traces the dip in my hips.

"Or are you wanting to go about your morning while I go back to sleep?" She bats her eyelashes as she toys with me.

I find myself loving to be the object she plays with.

"No, ma'am. I think—" In a blur, I have her pressed against the shower wall and blast the warm water.

She gasps, surprised by the change of location.

I love that look. I'll have to make sure I take her by surprise more often.

"—I have exactly what I want right here." I dip my hand between her legs, my fingers pinching the tampon string.

"Wait. Let me use the restroom."

"I don't think so. Hold it. It will make your orgasm more intense."

"Kentucky. I can't. I don't think I can do that." She tilts her head back when my thumb presses against her clit.

"I think you can, and you will. Want to know why?" I lick the water from her lips, my tongue dragging down her neck where her vein is. Every instinct is pushing me to bite.

I can't.

I groan the words internally, fighting every instinct.

"You can," she whispers approval. "Bite me. I want you to."

I scrape my fangs down her neck, pressing a single kiss to her jugular. "One day, but not right now, Beloved." I let the word slip. Lorcan told me it is a special term vampires use for their fated mates.

Beloved.

I can't believe I have one.

"But it can be today. You can bite me, Kentucky. I want it. I want you."

"I want you too," I growl, clamping onto her collarbone with very light pressure. The skin won't break, no matter how badly I want it to. "You have no idea how deep the craving for you goes." I fall to my knees, my hard, solid cock slapping against my stomach, and precome dribbles down my shaft. "Is this where you want me, Darlin'? On my knees for you. I'll do it every morning and night."

She runs her hand through my wet hair. "You do look good on your knees for me. It is a sight I could get used to."

"Well, I haven't ever been the praying type, but I'll pray to you." I lift her leg onto my shoulder, place my hands together, and peer up through wet lashes. "Bless this food for which I'm about to eat," I snarl. "Amen."

"Kentucky!" she giggles my name.

I pinch the string of her tampon and tug. Her hands slap against the wall, trying to gain some sort of leverage or support to hold on to.

"What are you doing?" The question ends on a high-pitched note, proving how horrified she is.

"Like I said, a man's got to eat." I tug again, slow and gentle, the tampon coming out with ease. I'd hate for her to be in pain just to feed me. "Does that feel okay?"

"Yes, but—oh."

I rub her cunt with my fingers, massaging her lips while keeping my thumb applied to her clit. Slow, hard circles cause her to moan, her thighs shaking from the attention. Her mouth parts when I bring the tampon to my mouth. Our gazes lock. Her heart rate increases. I hear it. A fast, uncontrolled beat by what she is seeing.

"Kentucky, are you going to—"

I sink my fangs into the warm tampon, groaning when her blood flows across my tongue. My sight zeroes in between her thighs. The smell of her blood has more saliva pooling in my mouth. Inserting two fingers, I slip them inside her, growling within my chest when rivulets of red flow down my hand, dripping onto the tile floor.

The water washes it down the drain, forever gone.

Wasted.

"Have you...have you done this before?" Her words tremble with a hint of sadness.

I toss the tampon on the floor and lift the other leg onto my shoulder, keeping her propped against the wall. "No. No one's blood has ever called to me the way yours does. I believe I've saved many parts of myself for you, and I am angry at the world for keeping me away from you for so long." I dive my head between her legs, my tongue parting her lips.

I moan when her flavor bursts through my taste buds. She's so soft and warm, like silk draping over my tongue. Her blood invigorates me more than the coffee from yesterday.

"Kentucky," she groans my name, her nails digging into my scalp as my tongue plunges inside her depths that I claimed as mine last night.

No other has had her.

No other will have her.

I'm the only man she will ever experience for the rest of her eternity.

The thought of that has my hand wrapping around my cock, stroking the length within my tight fist.

"Are you sore from yesterday?" I give her clit a kiss, circling the nerves with my tongue, then sucking the sweet cherry into my mouth.

Her passionate cries echo within the shower stall, her breath causing the clouds of steam to surround her. "Yes," she shouts. "Yes. Yes. Yes." Dru stretches one arm above her, shuts her eyes, and her thighs tremble around my neck.

Continuing the sweet assault on her clit, I sink two fingers inside, fucking her hard and fast, wishing it was my cock instead.

"Kentucky!" She tries to climb up the wall as her orgasm slams against her.

Heat pulses through my cock as I smother my face between her thighs, worshipping her altar as her holy water drips down my throat to quench my thirst. She feeds the starvation that has been gnawing at my soul. The softness of her skin beneath these calloused hands should be a sin.

"Come for me again, Darlin'. Don't let me go hungry," I growl, giving her clit another hard tug as I roll the bead between my fangs.

Her entire body shakes, preparing for another wave of pleasure.

Fuck, I'm so close to coming just from her taste, just from her pleasure. Knowing it's me who is having her become a fucking mess has me tightening my fist around my cock to the point of pain to stop the impending orgasm.

"Fuck—Oh, god! Kentucky!" She screams my name, curling over me as she loses her strength. Her nails rake up my back, using me to let her pleasure out.

When she's done, I ease her legs from my shoulders and stand. She's shaking within my embrace, her knees shake from how unsteady they are.

"I have…" She points to my mouth, rolling her lips together to keep from laughing. "You have a little bit of me all over your face."

"Good," I snarl, flicking my tongue to get the blood from the corners. "You're about to have me all over yours too." Grabbing her shoulders, I force her to her knees, grab her hair within my fist. "Be a good girl and suck my cock."

The water from the shower shines against her lips. I groan out loud for her to hear when her hand wraps around the base of my cock. I want to show her how good she makes me feel. I don't care that she is new to this. I fucking love that no other has ever had her. I love her uncertainty because of how sweet it is, how gentle she is, and how badly she wants to help me feel good.

What she doesn't understand is, it is her existence that makes me feel on top of the world. Not this.

Don't get me wrong, there isn't a prettier sight than my fated mate on her knees and her mouth an inch away from my cock.

"Hey, no pressure, Darlin'. You don't have to do a damn thing you don't want to do, okay?"

"I do want to. I do. I'm nervous. I don't think you'll fit in my mouth."

"Mmm," I hum with delight. "That's just fine. I know another place that takes every inch perfectly." I tilt my head, allowing my eyes to morph to red before her eyes. "And I love that fucking place."

The sound of her heart skipping a beat has my cock jerking in her hand.

"You'll tell me if it doesn't feel good?"

"Anything you do will feel good, Dru. It's you. You could read me the damn phone book, and I'd come."

The freckles on her cheeks become a deeper shade of brown as her face heats.

"It's okay. I'll guide you if you need it." I brush my knuckles down her face, marveling once again at her beauty. She's a goddess. *My* goddess.

Her fingers and thumb don't touch. I don't know if her hand is small or my dick is big, but she's making me feel on top of the world right now.

She takes her time, and I don't mind at all. I want this moment to last for as long as she wants it to.

Dru squeezes her hand tighter in an experiment, giving me a tight stroke that makes me gasp.

"Does that feel okay?" she asks, shy and bashful.

"Feeling fucking amazing," I tell her, loving the glow confidence brings to her face.

She kisses the head of my cock, her big hazel eyes peering up at me to seek approval.

I flash my fangs, wanting her to see how on edge I really am.

Wrapping her plump mouth around me, she sucks in the crown. Her teeth scrape against the flesh, and I punch the wall, shattering the wooden panel.

She slides me from her mouth. "Did I hurt you? I'm sorry."

"No. I love it. I love the slight pain. Do it again," I growl the demand.

She smirks, tracing the crown with her tongue, slow and easy for her first time. I tilt my head back, loving how she is experimenting, taking it slow, and wanting to please me.

"That's a good girl. You're doing so well, Darlin'. You feel so damn good. I could stand here forever watching you on your knees, my cock in your mouth with your hand around me."

Praising her adds to her confidence. Her tongue traces around the crown again, dipping into the slit to gather the precome. Sucking me down a few more inches, her tongue continues to massage my shaft while she hollows her cheeks.

I toss my head back, moaning her name, "Dru. Just like that, don't stop." Fisting her hair harder, I flex my hips, needing to slip down her throat a little more. "Oh, fuck, you feel so good. This mouth is dangerous. If you think for one minute I'm wasting my come down your throat, you're wrong. You're going to sit on my cock and take every fucking drop." I wrap a hand around her throat, loving the movement I feel in every finger from her head bobbing to take me deeper.

She hums around me, the vibrations sinking into my cock, and I shout my approval. She does it again, and again, bringing me closer to the edge. One hand begins to stroke in tandem with her warm, wet mouth, pulling me deep into her throat.

Dru lightly bites down on my shaft, and I rip her off me by yanking her back by her hair. Picking her up, I spin her around, press her against the wall, and sink as far as I can inside her.

She moans from the intrusion.

"Does that hurt? Because you're so sore?" I grip her thighs, my claws dragging across her skin.

"So sore," she replies, hanging her head as the water rushes down her back.

I slide out and then slam back in. "Good," I growl into her ear. "You'll always know I was there. That this pussy is all mine. That no other will make you ache the way I do. Isn't that right?" I kiss the side of her neck, wishing I could take a quick drag from her vein.

So tempting.

"Yes. Yes! That's right. Always." She turns her head, pressing her cheek against the wall, gasping as I take my fill.

I use her tight cunt to grip me, her warmth sending me over the edge. I roar her name, biting into my arm again to stop myself from binding our fates.

"Dru," I gasp her name on an unholy exhale, my cock jerking as every rope of come escapes me.

"Oh, god!" she cries, squirting all over my length while her spasms pull my come to her womb.

I knew her orgasm would be intense.

I stay lodged inside her, kissing her shoulder, wishing that she'd be bred with my child by the end of the day.

If only I could have kids. I know I can't. I'll have to talk to her about that. If she wants children, we can always adopt. I want to be a father more than I can put into words.

It's on the tip of my tongue to tell her I love her. To beg her not to go home. To stay with me here on the ranch. I want to tell her that I'd give her everything in this world. She'll never have to ask, need, or want for anything. If she never wants to work, that's more than fine by me.

A woman of her caliber deserves warm baths every morning and night, massages, gifts, attention, and love. I want her to have all that.

And I want to be the one to give it to her.

Easing out of her makes us both gasp. I hate and love

watching as I drip out of her. Blood and come washes down the drain, leaving no evidence of our time together.

I spin her around, slamming my lips down on hers, readying myself for round two. That's one positive about being a vampire. My endurance never ends, but my sweet mate is human, and she's sore. She needs time to recover.

"Let me take care of you." I maneuver her in front of me, tilt her head back so the water is soaking her hair, and steal another kiss. "I can't get enough of you, Dru."

"I can't get enough of you either," she mumbles, relaxed and sated.

She reaches for the shampoo Lorcan got her, and I reach for her hand, stopping her. I'm agitated that Lorcan got her everything she needed. That was my job. I failed her.

"I want to wash your hair."

"No one has ever washed my hair before."

I grin, continuing to separate her hair to get every strand wet. Dru's hair is so thick and curly. I'm obsessed.

"Lucky me for getting another first." I bend down, kissing her left shoulder, then her right. "The only man who is ever going to wash you, bathe you, and take care of you is me."

She turns her chin to her shoulder, a genuine smile twisting her plump lips that are as soft as suede.

They are an addiction I will never break.

Her kiss is hypnotic, a spell so strong that all I think about night and day is feeling her against me. I can't believe I've lived long enough to have someone destined for me for all eternity. I still can't seem to wrap my head around it.

"I think I really like the sound of that, Kentucky."

A purr of pure happiness fills my chest. I've never been this content in all my years. Feeling like this is so new to me that I'm not sure how to fully believe it. She's almost like a dream, too good to be true, and could be gone in the blink of an eye.

"It would be a little easier if you parted my hair into sections. Since my hair is so thick, it will be easier to get the sections wet."

"Tell me everything. I want to learn how to do your hair, so you don't have to. Anything you need for it, it's yours."

"I wouldn't mind a silk bonnet. It helps protect my hair."

"Consider it done, Darlin'. I'll buy you all the bonnets."

She giggles, a beautiful sound I want to record so I can have it on replay. "I only need one or two."

"You deserve as many as you want. One or two," I scoff, sectioning her hair like she told me to. "I'm assuming they have fun patterns? You should have your choice of selections."

"You're going to make me fall in love with you if you keep that up."

Warmth blooms through my body, my heart skipping a beat, and I hold my breath when I realize what it is.

Hope.

Because I do love her already. Loving her happened the moment I smelled her blood. Loving her happened when I killed those shifters to save her. Loving her happened when I finally had her in my arms, close to my chest, and my tears falling into her wound.

"Maybe you falling in love with me is exactly what I want and need." After sectioning her hair and wetting it, I reach for the shampoo, pouring a generous amount in my palm.

Taking care of her is my life's mission now.

Nothing else matters.

DEAD MAN'S
RANCH

CHAPTER
Sixteen
DRUSCILLA

After being pampered in the shower with amazing haircare products from Lorcan, including a lovely deep conditioning mask that I left on while Kentucky washed every inch of my body, I'm feeling better than I have...ever.

"What do you want, Dru?" Kentucky asks me as we sit on the rocking chairs on the porch while we have our coffee.

His just the way he likes. Black with an inch of blood inside. I like to give him extra rather than a few drops. I like knowing I'm feeding him, especially after what Lorcan told me.

It's been hard keeping that a secret. To not let Kentucky know that I know I'm his mate. I want to spill the truth to him. I don't feel right knowing this while he is respecting me enough to allow me to make my own decisions.

I have to. Lorcan is right. Kentucky won't think I made the decision myself if I knew the truth, but I think I've always known I was destined for him. Even on the first day, when I was scared, I felt in my soul that I had no reason to be afraid of him.

"What do you mean?" I take a small sip of my hot coffee,

careful not to burn my tongue as I watch the sun cast its brightness on the tall grass of the pastures where all of his cows graze. I can tell the sun won't last long. In the distance, storm clouds are forming.

It's rained every day I've been here, and I have to say, I don't hate it at all.

"Out of life? What are your goals? Is there anything you want to accomplish? Do you want a big family?" The spurs of his boots reflect from the sun with every rock of the chair; the sharp points could kill someone, the longer I analyze them.

I wonder if they have?

"I would love a big family. Both of my parents were only children, and after my mom died, I remember growing up wishing I had siblings. Then, after my dad died, I became focused. I didn't care about having a lot of friends because I didn't want to get distracted. I had a goal. I wanted to become a dentist. Eventually, I'd like to have my own practice."

"You could be a dentist here if you wanted. The town is small, and people have to go to the next town over to get dental work done. I think you'd be successful in this town. If you know, you want to think about it. And maybe, you could specialize in animal dentistry. I don't know anyone who does that, and there is a lot of farmland out here. A lot of animals need care. I'm just saying, I think you could be successful."

"I'm not a veterinarian. I could only focus on the teeth."

"That's perfect. There's a vet I know who comes when I need him. It's been a while."

"Can't you give the animals a drop of your blood if anything is wrong?" I ask. "Like you did with Romeo."

"Well, turning animals is kind of frowned upon in the paranormal community. There aren't laws against it, so Lorcan told me, but they don't celebrate it either. I got a pass because I have the rare gift of speaking to animals. Romeo let me know he didn't want to die. I had to give him a lot of blood, kill him, and then he came back as a vampire. I try not to use my blood to heal any of my animals if they need help. I know it seems cruel, but then I'd have dozens of cows with momentary enhanced speed and strength. I wouldn't feel comfortable selling my cattle either if they had my blood in them. I take pride in my farm. I believe life is sacred. The animal's life is sacred. You're born, you live, you die. I give them the best life possible."

"Do you only have cows and Romeo? Why not more? Have you ever thought of adding to your farm? Maybe even a sanctuary of animals who are like Romeo? Who want to live? They could be a big happy family."

His cowboy hat shadows his face when he dips his chin. "I've thought about it. It is only me here, so I figured that wasn't what was best for them. Is that what you would want? To save animals and they could have good teeth?" he jokes, adding a smirk before hiding it in the coffee mug.

I toss my head back, laughing. "I mean, that doesn't seem so bad, does it? Seems pretty great to me. We could have chickens, donkeys, peacocks, and dairy cows! We could sell milk. We could have more horses. Romeo is probably lonely."

Shadows darken the sky again, the sun vanishing as a storm trickles in. A light fog stretches through the pasture, covering the grass in a large cloud.

I love the weather here. I could sit on the porch all day to watch the rain fall, the greenery sway, and the sound of the leaves being pelted by the water. It's perfect.

It's no wonder Kentucky loves it here so much.

"I love the sound of that. If that's what you want, then I can make that happen, you know. I'll give you everything you want." He turns to me, placing his hat on top of my head. His eyes swirl into the ruby color I love so much. "You look cute with my hat on."

I pinch the brim like he does and give him a tilt. "Maybe I can get my own one day, Mr. Jones."

His nostrils flare. "I think I'd rather have you wear mine. It means you're taken. No other cowboy will talk to you, and if he does, well, they might find themselves in the grasp of my claws." He flexes his fingers, his nails growing and darkening to show his shift.

"What if I want to wear my own while you're wearing yours?" I place my hand on his knee, needing him to relax. I want him to know that no other could possibly take me away from him when I know there is no other for me.

"I'll have to figure out a way to show the world you're all mine, then."

The side of my neck heats with the thought of his mark there for all to see, for all to smell, and arousal soaks my new panties.

I don't even want to know how Lorcan got those, and I'm sure Kentucky won't be happy about another man buying me underwear if we talked about it, so I'm going to keep my lips shut.

A growl comes from Kentucky. "You can't be smellin' that good, Dru. You need to go inside, lie down, and I'll get a heating pad for your cramps. I'll get anything you need. I have to go out and do the chores. Later, I don't think I'll be able to wait. My body is on fire for you still." He stands, downs the rest of his coffee, and sets the empty cup on the arm of the rocking chair.

He cages me in, each arm gripping my chair, and he tilts me back. I gasp, worried I'll fall backwards.

"Don't worry. I won't ever let you fall. I'd catch you before you ever hit the ground." He leans in, his breath riddled with a hint of coffee and iron.

We fall into a sexual tension-filled silence. Seconds turn to minutes, our gazes locked, and his tinted eyes have a sparkle of happiness to them that I haven't seen before.

Without saying a word, his palm reaches for my face. His thumb glides across the edge of my jaw, taking his time drinking me in. Kentucky exhales, tilting his head while he traces the other side. It's as if he is memorizing me.

"If a constellation-decorated sky is what the world sees as beautiful, then they have never met you," he admires, never once taking his attention away from me.

"Kentucky." I become shy, breaking our gaze.

He lifts my chin up with his index finger, forcing me to look at him. "I'm serious, Dru. Never in my entire life have I ever seen someone or something so fucking breathtaking before. I need nothing else as long as I'm surrounded by you."

I lean forward, placing his hat on top of his head, and give him a long, soft kiss. Our lips move in slow, deliberate skims. I'm weightless. I'd float away if it weren't for his arm wrapping around my waist to pull me closer to him.

"I could kiss you until the sun goes down," he mutters, breaking the kiss so we can catch our breath. "I'd better go before I lock us inside this house."

"Can I come with you?"

He straightens, hooking his thumb through his belt loops. He looks like a cowboy. He has on dark jeans, a belt with a big, gold belt buckle that says, 'Dead Man's Ranch', and his button-up shirt is tucked in with the sleeves rolled to his elbows. His black boots round at the top, and the only speck of color on them is the silver spurs in the back.

"Darlin', I never expect you to work the ranch. I want you to have relaxing days. I want you to do whatever you want. If you want to work, great. If you want to stay home, great. If you—"

I stand next, grab the lapels of his shirt, and haul him in for a kiss to silence him. He groans, sinking into my embrace. He cups my face, then places his free hand on the base of my neck. I nibble his bottom lip, giving it a gentle tug, and lean away from him.

His eyes are still closed. His lips are puffy and a bit red.

I never expected love to find me like this, yet here I am, wanting to completely change my life.

"You better listen to me, Mr. Jones. And listen well. I will not ever stay cooped up in that house. I'm ambitious. I have goals. I like to work. That hasn't changed since meeting you, do you understand? It's important to me to work. I've come too far to give it all up now—especially for a man—no offense."

The muscles in his neck tense when he laughs, a big, bright smile taking over his face. His shoulders shake with all the humor he is experiencing. Kentucky even pinches the bridge of his nose, then wipes under one of his eyes.

"What is so funny? I'm serious."

"I know. I know, Dru. Hey, I don't mean to make it seem like you aren't or that I'm not taking you seriously. I am. I've lived through so many different times where women didn't have the same rights as you do now. I've been isolated, and it's refreshing to see how times have changed; that's all. I love that you have dreams and want to work. I support you always, no matter what you want to do."

I slip my arms around his waist and peer up at him. I have to bend my neck as far back as possible to even see his face. He is so tall. "That means I can come and do the chores with you?"

His happiness fades a bit, a stern tension morphing his face. "Yes, but you won't do anything that puts you in danger. Okay?"

I squeal with glee. "Yes! Yes. I promise. Okay, let me go get dressed."

"Okay, Darlin'. I'll wait out here for you. Go on." He

spanks my ass when I turn around, and I yelp, rubbing the spot he hit.

"Kentucky!"

"What?" He acts innocent, holding his hands up in the air. "I can't help it. You're too divine."

"Well, that's a good excuse. I'll let it slide," I wink at him, open the screen door, and rush through the house to get to his bedroom.

I change, taking one of his Dead Man's Ranch shirts to tie at the side so it fits me better. I could wear one of the shirts Lorcan got me, but it isn't the same. This shirt smells like Kentucky, and his scent brings me comfort.

Tossing on a pair of jeans that have a few rips across the thigh, I hurry to put on socks and my new pink boots. Sure, they might be a little extra, but they are so much fun. Plus, they are cute and would look good with most outfits.

Practical and impractical. It doesn't get better than that.

My boots thunder down the hall when I sprint. Right as I get to the door, I trip over the trim, slam against the screen door, and fly outside. The screen breaks, my arm scrapes against a broken piece of metal, and then I slam into Kentucky's chest.

I catch him off guard. I hear the air leave his lungs when I slam against him. The momentum, unfortunately, doesn't stop with him. He tumbles backwards, but he doesn't let me go. His arms are safety nets, holding me tight against his chest as we fall off the porch.

He hits the ground so hard, I swear I hear bone break.

"Oh my god. Kentucky! Are you okay? I'm so sorry. I can't believe I did that. I was so excited. I wasn't paying attention. I broke your door. I'm so embarrassed. What did you break? I heard it. Don't lie to me. Oh, no." Tears begin to form, blurring my vision.

I get off him, checking him over for injuries. His arm is in a funky position and is definitely broken.

"Your arm! What did I do? Okay, I'll call the ambulance. Or wait, no. We can take the work truck to the hospital. It will be faster and less expensive if you're worried about that. Are you? Worried about that? I don't mean to pry into your finances, but—"

"Darlin'. Hey, slow deep breaths for me. Alright? I'm fine. I don't need a doctor. Remember? I heal just fine. Look at me."

I can't even bring myself to look at him. I'm too embarrassed. Too ashamed. I don't break hearts. I break bones.

And I think that might be worse.

"Watch me, Dru. You don't have much time to see for yourself." He wipes the tear on my cheek.

I sniffle but do as he says. The dent in his arm straightens to normal, the bone snapping into place. Kentucky flexes his hand to show me he is okay.

"See? I'm as good as new. No need to waste those tears. Injuries like this don't bother me. I'm not in pain. This doesn't hurt. I promise."

I curl over him, pressing my forehead against his chest. "I'm so relieved. I forgot you had those nifty healing abilities. I still feel terrible. I broke your door."

"Doors can be fixed. I'm not worried about that at all." He sniffs the air, a scarlet curtain draping over his eyes. "You're bleeding." Kentucky zeroes in on the scrape against my forearm, his fangs peeping out from between his lips. "What happened?"

Gentle and calm, his hand circles around my wrist, bringing my arm closer to his face. "It cut you."

"It's not the door's fault I tumbled through it," I grumble with embarrassment.

He snarls, lifts his eyes to mine, then, without breaking

our locked stares, he flattens his tongue on the wound. An injection of lust warms my body, pooling between my legs. My throat becomes dry. I forget how to speak when I glimpse the red painting his tongue.

Kentucky's eyes roll to the back of his head when he groans. The sound echoes through the pastures, alerting anyone who is outside.

"You taste so fucking good," he growls, his hand reaching between his legs.

The movement draws my eyes down to his arousal, heavy and thick in his jeans. He readjusts himself, continuing to lick at the wound that has already healed from his saliva.

"Biting you will be my salvation on this earth." He presses a kiss against where the cut was seconds ago. "And when I do bite you, I'm going to fuck you wherever I fucking want, Dru. Over and over again, I'll claim you on every square inch of this ranch until other paranormals will be able to smell you for miles. They will know better than to come here. They will know better than to dare try to take you from me like those shifters did."

In a move I'm not expecting, he snakes his hand to my hip, flips me to my back, and hovers over me with the promise of death lingering in his eyes.

"If they do, I'll add their spines to the lasso I've made of your enemies. They will be my trophies, while the lasso will be your protection."

That shouldn't be so sweet. I shouldn't like the thought of him killing anyone, yet the thought of him protecting me, I'm obsessed with his idea of what protection means.

Grabbing his face, I smash our lips together. The mating heat begins to call again, screaming at Kentucky to bite me, to finish what he has started.

He presses his body against mine, lifting my leg to hook it on his hip. He deepens the kiss just as the clouds open up.

Thunder applauds when Kentucky thrusts against me, his denim-covered cock pressing against my clit.

A whimper flees me with every rough drag of jeans.

Rain begins to pour, soaking our clothes to our skin, and Kentucky never stops kissing me. His hand clutches my hip, using it as support to drive his hips. The girth of the crown rubs against my clit through my jeans.

His kiss becomes slick from the water, and somehow, even the rain tastes sweeter off his lips.

A growl from him travels down my throat and tingles my core. His claws hook around my shoulder, forcing his body harder between my legs. I cry out, the lightning cracking so loud, my climb to climax is silenced.

The ground becomes slippery; the dirt turns to mud and sticks to our clothes. I slide against the ground from Kentucky's need.

"Where do you think you're going?" He uses the hand that's wrapped around my shoulder to close the distance between us. "I didn't say you could go anywhere." He curls over me, and yanks my head to the side to show my neck. "Right here." His tongue licks the rain from my skin. "My mark will be here. Ruining you for any other man." Kentucky sucks my earlobe between his teeth, the tease of his fangs has me parting my lips, allowing the rain to quench the dryness on my tongue. "Your future is mine."

I slap my hand in a shallow puddle, dirt sticking under my nails. "Kentucky!" I cry out his name, the echo lost in the storm. Fireworks explode in my eyes, different colored spots dancing across my vision. This orgasm is different. I still feel like I'm pulsing, aching, a throb at my entrance for his cock.

"Druscilla," he moans against my throat, his teeth pressing against my vein. "Dru." He begins to tremble under me, and the harsh, monstrous growls take over every exhale. "Fuck. No one has ever made me come in my jeans like that before."

"You came?" I ask while kissing and sucking on his neck.

"It's you. Of course, I came." Swinging me into his arms, he blurs us into the house.

We're soaked. Dripping water onto the hardwood floors. Tossing me onto the bed, ruining the comforter with mud, he unbuttons his pants.

"Now, be a good girl and clean me before I make a mess again."

I crawl across the bed and sit on my knees.

"Open."

And like a good girl, I listen.

Chapter Seventeen
KENTUCKY

"You smell like death."

"That's not very nice, Romeo." I am finally trimming his hooves. I've been distracted in the best way. I'm a day behind on chores, and I couldn't care less. The cattle and Romeo are fine. There's food. There's water.

Dru has reminded me that the ranch doesn't need to be my entire life. Yesterday proved that. I don't think we left the bedroom. We laughed. We moaned. We napped. We fucked.

Not always in that order.

"I'm not trying to be nice, Kentucky. You smell like you're dying. Why are you doing this to yourself? Mate her already. You're already so close. I can smell it on you."

I pick up his leg, bend his knee, press my thighs together to keep him in place, then snag the hoof pick from my belt. Romeo is really great about his pedicure. He never gives me a hard time. He knows it's what is best for him. We didn't think he needed horseshoes at first since he can heal, but we were proved wrong one day when his hoof cracked in half and it wasn't healing.

I don't think his healing applies to his hooves. We don't

know why. We have a theory that it's because of the lack of blood circulation in the hoof itself. We might not ever know why.

Honestly, I think it helps bring purpose to me, and even if he won't admit it, this basic need brings purpose for Romeo too. It's hard to find what you have to have in order to survive after having these abilities to heal. This mundane task gives us that piece of humanity again.

"I'm fine, Romeo. You don't have a thing to worry about. I'll be okay." I continue to pick away at the debris stuck in his hooves.

When I'm satisfied, I switch to the trimmer to shorten the hoof itself.

"Of course I worry about you. You're my best friend. I don't want you to die. There's nowhere else I'd rather be than here."

I stop mid-clip, a burning sensation spreads across my chest and makes its damn way to my eyes.

Clearing my throat, I start to clip again. "I won't be going anywhere. I know it may seem like I am, but I'm not. I have a plan."

"Care to share?"

"I wanted her to fall in love with me without the idea of knowing I'm fated to her. I don't want to take her choice. That matters to me. I think the plan is working. She feels the pull, yeah, but it's more. It's more natural this way, without the idea of her knowing there's an entity at play."

"I admire that, I do, but you need to be realistic. You already smell of death to me, Kentucky. You reek of darkness. Death is near and closer than you think."

"Okay, fine." I toss the trimmer down and pick up the rasp, which smooths out the edges of the hoof. "I'm a little sore. The amount of blood she is giving me is not enough, not without being mated. I'm tired. My hips ache." I sigh, dropping his leg to grab a horseshoe from the bin. I keep it full of premade shoes I've made him over the years. They are the perfect fit.

Next, I heat the iron, shoving it into the hearth. I need to get it hot first so Romeo becomes more comfortable with how the shoes fit. Hot shoes help with the durability and fit of the iron itself.

"I knew it."

"I'll be fine. And you know, if I'm not, just talk to Lorcan." I pinch my brows together when I realize how that can't happen. Lorcan can't speak to animals. "Somehow." Snagging the shoe from the pit, Romeo bends his knee to give me access. "You'll be okay. You'll find another home."

"I don't want another home. Home is the person, not the place."

I begin to nail the shoe on, doing my best not to shed a tear. He and I have been through the grain over the years. It hasn't been easy. He's seen the worst of me. No one else can say that.

"I'll be okay. I promise." I set his hoof down. "Want a brushing?"

"Of course, I do. It's not like I can scratch myself."

I snort, nodding in agreement. "I guess so."

Romeo also likes to be pampered. He loves his mane brushed and for his coat to shine. He would love to be massaged every day, be fed his favorite hay, and sleep in a warm barn with a blanket.

He has two out of those three things. I don't know an animal massage therapist.

"Please talk to her soon."

"After I'm done here, I'm going to pick some wildflowers and ask her to the rodeo that Lorcan signed us up for. You up for it, Old Man?"

He flicks his tail, excitement brightening the pools of red ink. *"Who are you calling old? You've got a few years on me."*

"I think it will be nice to finally shake the rust off. After the rodeo, I'll tell her. If I'm feeling like this, I can't imagine how she is feeling. For humans, it has to be different. We'll make it."

We have to make it. Now that I've tasted what life could be like with her, the thought of the need to die fades. I want to try living for all eternity. I also want us to agree that if we both get tired over so many years, we agree to die together, in each other's arms, staring up at the night sky.

That will be my only request.

"I hope so. Don't be so stubborn. She'd love you with or without Fate."

"If Fate didn't exist, I'd already be dead." I sweep off the dust on his hide, the deep onyx color coming back to its brilliant shine.

Romeo stays silent for a few minutes. All I hear is the hay between his teeth as he chews.

"She's right, you know," he says out of nowhere, flicking his tail to annoy a fly.

"About?"

"Being lonely. I wouldn't mind some others."

"You heard that conversation?"

"Yes. I never told you because I knew you didn't want to be responsible for a lot of things, given your decision on life."

"I don't want you to be lonely, Romeo. You should have told me."

"I had you. That was enough. Things have changed. You are growing a family with Dru now. It made me realize I also want someone. I want a companion."

"Skew-dang ain't that cute."

Romeo and I groan in unison at the sound of Lorcan's voice.

He always finds the worst time to pop in.

I stop brushing Romeo and turn around, crossing my arms over my chest. "What do you want, Lorcan?"

He's dressed in the cowboy hat and boots again for some reason. Every step he takes, my annoyance grows.

"I'm here checking on my favorite cowboy." He stops in front of me, brow bones rising when he inhales. "And he's dying from the smell of it." Lorcan waves his hand in front of his nose. "What did I tell you, Kentucky?"

I'm surprised by the venom in his voice. Even Romeo turns his head to stare at the Void. His tail flicks back and forth with anxiety. Romeo might be a vampire, but he is also an animal, and animals always know when a predator is nearby.

Lorcan might be happy-go-lucky, funny, and unserious most of the time, but I've never been mistaken about the darkness he holds in. I know he keeps it balled up tight in his chest to not scare anyone. Lorcan described his power to me one day. He said the older the Void, the more powerful they are.

And my reaper friend here is one of the oldest. If he unleashed all the power he had, he could wipe out the entire country's population.

He disperses into smoke, vanishing before our eyes, before popping in front of me. For the first time since I have known him, he shows his sharp rows of teeth.

He's furious.

"You don't have enough time left. You're going to die. I'm here for you, you know that, right? Has that not sunk into your fucking mind?" He presses a finger against my chest, shoving me so hard, I fly backwards.

The air is knocked out of my lungs as I hit the wall, breaking the old wooden slabs with simply the force in Lorcan's damn index finger.

"I know you're here for me. You're a good friend, Lorcan. I need you both to listen to me—"

Lorcan morphs into dark spots, drifting through the air. When he is close enough, a weight of dread presses against my chest. It's as if I'm being drowned in a lake with cement blocks chained to my feet.

"Let me be clearer." He squats down, fire illuminating his orbital sockets. "I am here *for* you. Do you get it now? All this time, I've been warning you. You'd think you'd be able to read in between the lines." He flicks the middle of my forehead.

"Ow." I rub the sting away. "What the hell was that for?"

"I can't take your soul yet, and it is taking everything I have not to rip your skin from your body from the pure amount of frustration you make me feel.

"I'm Kentucky. I'm a big, bad loner man who doesn't need anyone or anything. I'm not even going to tell my mate the truth because she deserves to have control of her own choices." Lorcan mocks me in a high-pitched voice, prancing around in the cowboy boots. The spurs jingle with every step, and it's hard to keep a straight face given the circumstances.

"What do you mean you're here for me?" I stand, crack my back, then dust off my jeans. "I'm not dead yet."

He pauses, stopping next to Romeo. "Do you think I care about the technicalities when it comes to one of my best friends? I had to beg Death to let me be the one to come here so soon. He was going to send another Void because he thought I was too close to your soul. I couldn't allow someone else to reap my friend." He glides across the floor, floating closer to me. "I can feel the pull of death to you, Kentucky. The tug that pulls at my bones every time a soul calls for me to take them to another place, I feel it from *you*."

He goes to poke me in the chest again, but I take a step away. "No need to throw me like a sack of potatoes. I get the point."

"Do you? Do you understand what it means for me to be here early? I'm warning you, Kentucky. By tomorrow morning, you won't be here. You'll be lucky to make it through the night by the smell of it." The hatred is venom in every word he speaks. It's clear he is very upset with me. "Tell her. Now. Or I will."

"You wouldn't dare," I snarl, my hands falling to my sides out of habit to grab my gun for a quick draw.

"You'd be surprised at the lengths I'll go to make sure my friends stay alive. You've come so far. Don't you care at all about that? You now want to live forever, and you're leaving it up to the last second? How is that fair to her? You aren't being the man I know you to be. You're being a coward."

Romeo blows out a loud snort, pawing at the ground. He's agitated. He won't be able to keep it managed without being set free to run.

"I'm being a coward? How is giving my mate the choice that I didn't have a cowardly thing to do? If anything, I'm thoughtful. I'm being a good man and a good mate."

"Coward!" His yell brings force from the pits of Hell, shaking the barn and ground we're standing on.

Romeo raises on his hind legs, neighing from being scared and confused.

"It's okay. You're okay. Lorcan might be a dick, but he won't let anything happen to you." I pat Romeo's neck, stroking the sweat-soaked hide. He is beyond stressed. "I won't let anything happen to you."

"Coward," Lorcan repeats. "You're already letting something happen to him. *You*. I think you're using your mate as an excuse. I think there's a part of you that still wishes for death, that thinks you'd be doing Dru a favor by not allowing you two to live. Maybe you've even thought about my offer? I can make sure she is in a new dimension with a mate who won't be terrified of living. Is that it, Kentucky? Scared of a little life?"

I know what he is trying to do. He's taunting me, trying to get me to react. I won't let his attempt work.

"She is very pretty. Have you noticed how the sun glistens off the apples of her cheeks? I mean, it would be hard to see, considering it's always so cloudy here. If you blink, you'd miss it. She glows, doesn't she? Imagine her with someone who would appreciate that. Another man having his hands on her body, claiming her as his. He wouldn't be afraid to bite."

I curl my fist into a tight ball, my breathing turning rough and ragged as the images of her with another assault my mind. Her laughter, gasps, moans, orgasms—they all belong to me.

"Imagine her begging for someone else's bite," Lorcan cackles, showing the cruelest part of himself. "I'm sure in another life, her mate would be more appreciative."

Flexing my fingers out, my claws unsheathe, my fangs lengthen, my eyes flip crimson, and I launch myself at Lorcan. I use every bit of speed and strength I have to take him by surprise.

He can anticipate my every move. Lorcan dodges left, missing the swipe of my claws through the air. I pretend to repeat the same move, only I lift my other arm, trapping him against the wall by his cervical spine.

"You might have more power than me, but you will not win against a vampire whom you have threatened. You will not take my beloved away from me. She is mine. She will have my mark. And it might not be happening in the fucking way everyone else wants because I give a fuck about what *she* wants." I lift him off the ground, debating on snapping his neck.

It's not like I can kill him. Only a reaper can kill another reaper.

"I plan on telling her everything after the rodeo tonight. I do not appreciate being spoken to like a child. I am over one hundred and fifty years old, do not patronize me with your fucking lectures!" I shout so loud, my own voice changes to the monstrous depths. "I will respect her choice until the very last fucking second of my life. Do you understand that? You can go tell Death that I won't be needing your assistance. My soul will not be getting reaped."

"You have that much faith in her?"

I lean in close enough to smell Hell's smoke on his breath. "Yes," I clip. "I have more faith in her than I do in myself. If that isn't enough for you. Get the fuck off my ranch and don't bother coming back." Using my speed, I have the hammer clicked back on my gun, the barrel pressing under his chin. "You might not be able to die, but finding every piece of your fucking skull would take an awfully long time, don't you think?"

Fire ignites behind the lifeless sockets, he used to call eyes. "You make a good point," he concedes, tapping my hand. "You can let me go. I'll back off."

I give him a once-over, growling to show I'm not ready to forgive him yet. I don't set him on the ground.

I drop him.

And I pull the trigger.

The bullet pierces the floorboard. A hole signifying how his skull could look if I didn't have mercy.

"Don't ever mistake my kindness as weakness again, Lorcan. I won't be so kind next time." I spin the gun around my finger and tuck it in my holster.

The blaze diminishes and leaves an abyss of swirling darkness in the sockets. "Noted, Kentucky." He begins to walk away, stopping behind Romeo. "Don't make me come back here tomorrow. Please. I do not wish to see a friend die."

"I'll do my best."

Romeo blows a raspberry and kicks his back leg out, landing his hoof in the middle of Lorcan's torso.

"Skew-dang!" His head tumbles from his body first, followed by a few ribs soaring through the air.

One slings by my head with a comical whoosh, piercing the barn wall.

His leg flies a few feet, and the kittens pounce on it immediately.

"Oh my god, get them away from my body! This...this is abuse. Torture, even. I'd go as far as to say cannibalism. Get my bones! Don't let their nasty little teeth ruin my structure. Do you know how much milk I drank as a human for these bones? Unbelievable. You creatures don't appreciate science!" He is beside himself, scurrying to gather every piece of himself.

There's always one thing I can count on when it comes to Lorcan—his theatrics. Sighing, I tug the bone from the wall and toss it to him.

"Romeo, I think you owe Lorcan an apology."

"Yeah, Romeo," Lorcan mocks like a child. "I think I'm owed one too."

"No."

I clear my throat and lean in, whispering, "You should apologize. That was pretty mean. I didn't shoot him to avoid this mess."

"He deserved it. I won't apologize. He needs to apologize. Tell him I'll do it again, too."

"Romeo isn't going to apologize. He thinks you're the one in the wrong."

"I'm sorry. Is that better? Jeez. It's not like I removed your hooves." He twists his head back on, moaning when it snaps into place. "That's better." Placing all his bones back into his body is like a puzzle. Seems he has done this more than once, considering how he knows where all the ribs need to be placed.

"Are we done? I have a woman waiting for me to ask her to the rodeo tonight."

Lorcan brightens, forgetting the spat we just had. "You're going? Phew." He wipes his hand across his forehead, swiping away fake sweat. "I have a few hundred bucks placed on you to win. I lose every year since you never go. Barrel racing? Bronco riding? Bulls, maybe?"

"Depends, what did you sign me up for?"

He laughs, but it's the kind of humor that's full of nerves. "All...of...them?"

"Damn you, Lorcan. You're going to get me killed. I haven't ridden a bull in—" I try to think of the time and year, but I can't. It's been too long. I sigh, shaking my head, "—I'm going to withdraw from bronco riding. I'm not getting on another horse that isn't Romeo."

"But I'll—"

I arch my brow at him, daring him to continue that sentence.

"I understand."

"Good."

Romeo tugs on the rope, keeping him tied to the post. He's tired of standing here listening to Lorcan and me bicker.

"Alright. Alright. Keep your shoes on." I unravel the knot, unhook the rope from his halter. "Go on." I slap his side, and he neighs, bolting out of the barn in a blur.

He must be hungry.

I hold out my hand to Lorcan to help him up. "Come on. I have a mate to swoon. Get off your ass."

He slaps his palm into mine and jumps to his feet with the smile on his face that I prefer to see. I don't like my friend mad at me. It doesn't sit right. Life is hard enough doing it alone. Then, there are some people who refuse to leave you to that loneliness, wanting to prove to you that there's someone who cares about your existence. A friend like that is hard to find.

Having Dru, Lorcan, and Romeo, I'm realizing my loneliness was a disease. I was dying from it, a sickness that always lingered and weighed me down until getting out of bed every morning felt like a chore.

My loneliness had turned into depression.

Even with Lorcan and Romeo, I don't think anyone could have saved me. No one could have changed my mind about dying.

Until Dru.

She is the answer to my disease. The cure.

My mate breathed life back into me. I owe her whatever she wants. Whenever she wants. *However* she wants.

"Skew-dang." He waves his fingers at me. "Tootles, Darlin'."

I groan, reaching to take the damn hat off because the attire is getting to his head. He fucking giggles before disappearing, leaving me in an empty barn, and doing my best to ignore the smell of a rotting corpse.

Only paranormals can smell it. Dru won't be able to tell.

I stroll outside the barn, staring at all the land that goes on for hundreds of acres. Dru's idea whirls around in my mind as I take in all the pastures. I realize she's right. There's so much land here that can be put to good use. I really have been waiting to die if I haven't been utilizing my ranch properly.

Only focusing on the cattle side of the business, I've made great money. I'm a millionaire. If I wanted, I could hang up my hat and call it a day. I can't turn my back on this ranch. It's the one thing that has kept me going for over a century.

If anything, I need to stop neglecting it and breathe life into it like Dru did with me. It's time for a change.

Horses. Cattle. Chickens. Dogs. Whatever she wants. I'm ready for the quiet not to be so loud.

I hop over the pasture's gate, waving to the cows chewing on the grass.

"Ladies." I tip my hat as I always do to the ladies.

"Kentucky!"

"Hi!"

"Hey, Kentucky."

I squat next to Mable, petting her stomach. "How are you feeling? Any day now and you'll have that baby."

"I'm feeling like a whale."

I snort at her joke. "Funny, Mable." The baby kicks her side, and I'm able to feel it in my palm. "Healthy. That's what I like to see, Mable. You better call me if you need me, okay?"

She moos in return, bending down to chew on more grass.

I leave them be, taking my time to enjoy the view. The pastures roll with hills, long miles of fresh green grass. Tall pines fill the woods on either side, where I know a creek flows through the middle.

I pause when a fox dashes to the other side of the woods, the bright red fur impossible to miss. There's plenty of wildlife around here. I have a few cameras set up to check for large predators that I don't want getting too close to my cattle. Last year, a mountain lion ignored all my blood markings on the trees. Usually, the scent of a vampire deters the big game, but this mountain lion was determined.

I was too late to save my cow. It was a horrible loss, and I had the mourning of a hundred cattle in my head. It was heartbreaking that I couldn't do anything for them.

We haven't had another incident since. Still, my guard isn't down. I'm protective of my land and what is on it. I understand animals have to eat. It's the way of life.

Regardless of mother nature, I have to do my best to protect my herd. If they choose not to trust me because they feel unsafe, my job would become much harder, dealing with unruly cows. They could try to leave, or worse, kill me.

Checking my watch, I curse. I'm taking too long. We don't have much time before the rodeo, and I need to get there for registration. Turning on the vampire speed, I cut through the long grass that grows more towards the back of the pasture.

The meadow comes up fast, and I stop at the edge to appreciate the beauty of it. Wildflowers grow as far as the eye can see. The Black-eyed Susans, Virginia Bluebells, Purple Coneflowers, Little Evening Primroses, and my favorite, the Goldenrods. I love their bright yellow color.

I stand there for a moment, closing my eyes, and inhaling the sweet scents coming from the meadow. I'm reminded of something Daphne said.

"One day, you'll pick flowers for a woman who isn't me, so promise me, you won't ever pick flowers from the meadow for me."

Gasping, I open my eyes, wondering how Daphne would know I'd be standing right here.

I promised her too. I remember thinking how ridiculous it was. Now, I'm starting to think Daphne wanted me to have so many firsts with Dru. She saved them for me. I don't think I'll ever know how to repay her for what she has done for me.

Taking off my hat, I flip it upside down and begin plucking flowers until there's no more room left.

"Thank you, Daphne," I whisper, knowing damn well she can't hear me, but I do hope she can somewhere. And I hope wherever she is, she's happy. She deserves it more than anybody.

It's time for me to start thinking of my future. What I want and need for this life that will never end. Every thought, every want, every dream, they all lead to Dru.

Gripping the bouquet in my hand, I sprint home, stopping at the front door. I'm nervous. Dru could say no to the date, which would put a damper on the plans I have.

Opening the door, the mouthwatering scent of roast hits me. I hear Dru in the kitchen, tinkering with the dishes. I try to be as quiet as possible with my loud footsteps walking towards the kitchen.

I lean against the door frame, crossing one ankle over the other. She's singing a Chris Stapleton song blaring on the speaker while she plates the food.

I can't help the smile that takes over my face. Happiness is her soul, and mine drinks in her joy.

She finally sees me after a few minutes. "Kentucky!" She dashes around the counter and jumps, wrapping herself around me.

"Mmm, Darlin'. I missed you today." I drop the bouquet on the counter so I can wrap her in my arms properly.

"I missed you too." Her cloud-soft lips press against my cheek. "I hope you don't mind; I made lunch." I love how she slides off my body, rubbing me in all the right places on the way down.

"I'm starving after the day I had."

"Sit. I'll get your plate."

"Nonsense." I pick up the flowers and hand them to her. "You sit down, and I'll serve you."

"For me?" Her smile reaches her eyes, brimming with surprise and glee. "I've never had anyone get me flowers before. They are gorgeous, Kentucky. Thank you. I need to put them in water. I don't want them to die."

The word 'die' hits a little too close to home. "I'll handle all that. Right now, I need you to dance with me." I hold out my hand for her to take. "Will you do me the honor, Ms. Whitley? And be by my side at the rodeo tonight?"

Her cheeks plump with her smile. I always want to be the one to put excitement on her face. I notice I do that often, and it makes a man like me feel real fucking good.

She slides her hand in mine, and I tug her close, dancing to the next Chris Stapleton song, *"Think I'm In Love With You."*

"There isn't anything else I'd want to do more," Dru replies, blinking up at me with those big hazel irises.

I want our children to have her eyes.

If that's even an option.

"You are the prettiest woman I have ever had the privilege

of my gaze falling upon." I trace her jaw, cupping her cheek in my palm. I need to be closer somehow.

"I don't know about that." She turns away, becoming coy.

I pull her in close as close as possible so our chests are touching, our hands are clasped, and there's nowhere else to go except to get lost in the kitchen to the low baritone serenading us through the speaker.

We sway, dancing slowly with no hurry in the world. The tension becomes palpable the longer we stay close. The invisible urge to confess love or want. I hold my breath when we lock eyes. She trusts me. There isn't the faintest scent of fear. Not anymore.

I smell something sweet invading our space. I'm assuming it's peace. She turns her head, resting her cheek in the middle of my chest, and I bend down, kissing the top of her head.

I never want this to end. I want these moments forever. With her. No question.

The song is wrong.

There's no 'thinking.'

I *know*.

I'm in love with Dru.

To the point where death is no longer what I look forward to the most.

DEAD MAN'S
RANCH

CHAPTER EIGHTEEN
DRUSCILLA

"Don't you dare think about climbing out of the truck. Wait for me," Kentucky orders.

A girl opens the truck door one time and is in trouble for life.

"Yes, Mr. Jones. Whatever you say." I bat my eyelashes at him a few times, teasing him. "I'll be good."

He leans across the console, wrapping a hand around my throat. His lips are millimeters away from mine, the anticipation of his kiss a phantom taunt.

"You could choose to be bad." He nips at my lip. "It just means I'll have to bend you over my knee when we get home. Or maybe I'll do that, anyway."

Kentucky leans away from me, leaving me dying for his kiss, and he knows it too. Even walking around the front of the truck, our gazes are locked. I follow his every step until he is at my door and offering his hand to help me out.

I didn't know men like him still existed. In a way, I suppose they don't, considering Kentucky is from another time.

"Let me help you, Ms. Whitley," he drawls, waiting for me to take his hand.

"Don't mind if you do." Slipping my hand in his, the world rights itself again. The strings that bind us twirl together, tying our hearts into one. My heart slows to a calm beat, a rhythm belonging to Kentucky and Kentucky alone.

Only he has the ability to bring peace to my heart.

"God," he seethes through his fangs, trapping me against the side of the truck. "You look so fucking good in those tiny shorts." He tugs at the frayed ends, slipping his finger under the dark blue denim. "Wouldn't take much for me to slide these to the side and take what I want."

His finger inches closer to my pussy, the callouses scratching the most sensitive part of my inner thigh.

"Right here. Right now. No one would need to know. I could have you drench my palm so I can smell you on me when I compete."

I bury my face in his black coat to muffle a moan when he pinches my clit. "Kentucky. You need to go get ready. We don't have the time. Plus, you can't. I'm wearing a tampon."

"Darlin', if there's one thing I'll always do, it's have enough time for you." He tugs on the string, stealing my breath. "You're already getting wet for me." Kentucky circles my clit, slow and steady to drive me insane.

"Last call for registration. Come get your numbers. You will be disqualified if you do not register." The announcer's voice spreads through the speakers.

Kentucky curls his lip in annoyance, showing his fangs. "Well, that's too bad, isn't it?" He slips his fingers free, a shine glistening off the digits. I ache for him now. "Taste yourself so you know why I'm so addicted to eating this pretty pussy." He rubs my juices across my lips as if he is applying lipstick.

My tongue flicks out, tracing my lips in a slow stroke. His attention is locked on my mouth, desire etched across his face.

"Later tonight, you're mine, Dru. I'm warning you now." He

sucks his fingers, eyes flashing with the lack of control. "Mmmm," he hums as if I'm the best food he has ever tasted. "I'm going to bury my face between your thighs." He cups me between my legs, another growl vibrating his chest. "And then right here —" Tapping the side of my neck, I naturally tilt my head to the side to bear my throat from him. "If you'll allow me—"

"Last call. We are still missing three competitors. If you have not registered, you have three minutes to make your way to the booth."

He groans in frustration towards the sky. "Okay, Darlin'. I've got to go. Impressing you tonight will be for nothing if I don't get my number." He bends down, kissing my cheek. "Tonight, Dru. Think about forever with me."

The loud conversation of people returns when he backs away from me, seemingly starting time again. When he touches me, everything, everyone fades away. Nothing else matters. He steps back, our hands clasping onto one another. I don't want to let go.

I have no choice when he's too far. Our fingers slip from one another, and in the blink of an eye, he's gone.

"Skew-dang, I'm so excited to win money."

I scream when Lorcan pops up next to me. My hand flies to my heart from the momentary rush. "Lorcan, you can't scare me like that. I'm human. You could give me a heart attack and Kentucky—" I fall silent when I turn to Lorcan. I do not recognize him.

Holy crap. This man is a giant.

I didn't know he had a human form. To even see his face, I have to crane my neck back to stare up at him.

"Lorcan?"

He grins. "Don't sound so surprised. I clean up good, don't I?" He is perched against the side of the truck, using his leg to push himself off. "See? I know how to look like a cowboy." He gives me a cocky spin, adding a little sway to his hips that he doesn't need to do.

He's wearing black jeans with rips across the knees, a tucked-in black shirt, a belt with a big matte black metal buckle that has swirling souls on it, as if they are crying out for help, black boots with silver chains hanging from the side, and a cowboy hat that matches the one Kentucky wears.

His nails are painted black too, and he has smudged eyeliner around his eyes.

I'm speechless. "Your eyes, though," I whisper, darting my eyes left and right so I know we are alone. "They are orange."

He clicks his tongue, scratching the back of his head. "Yeah, I can't hide that, unfortunately. Only so many things can be maintained in this form." He holds out his elbow. "Let's go find a front row seat. Shall we, ma'am?" He lays on a bad southern accent that has me laughing.

"Are you wearing a gun?" I steal a glance at his hip.

"Death won't let me carry a real weapon."

I loop my arm through his, and we begin to walk to the bleachers. We zigzag through crowds of people. Every person I see, I'm curious if they are vampires too, or maybe werewolves. The thought is terrifying and exhilarating. We could be surrounded by other creatures, and I'd have no idea. Lorcan would, and I doubt he'd tell me.

"What? Why not? I don't think that's fair."

"I agree, but being a Void and all," he scoffs. "I'm more powerful than a gun. I don't need one. They look so cool though. I love how Kentucky wears one on his hip. He's ready for a duel." Lorcan pretends to snag a weapon from his side, pulls his thumb back to 'cock' the gun, and fires. He even goes so far as to make the 'pew pew' sounds.

Like a responsible cowboy, he tucks his ghost gun in the holster. "I bet he has had many duels back in the day."

"You think so? What was he like all those years ago? When you first met him?"

"He hasn't changed much. He's always kind of been who he is. He's gotten a little more stubborn over the years, more of a recluse, but what never stopped was the genuine nature of his soul. Granted, he has changed since meeting you."

"Really? How so? He still seems set in his ways."

"And he always will be." Lorcan steals a bucket of popcorn from a man walking by. He whispers, "You dropped your popcorn. Go get another."

The stranger in the brown cowboy hat listens, not questioning Lorcan in the slightest. Nodding his head, the guy turns around to go to the concessions again.

"Anyway." Lorcan throws a handful of popcorn in the air, somehow managing to catch every piece. "He's better with you. Happier. I've never seen him truly happy. He always felt cursed, and he doesn't feel that way with you. He's lighter. In here." Lorcan taps the middle of his chest. "He hasn't done a rodeo in decades, Dru. He is doing this for you."

"The rodeo? Why? If he doesn't want to do it, then he shouldn't. Plus, he could get hurt, healing abilities or not. I don't like to see him in pain."

We take a seat in the front row. I'd prefer to sit a little higher, but I also want to be as close to Kentucky as possible.

Lorcan offers me the buttery snack. One thing to know about me, popcorn is one of my favorite food groups.

It's a grain, so I consider it an important part of my diet.

"You don't get it yet, do you?"

"Get what?" I ask through a mouthful of popcorn.

"He wants you to see him compete. He wants you to be impressed by him. He wants to win and show you he is better than all the other fools here."

"I already think and feel that way. He never needs to put himself in danger for me."

"That's exactly why he is doing this. Do you know how long it has been since he has put himself in danger? He's a man at the end of the day, Dru. He wants you to see him *be* dangerous."

"Men make no sense. That is a ridiculous way to think."

"Men are ridiculous. Good thing I'm not like them."

My brows must reach my hairline when I hear those words come from *his* mouth. "Lorcan, you might be the most ridiculous one I've ever met."

Popcorn flies in the air again, and this time, he misses every piece. "Sounds like I'm special."

I pat his shoulder. "That's exactly right."

His irises are fire-lit lanterns in the middle of the night, glowing a color that can only belong to Hell.

Lorcan wipes a fake tear away from his cheek. "That might be the sweetest thing anyone has ever said to me."

I knock my shoulder against his, and he misses another airborne piece of popcorn. The lights surrounding the arena become brighter. I'm able to see beyond the gates where all the cowboys are, and I know somewhere out there, Kentucky is with Romeo.

He'll be fine. He has to be.

A group of toy cars comes flying from one of the chutes where they keep the livestock. The cars range from bright pink to purple. The clowns' bodies are too big for the children's vehicle. I remember I had one like it when I was little, and I loved driving it. In that driver's seat, I was an adult.

Or I thought I was.

Another clown pops his head out from a barrel. When he notices the minicars coming at him, he dips down to protect himself. A pink car smashes into him, tilting the barrel over. Another car comes, and together, they push the barrel around the area with the clown inside.

Each of the clowns has different expressions painted on

their faces. A few are wearing smiles while the others wear frowns. All of them are wearing cowboy hats, shoes that are too big, and red noses.

"They are funny, but want to know what I would have done? Instead of using toy cars, I'd use Hellhounds to chase them around. I feel like the screams would be more authentic."

I don't have a response to that. I blink at him, dumbfounded.

"Well, yeah, Lorcan. The clowns aren't supposed to be afraid for their lives while they entertain us."

He scoffs, gesturing towards the arena. "Then, it isn't entertainment. You haven't seen nothin' until you see a Purgatory fighting ring. They have to fight to the death."

"You scare me sometimes," I mutter, chomping on more popcorn.

"Eh, you'll get used to it." He shrugs.

The speakers cut on, and static pours through. "Good evening and welcome to the—"

The announcer's voice fades to nothing when a tug in my stomach begins to turn and cramp, sending pain shooting through my chest. I hiss, doubling over as I hold onto my stomach. "I think I'm going to be sick."

"My god, he is as dusty as a granola bar, isn't he? I think I'll go up there to spark some life in these announcements."

"What?" I wipe the sweat from my brow, hoping the pain passes soon. "No. I don't care about him. I'm in agony. What is going on, Lorcan?"

"Take my hand."

I do as he says, whimpering as another wave of pain cramps my abdomen.

His veins flow black, pumping his body full of pain that doesn't belong to him.

"Lorcan. No! Stop! What are you doing?" I try to pull my

hand away, but he grips harder, leaving a black outline where his fingers are clutching onto me. "Let go, Lorcan!"

The orange irises that glow burst into flames when the blackened veins reach his face. I take a sharp breath when I'm able to breathe again. The pain is faint now. It's still there, tingling my stomach, but I can manage it.

"People are going to see you. You have to let go. Let go, Lorcan!"

He finally releases me, tilting his head down to hide. Black smoke billows from his nose and mouth, reminding me of an angry bull waiting to charge.

His tainted veins return to normal, and I'm met with a brilliant smile, even if he looks like he has been hit by a truck. He has sweat dripping down his face and dark circles under his eyes. I'm not sure how he is able to stay so positive.

"Whew. That kicked my ass. You and Kentucky are literally trying to kill me. Lit-er-ally," he pronounces with a snap of his finger. "What I did is only a temporary fix, Dru. I took your pain. For now." He leans in so no one can hear him whispering, "The only solution is for him to complete the bond by biting you. You're running out of time. The pain you're feeling? It's parts of your body decomposing on the inside. Eventually, it will overtake your heart."

"How do you know for sure? Maybe I'm cramping."

He narrows his eyes at me and stands, shoving the half-eaten bucket of popcorn at me. "I'm going to pretend you didn't just insult a reaper. Would I not know how death feels and smells? The audacity."

"I'm sorry, Lorcan. You're right. I just hoped you were wrong."

"Sorry, Dru." His finger lifts my chin. "Not in this case. I'm going to the announcer's box. This guy is a snoozefest."

"You're going to leave me here? Don't—" I grip his wrist and hand when he walks away. "Don't leave me alone. I don't know anybody! And you just told me I was dying. It's rude to leave someone after dropping news like that."

He lifts up one finger. "Okay, first off, this isn't news. I warned you both about this little side effect." He holds up a second finger. "Secondly, you know Kentucky. Come on, let me have fun, Mom. I'll be right back. Please," he begs, sticking out his lower lip in a pout.

I can't argue with his logic, even if it scares me. Parts of me are dying on the inside. Kentucky isn't going to go another day without those damn fangs in my throat. I don't care if it means I have to bite him first.

"Fine. Go." I release him, grabbing a giant scoop of popcorn and shoving it into my mouth. "I didn't need you anyway," I huff.

He vanishes in front of my eyes, and I analyze the crowd to see if any of them are watching. No one seems to be questioning how he was there one second and gone the next.

A loud, high-pitched frequency pierces the microphone. The entire crowd groans in protest. A few people begin to peer up at the announcer's box to see what is going on.

All I see is Lorcan waving down at me with the microphone in his hand.

"Skew-dang!" he shouts into the mic. "Ladies and gentlemen, welcome to the county rodeo, where wild riders always make their way to our hearts. Awwwww. Say it with me now."

I slip another piece of popcorn in my mouth, staring at people who are actually listening to him.

"Awwww," they say in unison, and it's followed by the entire crowd erupting in applause.

"Excellent. I know we are all excited to be here to see the best of the best in the county compete! Qualifying in these events will get you to the championship. While we would all love for these cowboys and cowgirls to see themselves in the championship round, that just isn't on the table. Competitors who are the fastest, have the best accuracy, and have the least amount of penalties, will move on to their dreams while the others will cry themselves to sleep."

"Oh my god." I bury my face in my hands, hoping no one remembers I'm here with him.

Everyone laughs too. I know Kentucky is hearing this and wanting to kill Lorcan. This is feeding the Void's ego so much.

"Up first, we have the steer wrestling for the big, strong men who need to prove themselves. Isn't that cute?"

"It's a good thing he can't die or he'd already be dead," I say to myself.

"Our first competitors are a championship duo, holding a record time in this event. I hope they don't think they are untouchable because that's when egos become dangerous."

"Who are you? Why are you in this—" The second announcer's voice vanishes from the mic.

I can only imagine what happened to him.

"Steer wrestling is a team event. One needs to keep the steer in a straight line while the other jumps on the steer by grabbing it by the horns and wrestling it to the ground. All four legs of the steer have to point in the same direction in order to stop the clock for an accurate time." Lorcan whistles. "You humans are off your rockers. I don't even think Lucifer would do something this insane. You really have no care for life, do you?"

I pinch the bridge of my nose from Lorcan-induced stress. I truly think the only person who can handle him is his fated mate. Bless whoever she is. He will keep her on her toes. I hope she is preparing herself for constantly being surprised.

"The chute releases!" Lorcan shouts. "Followed by our team, Cal McCartey and Oklahoma Richards."

I whip my head to the arena so I don't miss anything. It's my first rodeo, and I want to be able to enjoy it. The steer is fast with a tan body and white horns that curl upwards, the perfect handles for a cowboy.

"Skew-dang! This team is fast. It's no wonder they are champions. Cal manages the direction of the steer, doing his best to keep him in a straight line. Oklahoma jumps from his saddle!" Lorcan announces with excitement. "He brings down the steer! Their time is three point two seconds. Damn, that's going to be a hard act to follow. The record is two point two seconds, and I believe they will be able to break that as their competitive days go on."

A few more steer wrestlers compete, and none of them are able to get close to the time Cal and Oklahoma did.

"Next, we have my personal favorite event, barrel racing. My buddy is one of the competitors, and I just know he is going to smoke all your asses. You stand no chance. Let's go, Kentucky!"

By the time this rodeo is done, Lorcan is going to make an enemy out of every single cowboy and cowgirl here.

I snicker to myself, loving how much fun I'm having, and most of that is due to Lorcan being himself. As I sit here waiting for the next event to start, my thoughts wander to Carmen and the dental office I work at. A stab of guilt hits me, ruining my appetite for my favorite snack.

Carmen has always been by my side. Through thick and thin, ups and downs, she's been there. She deserves to know where I am and would love the rodeo. She's the adventurous type, more than I ever was. Maybe I can convince her to come visit or move out here. I'd love that even if it would be selfish of me to ask.

I can't fathom the idea of leaving Kentucky.

As for my job, I'll get another one or create my own by opening my own dental practice, like Kentucky and I talked about.

The twist in my gut returns, and the hair on the back of

my neck stands up. I narrow my eyes, sliding my attention over every corner of the arena. Someone is watching me. I don't know where they are or who it is, but my instincts are screaming to run away.

I can't. I couldn't do that to Kentucky.

The loud crash of the chute opening startles me. The crowd roars as a cowgirl finishes the first barrel race. I clap slowly, staring across the arena at the other set of bleachers. I scan every face, trying to pinpoint who is out there.

Goosebumps arise on my skin. My tongue and throat become dry. A stampede replaces my heartbeat. Any faster, and it would gallop out of my chest.

"Ladies and gentlemen, the moment we have all been waiting for, my friend, Kentucky Jones! He is a world champion and has countless records. It's been a while since he has competed though, and he is going to have to brush the rust off if he wants to beat the cowgirls who were before him. And before you go giving him shit about choosing to barrel race, you'd better remember it's a unisex sport, and if you love it, that's the reason to do it. Fuck everyone else."

"There are children here!" someone yells up at the announcer's box.

"I don't care," Lorcan replies, sticking his head out of the window. "They won't be going to Hell. You know that, right? I've been there, and no one has ever been sent to the underworld for cursing. My gosh, humans can be so dense."

"Okay, you're out of here, buddy. Go sit down before we kick you out of the event." A booming security guard's voice blares into the microphone for all to hear.

Half the crowd claps, happy for Lorcan's demise, while the others boo.

"I'm going, I'm going, but don't come crawling back to me when you realize my worth."

My lips vibrate together when I blow out a tired breath, that is all caused by Lorcan's antics.

"Can you believe them?" He pops next to me, placing two fingers in his mouth and ripping a loud whistle. "I was doing better than the other guy. They'll ask for me back."

"How do you know how to announce everyone?"

"They have sheets up there. It's easy to read."

"Oh." I expected more of an explanation from him. A statement of some sort about researching rodeos, best times, and competitors. I guess his reason is as good as any.

"Kentucky is up. Oh, I'm so excited. He'd better not lose. I'd have to release a pretty terrible person from Purgatory."

I dislike how high-pitched his voice is around the words 'pretty and terrible'. He reeks of guilt, and he hasn't even stated what this person has done.

And you know what? I don't want to know.

"Don't tell me more information. Leave me in the dark this time. I already feel on alert." As much as I want to continue to examine my surroundings, my anxiety fades when I see Kentucky in the chute.

My heart eases with our gazes locked. From here, he pinches the brim of his hat, tilting his chin. Putting his finger into a gun gesture, he kisses the tip of his index finger, aims it at me, and shoots.

I catch it, placing the phantom kiss on my lips.

"Yuck. You're sickening. Like two teens in love," Lorcan gags.

Ignoring him, I lean against the rails, my focus never leaving my mate. Romeo neighs, raising on his hind legs from being in the chute. Kentucky strokes his neck to calm him, bending down to whisper into Romeo's ear. Whatever is said, the vampire horse calms to an eerie standstill.

"Kentucky Jones is riding Romeo, a Friesian horse, not a horse that is too common to ride in the rodeo," The announcer informs. "While not too common, his record has proven him worthy to be here."

"That reminds me. How does he have a record if it has been decades since he has competed, Lorcan?"

The Void takes the spot next to me, leaning his elbows against the rails. "You need to remember Kentucky is a lot older than everyone here. He's had to forge documents before, so this event was easy. Well, I forged them, then I signed him up, but he knows how. He did have to mystify a few people when he got here, but no questions will be asked of him. He doesn't use any of his abilities out there. Neither does Romeo. They play at the same level as all the others. If he wins, he always donates his earnings. He never feels right about keeping them."

The chute opens, which ends our conversation. I couldn't care less what he has to say. Romeo launches forward, his long legs eating up the distance between them and the barrels.

I jump, clap, and shout. I can't seem to stay still. "Go, Kentucky, go! Let's go, Romeo! Woooo!" I scream by cupping my hands around my mouth, hoping he can hear me over all the other spectators in the crowd cheering him on.

Romeo is quick and agile, keeping the turns around the barrels tight and clean. Kentucky holds the reins with one hand, keeping the other free. Kentucky and Romeo together seem effortless. They have done this hundreds of times. There's no doubt that they make the perfect team.

They round the last barrel, bolting to the finish line with a time of seventeen seconds flat.

"Yes! Oh my god, that was phenomenal! They were so fast. Is that a good time? That has to be, right?"

I scream as loud as I can, capturing Romeo and Kentucky's attention. I blow them kisses, waves, and jump with so much excitement, I'm ready to hop over these rails and run to them myself. Something about Kentucky in his black coat, black shirt, jeans, and hat. I want him to wear this exact outfit later and use me to the point where I fall unconscious, hopefully from his bite.

"No one will be able to touch them. Eighteen seconds for barrel racing is pretty standard, so I don't see anyone else beating their time."

The eerie sensation is back, sucking all the joy and excitement from the moment.

I search for the reason for my paranoia again by scanning the bleachers up and down, left to right. Most people are taking the time to go to the concession stands between competitors. The lines are long. People are waiting for the best BBQ in town. The food truck is to the left of the concession stands, painted a bright red.

It's who is on top of that truck in a crouched position who draws my attention. He has a smirk on his face. He points at me, slashing his finger across his throat.

It's Louisville.

I'd know that evil curl of his lip from anywhere.

The validation of fear has me tugging on Lorcan's arm. "Lorcan! Lorcan, it's him. That's the vampire who kidnapped me."

"Where? Who?" He straightens, readying himself for a fight.

"At the red truck. He's on top of it. He's right there." I spin to see him again, my heart in my throat, and terror in my bones. Everything is telling me to run, but I know the safest place I can be is here with Lorcan, Kentucky, and Romeo.

"There's no one there, Dru. You're sure you saw him?"

I flinch, rearing back as if he slapped me across the face. The sting of his doubt is fresh. Being doubted by someone you thought trusted you is a new kind of disappointment. This is why I stayed focused my entire life and didn't get distracted by friends. I didn't have time for anyone doubting me then, and I sure as fuck don't have time for anyone to doubt me now.

I don't care if Lorcan could kill me with a snap of his fingers.

"Of course, I saw him! I can't believe you're asking me that. Do you really think I'd imagine him in a place like this? He's here. I *feel* him. I felt him earlier. You know that sensation of someone watching you? It was him. Lorcan, please." I dig my nails into his arm, pleading with him to help me. Tears brim in my eyes. "I can't be the only one fighting for my life. I won't win this fight without you or Kentucky."

"Stay here. I'm going to go tell Kentucky. We're getting out of here."

"Wait, but the competition. He's doing so well."

"When it comes to you, he won't give a fuck about this rodeo, Dru. Your safety means the world to him. I promised him I'd protect you while we were here. I'm going to keep that promise, okay? You aren't alone."

"Don't leave," I plead, breaking the skin of his arm, and he begins to bleed smoke. The dancing clouds swirl from the small cuts. "Don't leave me alone. We're better off staying together. He probably wants you to find Kentucky, so he can make his move."

"Okay, you're right. You've made a good point. I won't leave you. I promise."

I press my head against his shoulder, wondering if this is what it is like to have a brother. Growing up as an only child, having siblings was out of the question. My father never wanted to remarry or have more children after my mom died. I grew used to the idea of being alone.

Then, I met Carmen.

And now, I have Kentucky, Romeo, and Lorcan.

"Our favorite events are coming up! Prepare yourself for the Roughstock events! We have saddle bronc, bareback, and bull riding. These are some of the most dangerous events. Cowboys have been killed or severely injured by trying to stay on for the wild and untamed eight-second ride. Hold your breaths and keep your hopes high that everyone comes out of this unharmed," The announcer's voice is monotone and would put me to sleep if I wasn't wired from Louisville being here.

I keep my eyes set on the red BBQ truck, waiting for him to make his return.

This night has turned into a competition for survival.

I've beaten him once, and to do it again would be a miracle.

CHAPTER NINETEEN
KENTUCKY

I find something very odd about being here. My hackles are raised, and I don't want to alarm Lorcan or Dru, but I can't speak to any of the animals here except Romeo. I would never use my power for my advantage. But usually, I hear their thoughts about being here at the rodeo. They love to bitch and moan about their owners or how much they hate their pastures. Some actually enjoy the rodeo and taunt the other livestock.

It's quiet this time, as if something is blocking me from speaking to them.

"Romeo, do you hear anything from any of the animals? What's going on?" I ask him as I swing my leg over this giant crossbred bull.

He's half Brahma, half Longhorn, which is commonly known as a Plummer Bull. They are known for their strength and bucking abilities. There aren't many bulls that cause my nerves to fire, but this one here is definitely one of them.

"Nothing out of the ordinary. A few horses hate their owners, and the bull you're riding is plotting your death. You

can't hear them?" Romeo responds from the trailer I brought him in.

Typically, there are stock farms for the competitors to keep their livestock at. Romeo doesn't like them. He says they are "Too crowded" which is fine. I don't trust most people when they see a horse like Romeo, anyhow. He's unique. Different from any horse anyone has ever seen. Red eyes, a sculpted skeletal face, he's terrifying.

He's the type a human would try to kill so they can have a trophy to mount on the wall.

No way in hell am I letting that happen.

"No. I can't hear a damn thing, Romeo. Something is going on. Stay focused for me."

"I'll do my best from the trailer."

"The sass isn't needed. You know I can't have you walking around. You'll get attacked."

"I can take care of myself."

"Another reason why I'm keeping you in the trailer," I state in finality, leaving zero room for argument.

His silence means he knows I'm right.

The bull jostles, slamming my leg against the metal chute I'm trapped in with him.

"I can't believe you're the first to ride Gunpowder tonight. He's wired," the chute boss says to me.

"Can't wait." I tighten my legs on his side when he starts swinging his head left and right.

His horns are huge, towering over his head to the sky, and are as white as the moon without a single spot on them.

I take one last glance at my mate, not wanting her to notice how nervous I am. This bull is strong, weighs thousands of pounds, and seems like the type to charge, stomp, and run you over after throwing you off. If I could use my vampire abilities, I wouldn't have to worry about potentially dying or getting away from Gunpowder.

Tightening the braided rope around my hand, I keep a firm grip. I'm careful not to use my enhanced strength. I'm just a man out here, and that's what I love about this sport.

As I wait my turn, the rider ahead of me just gave permission to the chute boss to open the gate.

"Cal McCartey is off to a powerful start, riding Heaven or Hell, a bull who hospitalized a rider only last year from a severe head injury. Hopefully, Cal will survive this monstrous ride," The announcer informs.

Heaven or Hell is slate grey Brahma with mismatched horns. One curves up like normal, while the other points down.

One to Heaven.

One to Hell.

The name is fitting.

The bull jumps and twists higher than I've ever seen before. Silence falls over the crowd as they watch with a held breath if Cal will come out of this unscathed.

The rider's hat soars off his head. Heaven or Hell stomps on it, flattening and retiring it for good.

Another harsh buck and twist, Cal flies off, landing hard on his back. Even though I'm on Gunpowder, Cal's groans can be heard from where I sit when he tries to get up after getting the wind knocked out of him. He isn't moving fast enough to get out of the arena. Cal holds his side, limping to the rails to exit.

But Heaven or Hell is not done by how he is pawing the ground, lowers his head, and releases a violent grunt. It's as if Cal is a huge red flag by how the bull has set his sights on him.

Heaven or Hell charges.

The rodeo clowns try to intervene by distracting the bull to chase them, but it's too late.

I hold my breath for the guy, knowing it's far too late to save him.

The bull rams his head into Cal's back, the horn hooking onto his shirt. Cal somersaults through the air, and his being attacked leaves me helpless. On any other day, I'd be able to save him.

Not here. Not now. I wouldn't get to him in time before he hits the ground, anyway. Injuries are part of the sport. All riders at some point in their career have been injured.

Including me. Before the advancement of medicine and my vampire abilities, there was a time I stayed in the hospital for a month from a head injury. Being stepped on by a two-thousand-pound animal will do that to a man.

Cal lands on his side with a hard and audible *whack*. Everyone, me included, groans in unison. He screams in agony, clutching the arm that is broken, judging by the piece of bone sticking out of it.

If only I could talk to this bull to tell it to stop its rampage. I can't, and it is so fucking frustrating.

"Damn, I don't know if they will be able to get him out of there in time," the chute boss states with heavy sadness in his words. He takes off his hat, pressing it over his heart to show respect.

Cal manages to roll to his good side, missing another savage step by the bull. Heaven or Hell doesn't like to lose, it seems. He spins around and bucks, hitting Cal in the chest.

The snap of his sternum has me turn my head away. I don't feel comfortable watching a good man's death.

"Folks, this is hard to watch. Cal McCartey is a worldwide, three-time bull riding champion. There's always that one bull that people will remember, and I'm afraid today is one of those days."

I'm going to break the announcer's neck when I'm done here. Who says something so insensitive to a man fighting for his life?

"Please keep Cal McCartey in your thoughts while Heaven or Hell gets back in his pin."

I suppose that's better. Not great, but the announcer saved his own life by adding that sentence to his statement.

"Looks like Heaven or Hell has been successfully removed from the arena and is secure. The medics are on their way to McCartey now. Let's hope for the best."

One tear drop. One drop of blood. Cal would be cured. He wouldn't have to fight for his life. I hate the rules Lorcan told me about. So much good could come of vampire healing abilities. I understand why the rules are in place. It protects all paranormals.

Can't the rules be broken sometimes?

"Let's give a big round of applause to Cal, Ladies and Gentlemen. He is on the gurney and on his way to the nearest hospital. If there are any updates, I'll be sure to give them to you."

I hate to say it, but Lorcan was a better announcer. I don't know if I'll tell him that because it will go to his head, and he'd volunteer to announce at every damn rodeo.

"Our next rider, Kentucky Jones!" The audience erupts in applause and cheers, already forgetting about Cal.

Even with a near-death experience, the show must go on.

"Ready?"

In bull riding, one hand must be raised in the air at all times. It can not touch the bull, or it is an immediate disqualification.

Blowing out a breath, I give a curt nod, putting Cal in the furthest corner of my mind. A second later, the chute opens, and Gunpowder flees with the power of a million pissed off cattle.

"Ladies and Gentlemen, Kentucky Jones is riding Gunpowder, one of the craziest, strongest, and heaviest bulls.

Gunpowder is coming out of the gate with a purpose, and he doesn't seem to be losing any steam."

I wish that announcer would shut the fuck up.

Gunpowder lifts his back legs, twisting his hind end before landing. He spins faster, gaining speed and strength to buck me off. My chaps rub against the bull's hide, the leather keeping me as stable as possible.

Dirt is tossed in the air by his furious hooves, sending clouds around me. I dig my spurs into his side, taunting him to do more wreckage. Bull spurring can give me extra points. Not many do it, but I've been told once or twice that I have no care for my life.

Gunpowder stomps, grunting with fury to get me off his back. Out of the corner of my eye, I notice all the bleachers begin to empty. I'm holding onto the rope for dear life with every buck Gunpowder gives me. My vision of the stands blurs with every kick. I'm not able to see what is going on.

The buzzer rings when I hit the eight-second mark. Using the momentum from the bull during his next buck, I jump off, tucking my knees to my chest to roll safely onto the ground.

No cheers. No claps. No annoying announcer to inform everyone I've moved to the number one spot.

Brushing off my chaps, I stand, peering into the bleachers to find Dru. I don't give a damn about anyone else here. If Dru isn't here, something is wrong.

I forget about Gunpowder being in the arena and that no one is here to put him in a chute. I'm too focused on Dru. If I had bitten her when I had the chance, I'd be able to find her. I feel her. I can't place where though.

"Romeo. Get to the area now—" Gunpowder's horn plunges into me through my back, spearing through my chest. He raises his head, forcing me to hang in the air. I gasp, trying to push myself up and off the horn.

I can't.

I'm too weak to save myself in this condition. Blood pours from the wound, gathering in a growing red pool on the dirt. Iron saturates my tongue, the metallic taste warning me that I could die here.

If I had just bitten Dru, if I had been honest, none of this would have happened. I would have the strength a vampire should. I wouldn't be decomposing from the inside out.

Choking on my own blood, I gag when it is lodged in my throat, spitting the wad onto the ground.

"Is that any way to greet your son?"

My eyes are heavy from the pain. My hat falls from my head, drifting to the blood-ridden ground. I manage to turn my head to see a tall man standing there with Dru in his grasp. He has her by the throat, claws drawn, and sinking into her beautiful, soft flesh.

A scarlet haze overcomes my sight. My fangs unsheathing, wanting to protect her from this stranger who dares to put his hand on my fated mate.

"Dru," I rasp, reaching for her with my body.

I raise myself a few inches on the horn, using every bit of strength and energy I have to break free from this spear of a horn.

I can't.

I sag onto the bull's head, urging my body, my molecules to heal.

I need to get to her. I need her.

I *need*.

"Kentucky! Stop! Sweetheart, please, stop. Don't move!" she cries, a constant flow of tears wetting her angelic cheeks. "Please."

The scent of her fear is bitter. I'm taken back to when I found and saved her from the shed. She was so afraid of me and had every reason to be. I hated the smell of her terror then, and I hate it even more now.

"Get your fucking hands off my mate." The words are broken with a wheeze after every breath. "Your issue is with me. Let her go." Deep crimson rivulets flow down the horn, and the putrid scent of dying clings to the cells.

"My issue is with both of you, Dad. Can I call you that?" He dares to lick the side of my mate's neck. "She's delicious. Something about her calls to me. I finally figured it out."

"I don't have kids. I can't have children. You have the wrong man. Let my Beloved go. Or I swear, I'll fucking kill you!" I roar at a monstrous volume, the timbre vibrating the bleachers.

"Tsk, tsk. You might want to be careful and reserve your energy. From the smell of things, the two of you aren't doing very well, are you, Dad? Papa? Father? What do you prefer?"

I sneer, trying to launch myself off the horn again. "Where is Lorcan?"

"Kentucky, don't. Calm down. You must. The more your blood pressure rises, the quicker you'll bleed out. With us decomposing, Kentucky, you have to be careful."

I gasp again. Blood drips off my bottom lip in thick strings. I don't have the energy to spit. "We're fine, Dru. Everything is okay. We will be okay." She knows the truth. She's being too cavalier about decomposing. It isn't the time to talk about it, given the circumstances.

When we get out of here, I'll tell her everything I've been keeping from her.

"Don't lie to her, Dad."

I cut my eyes to him, groaning when the bull adjusts his stance. "Don't call me that. I don't fucking know you. I have no idea who you are or why you have the delusion that I'm your father. I'm not. I have no kids. I can't have kids. I don't know how many times I have to tell you that. Please," I hang my head in exhaustion. "Let her go. She's innocent in this. If you're problem is with me, let's handle this like men."

"Come here." The stranger tugs Dru by the throat with his hand, forcing her to follow him as he steps closer to me. "I said, come here!" he yells, throwing her onto the ground.

"Dru!" I roar for her, causing more blood to seep from the wound.

With a tight grip on the back of her neck, he lifts her again, leaving four superficial marks across her throat.

If only I had bitten her. She'd heal. I'm a stupid man. I should have protected her. I failed my mate.

"Okay. Let's turn back time a little. Shall we? Your friend Lorcan? He got called away to reap the souls in the next town over. All one thousand and twenty-two souls. It might take him a bit."

Dru sobs, covering her mouth with her hand in horror.

"You killed a thousand people? Why? What did they do to you?" I ask, realizing I'm staring at a vampire whom I was afraid of becoming. The longer I stare at him, the more I begin to notice the resemblance between us.

He has lighter hair than I do, but the same eyes as me. Our facial structure is similar. Same jaw. Same eyebrow shape. Same eyes. People look alike every day and aren't related—that has to be the case here.

I do not have children, and I refuse to acknowledge that I do from a vampire such as himself.

And if I did, I sure as Hell wouldn't accept a son like him. No one touches my mate or disrespects her. I might be impaled now, and I might not have the strength to heal, but I refuse to die without having her in my arms. I don't know what I have to do to make that happen.

Dying alone is no longer an option when my heart is being held by the best company there is.

"How else was I going to get you alone without alerting

the Void? You know he can never deny a call for souls. As for Dru, I realize why I'm so keen on her. It's because she—" he tucks her hair behind her ear, and she flinches away from him, whimpering when he digs his nails into the canvas of her throat even deeper than the last time. "—Is your fated mate. I've heard of bloodlines being attracted to another's mate, even feeling drawn to them in a way. She isn't my fated mate. Don't get confused. The obsession with her though is intoxicating, Dad."

"Stop! Stop calling me that. Enough. Let her go. She isn't yours. You admitted that yourself. She's mine. *Mine.*" I shout when Gunpowder slings me to the left and right, jostling the horn through my chest.

"You might want to watch how you speak to me. I'm controlling him. I have this nifty ability to speak to animals and people. I can control their every thought. See, the bull you're impaled on? The only thought he has right now is killing you, and he will if you somehow get yourself free from that horn. No one is coming back. Everyone thinks the rodeo is canceled after that poor bull rider got kicked in the chest. He'll live. I thought you'd want to know."

"You controlled the bull to target him? For this? Why?" I spit out another wad of blood. If I were human, I'd already be dead from this type of wound.

"It was...fun," he chuckles into Dru's neck, moaning when he inhales her scent. "How have you denied her? How have you denied yourself? It's a shame both of you have to die because of your mistake, Dad."

I grit my teeth when I hear him call me by that title again. "It was the hardest thing I've ever had to do. I wanted to give her a choice—Ah! Fuck!" I yell when the bull moves again from his command.

"Don't move," Dru whispers in a shaky voice. "Please. Please, I'm begging you. Stay still. Seeing you in pain is making me ache in my soul, please." She sobs so hard, her shoulders shake. "I can feel you dying." A dam of tears breaks away from her lash line, and the reflection of the neon lights shining down on the arena shines off her sadness. "It's killing me."

My own sadness almost breaks me. Tears burn my eyes, but I refuse to look any weaker in front of this crazed vampire.

"Romeo. Where are you? I need you. Someone has me and Dru hostage."

I figured he'd be here by now. Something must be wrong.

"If you're looking for your horse, he's currently a statue inside your trailer. Did you know that 'Cemetery Ophids,' also known as 'Stone Snakes' thrive in Purgatory? It isn't hard to find someone willing to smuggle out things that don't belong here." A sick grin spreads across his face, one of manic and instability.

"Don't worry, Romeo can come back once he meets his Beloved. Stone Snakes are rumored to have been born from Medusa. I don't know if I believe all that, but I thought, 'How perfect. I only needed to use them on Romeo.' Look how lucky I am? You proved yourself weak and useless. I thought you'd put up a fight. I didn't have to search for any other method to kill you. All I needed to do was show up."

No. I didn't know that about Stone Snakes. I didn't know fucking anything, and now it's biting me in the ass. Mourning is proof on my face this time, knowing my best friend is a stone. I refuse for that to be his life. I'll buy every horse in the world if it means there's a chance he can wake up.

There are two things in this world that are off limits to others:

My mate.

And my horse.

"I'm going to kill you," I seethe. "I'm going to rip your fangs from your fucking mouth, tie you to the back of my horse, and drag you across hot pavement until your skin is peeled from your bones. You won't be able to heal because you'll be wrapped in fucking silver!" I roar, almost pushing myself off the horn when he drives it back through.

"Kentucky!"

"Ah. Ah." The stranger tsks, tightening his hold on Dru.

"It's okay, Darlin'. I'll be okay. We'll be okay." Somehow, I know that. I don't know how or why, but I refuse to die now when I'm so close to living for the first time. "Who are you?" I finally ask him, hoping his name will tickle a memory.

"Oh, that's right. I've made an entrance but not a name for myself. Apologies, Dad." He pushes Dru forward, keeping her as a barrier between him and me.

She'd be the first to get gutted if he ordered the bull to attack. I have to remain calm. I have to be everything she needs. She deserves someone who can protect her, and I refuse for it not to be me.

"Louisville Reese."

I can't tell if I stop breathing because of what he said or if the wound is so bad, I'm dying.

"Oh, that last name rings a bell, doesn't it? I see you wondering how it's possible. Your thoughts are whirling." He twirls his finger next to his temple.

"That's not possible. She couldn't have. Audrey wouldn't have—" I stop myself from completing that sentence.

She would have hidden that from me. That's the harshest truth of it all. If she could hide the most important part of herself, the part of her being a vampire, then she would hide if she were pregnant.

But why? Why would she hide that? She knew I wanted kids.

I'm so tired of her betrayal seeping further into me. If I had known about him, he would have had a chance of being a decent man.

Not...this.

"Audrey Reese, you know her, don't you?"

"Audrey? Your maker?" Dru asks.

"Shut up. No one is talking to you. Be a good woman and keep your fucking mouth shut."

"Don't talk to her like that!" I snarl, the bull slinging me to the left for punishment.

"Don't talk to me like that, and maybe your death won't be so painful."

Dru covers her mouth to catch a loud sob.

"Get me free from this bull, and we can talk, okay? I don't have much time left. You obviously want answers, and I want to give them to you—" I try to stay as still as possible, the agony becoming more unbearable. "Son."

I add the term of endearment in hopes it will ease his vendetta against me.

"You don't have the fucking right." He shoves Dru across the arena, and she slams against the railing, falling unconscious.

"Dru!"

Louisville stands in front of me, clutching the bull's other horn to have more control. "You killed my mother." He leans in, swiping blood off the horn. "You killed her before I knew her. Do you know my grandfather lost Reese Railroads? He went bankrupt trying to figure out what happened to Audrey. No one knew until I ran across a demon and a warlock who had a fortune teller in their custody. She painted a pretty picture of you staking my mother through the heart. She hadn't turned more vampires or brought more kids to him to raise as bloodborns. Do you know how much more powerful bloodborns are than someone like me? Because she had to settle for a pathetic human like you, and you turned her down! You turned down the chance for us to be a family!"

Spit flies from his mouth with every hatred-filled word twisted from his tongue.

"I didn't know about you. I had no idea she was pregnant. She must have kept it from me. She—" It dawns on me, a memory reawakening in the forefront of my mind when I asked her if she ever mystified me.

She had.

She had altered my memories.

The hit to the soul has me coughing up my blood.

"I didn't know," I wheeze. "She manipulated me. She used the ability to mystify. Audrey altered my mind so I wouldn't know she was pregnant. She hid that from me."

"Liar!" Louisville wraps a hand around my throat. "She wouldn't do that. She was a good person. She would have been a good mom."

The agony of missing what he never could have fills his eyes as he stares at me with daggers. Tears race down his face.

He's just a boy missing his mom.

"I wish I could tell you she was a good person, Louisville. I really do. I want to be able to say that."

"You should, since you're on your dying breath. Why aren't you lying? Why aren't you trying to save yourself? Are you so self-righteous that you can't even do that?" he yells so loud his voice breaks.

"I killed her because she turned me into something I never wanted. I never wanted to be this creature. I longed for death." My eyes dart to Dru, who is pushing herself up into a seated position, leaning against the rails that surround the arena.

Blood drips down her temple, face, and neck, gathering at the collar of her shirt.

"Until now," I add, longing for my fated mate. "I don't want to die now. I want to spend eternity with my mate."

He steps back, looking me up and down. "The audacity you have to ask me to save you for another woman. You hated my mother so much for the gift she gave you, killed her, and now you appreciate what she did? So you can live happily ever after? Something you took away from my mother?"

"I didn't know how to appreciate it then, but I do now." I tilt my head back, needing one deep breath.

The night is painted in a billion constellations, giving me what I've always wanted—to die under the star-filled sky.

I'm not dying without a fight.

"You could have been my father, and I'm so happy you're not." He stares at the bull; the poor animal has my blood dripping down his chest from being forced to carry the weight of me. "Kill them," he orders.

Gunpowder paws the ground, snorting a fuming breath, and charges at Dru. Time slows when the bull gains speed. Every thunderous step brings more pain, but I don't care about that. Dru is seconds away from dying.

The bull tilts his head to plow into her, and it's enough for me to use his momentum and the rest of my strength to become freed. Nothing else matters except getting to Dru.

I dig down into the roots of my soul for energy, speeding to her, and curl over her, taking another spear through my shoulder.

"Ahh!" I scream, shouting my agony to the sky.

The bull pulls away, wanting enough distance to charge.

"He will never stop trying to kill you. He has no other thoughts anymore. His brain is wiped clean."

"Kentucky. I love you. I love you so fucking much," Dru says, pressing her shaking hands against my wounds. "You'll be okay. You have to be. You have to be okay. We aren't done. We can't be done. I just...I just got you."

I cup her face with my bloody hand, pressing my forehead against hers. "I love you too, Darlin'. From the moment I saw you, I loved you."

"I don't want us to die," she whispers, peering over my shoulder to the bull. "Bite me. Complete the bond."

"Not like this. I won't take advantage of your will."

Dru's murderous scream causes my ears to ring when Gunpowder's horn pierces my other shoulder.

It doesn't hurt anymore.

"My will?"

The bull backs away again.

"I don't give a damn about my will!" Dru palms the back of my head, forcing me to her neck. "You carry my will in your hands every day. My will means nothing without you. Bite me so we can have a chance of that happily ever after."

I hate the circumstance. I'm too weak to deny her offer when I want it so badly. Sinking my fangs into her vein is more than I've ever dreamed. Her skin gives without resistance, her blood pouring down my throat to heal the deepest wounds that have stained my bones.

Wrapping an arm around her, I groan from how fucking good she tastes. I pull her close, her hands still applying pressure to my wounds as she gasps with every drag I take.

My enhanced hearing begins to work again, and I can hear the pounding of the bull's steps closing in.

Danger is close, and it isn't enough to stop my body's reaction to having my fated's blood for the first time. My cock is hard. Her body is warm. Her blood is weighed with oxytocin, fueling every chamber of my heart with her desire.

I blur us out of the way in the nick of time, the bull's head bending the metal railing from his power. His horns become stuck, which only piss him off further. He bucks and wails, doing his best to free himself.

Instincts have me biting into my own wrist and pressing it against her lips. Her eyes round in surprise, but she doesn't question me. She holds onto my forearm, drinking to bind us.

The final step.

An orange glow lifts from my chest while a neon purple

swirls from hers. They twist together and become one, floating back into our bodies.

We sit there staring at one another, my arm still wrapped around her tight, pressing our bodies together so I know she's safe. The wound on her neck scars over, and the scent of death vanishes.

"Well, isn't that unfortunate."

Faster than he can take another step, I draw my gun hidden in my boot and fire.

Sinking a silver-plated wooden bullet through his heart.

His hand is slow, pressing against his bleeding wound, before he pulls it back to look at it. "You shot me?"

I stand, my strength renewed. My wounds need another few hours to fully heal, but they are well on their way. I keep Dru at my side as we walk to him, my gun still heavy and at the ready in my hand.

"You never threaten a cowboy and live to see another day, Son. Especially one who is quick on the draw."

"You'd shoot your own son?" He falls to his knees, struggling to stay alive when his skin begins to flake into ash.

He falls onto his back, staring up at the same night I've dreamed about dying under. I didn't have a choice. I had to kill him. Dru would have never been safe with him lurking around.

His hate, his need for blood, for violence, that's what killed him. I simply pulled the trigger to finally put him out of his misery.

I do what any parent does. I sit down, pick his head up, and place him in my lap.

"I'm sorry I wasn't around, so you wouldn't hold so much anger inside you. You and I are a lot alike in that sense. If I had known about you, I would have been there."

He lifts his hand for me to take. The angry man has

vanished, and now all I see is a lost little boy. I hold onto it, my own tears bursting free, knowing I killed my own boy.

"I'm sorry, but I had to protect what's mine."

"It's okay," he rasps. "I can be with Mom."

"I can take him from here." Lorcan arrives, covered in the blood of all the lives my son killed. "His soul calls to me."

"No. I want to be with him. He doesn't deserve to die alone." The breeze drifts in, carrying away ash peeling from his face.

"I bet you would have been a good dad," Louisville says with tears in his eyes. "I'm sorry."

"It's okay. You're okay." I choke on a sob, running my fingers through his hair until there's nothing there but piles of ash.

He's gone.

DEAD MAN'S
RANCH

Chapter Twenty

DRUSCILLA

Kentucky stares at his empty hands as the wind carries away his only child. What I love most about Kentucky is how honorable he is. He could have done a lot worse to Louisville, yet even through his anger for revenge for what Louisville had done, he stayed with his son until the end.

Now that the bond is complete, his every emotion courses through me, and he is devastated.

"I didn't know," he whispers, looking up at me with bloodshot eyes and my blood still lingering on his lips. "I promise, I didn't know."

I kneel next to him, forcing him to look at me by palming his jaw. "I know you didn't. I know."

"I took care of his soul." Lorcan appears again, freeing the bull that was stuck. Gunpowder runs away from us, and not in the way that gives him more room to charge. "The bull will be okay. I'm just sorry you had to go through all that pain, Kentucky. I'm sorry I couldn't be here. There were too many souls that needed me."

"I understand, Lorcan. I ain't mad. Is he in Purgatory? My son?"

"He is," Lorcan replies with a frown. "I'm sorry. He will never be free. His crimes are too severe."

Kentucky reaches for his hat and begins to put Louisville ashes inside it.

"What are you doing?" Lorcan asks with big, round eyes.

"He deserves to be cared about in death. I couldn't do that for him in life, but I can do it now."

I help him, fisting piles of ash until his hat is full. "I love you even more because of this." I kiss his cheek. "Even after everything he did, you're showing love."

"It's not his fault he turned out the way he did. It's mine for not being there, and it's his mother's. He's at peace. I know I did the right thing."

"You did. Rogue vampires never last very long." Lorcan places a hand on his shoulder, shooting me with a worried expression. "He wasn't going to last, Kentucky. Find peace in knowing it was you in the end to give him peace and not The Horsemen—War, Death, Famine, and Conquest with their leader Abaddon." His attention redirects toward me. "I don't know how much you know, but The Horsemen are called The Hell's Harvesters. Any paranormal who commits crimes that are deemed unforgivable is typically captured by them. They travel where they are called. They are on their way here. I couldn't...I couldn't get all the souls by myself. I have to go back." Lorcan coughs to clear the emotion in his throat. "I've never seen anything like it. I'm sorry for your loss, Kentucky, but the world is a better place without him. I know how much you wanted kids."

"I'm sorry for what he did," Kentucky sighs, wiping his cheeks with the back of his hand. "I need to get to Romeo. He turned him to stone with Stone Snakes. Can you reverse it, Lorcan? I need my fucking horse. Please," he essentially begs.

Lorcan's eyes turn downward, his brows pinching together in sorrow. "I'm sorry, Kentucky. The only way for someone to come back from Cemetery Ophids is if their Beloved finds them. In Purgatory, there's an entire forest of statues that will never meet their mates. We call it The Cemetery. I'm sorry for both your losses."

Kentucky hands me his hat and, without a word, begins to walk away. His clothes are drenched in blood, his wounds faint as if he wasn't just bored by a bull, and that isn't what weighs him down the most.

It's heartache.

I place a hand against my chest and take a deep breath when the pain seems to buzz inside me.

"You'll always feel what he feels. That won't change. Go. He needs you more than ever. I need to go. Abaddon is calling me."

"Be safe." I throw my arms around his neck to hug him.

"Look after my friend for me. He feels deeply. I'm not sure how long it will take for him to come back from this. Congratulations, by the way."

"On completing our bond? Finally, right? Just in time." I'm careful when I take a step back with Kentucky's hat. I don't want to lose one single ash of the son he never knew about.

"My god, he really knows fucking nothing, doesn't he?" Lorcan rubs his temples. "He makes my head hurt so much. You're pregnant, Dru. It's early. You wouldn't be able to tell. He should have noticed a change in your smell."

"But..." I press my hand against my stomach in disbelief. "I'm on my period."

"And? You met a vampire. Do you really think that matters?"

"But Daphne..."

"Daphne was a Dimseer. The moment she decided to be with Kentucky, not only did she sacrifice herself to a half-life, but also the ability to have children. Dimseer children cannot be born to anyone else except another Dimseer. It's how their power is so strong," he explains. "I'll leave it up to you to tell him the truth. He doesn't know any of that. Daphne didn't want him to. For good reason. Kentucky is hard on himself, and he was struggling with life up until he met you."

I don't like hiding anything from Kentucky. That's something I'll really need to think about. I'll tell him the truth, but I won't right now. We are still strengthening our bond, and I don't want anything to jeopardize that. I'm jealous Daphne got to love him first, and I want my own time to build our trust and truths before spilling hers.

He tilts his head to the side and rolls his eyes. "I'm coming! No need for the sass, Abaddon," he yells. "I need to go. Holler if you need me."

He's gone in the midst of smoke.

I'm standing alone in the arena where this was supposed to be a fun night, where Kentucky got to bring home a trophy. Instead, I'm holding the ashes of his dead son while pregnant with his child. Would he even want another child after what has happened today?

"What's wrong? Are you hurt? I felt it. You're uneasy. You're sad. Talk to me, Dru." Kentucky is at my side in the blink of an eye, his tear-stained face red and blotchy.

"Is it true about Romeo?"

"It is, but I'll figure that out. Since Louisville is dead, I can hear the animals at the stock farm again. They've been talking about a kill pen near here where the owner takes their animals if they don't win. I'm going to start there. I'm going to buy every single horse at every single kill pen. If that doesn't work, I'll adopt from every shelter. I'll find his mate. He has been loyal and by my side. I won't fail him now." His hand fits with mine like a missing puzzle piece. "Talk to me, Darlin'. Besides what happened tonight, what's wrong? I feel it." He brings the top of my hand to his soft lip to place a kiss.

"It's just a long night. Let's go home and get Romeo set up in his stall where he will be safe." I begin to walk away when Kentucky snags my waist and pulls me close.

My back is against his chest, a place that envelopes me in comfort.

"You just lied to me. I'll let it slide since the night has been so heavy. I feel your emotions. They are all over the place. Talk to me, Darlin'."

"I'm fine. I promise. Let's go home."

"You just lied to me again."

In one swoop, I'm at the truck, the passenger side door open, and I'm tucked into the seat with Kentucky bracketing me in with his arms.

"I'm sorry about everything tonight. The way we had to finish our bond—"

I silence him with a finger over his lips. "I'm happy. I don't care how we had to complete the bond. I'm glad I was able to get through to that stubborn head of yours. Plus, you can always make it up to me with a special date, and we can recreate what you had in mind. Saving our lives tonight doesn't seem like a bad way to complete the mating, right?"

"I waited too long. None of this would have happened if I had been honest with you. How long have you known that you've been my mate?"

"A few days. Lorcan told me because he knew how hard-headed you are."

He stares into the ashes in his hat, a heavy sigh drifting the ashes in a circle. "If I had listened, maybe I could have saved my kid."

"Don't go down that road, Kentucky. You'll torture your-self with thoughts like that. Louisville was a terrible person. I'm sorry he was your son. I'll never forgive him for what he did to me."

"I won't either. I just hate that something that was a part

of me could ever think of hurting you. I can't help but think of what could have been."

"You gave him more grace in the end than he would have ever given anybody. Don't be hard on yourself. It isn't your fault you were not around. It was your maker's. Louisville made his own choices, and he could have chosen differently. This is his fate due to his own wicked deeds. Stop punishing yourself for something you had no control over." I kiss the middle of his forehead.

I debate on telling him the truth. The words are on the tip of my tongue, and yet I can't seem to speak them. I'm nervous. I think he needs more time. Too much has happened tonight. He went from thinking he couldn't have children, to having a maniac son, to killing him, to being with him in his final moments.

If I say I'm pregnant right now, would he be happy, or would it feel like a burden?

"I'm not going to bring his ashes into the house. He won't ever step foot inside our home. I'll bury him somewhere on the property. I don't see his wickedness fading in Purgatory."

"Good." I run my fingers through his hair. "Wicked deeds belong in wicked places."

Nodding, he places his hat down on the floor of the truck and grips the doorframe, his muscles bulging as he leans forward. "How are you doing knowing the man who kidnapped you, bit you all over, and messed with your mind was my kid? Does that make you scared of me? I know before you were scared because I was a vampire, but it's different now, right? This time, not only was that vampire horrible to you, but he was related to me. Doesn't that make you fear me?"

I scoot to the edge of the leather seat, my legs swinging out of the door, and press my hand against Kentucky's heart. "No, that doesn't scare me because you aren't him. You've done nothing but show how much you care about me. You've protected me. Kentucky, how could I be afraid of you when you killed your son for me? You could have let him live somehow or have Lorcan deal with him. You decided to. Why?"

"No one hurts you and gets to live another day, Darlin'. Son or not. Blood don't mean nothin' if it flows with cruel intentions."

"Does it change anything for you? Do you see me differently?"

His hands fall to my thighs. "What? No. Nothin' could ever make me see you in a negative light, Dru. Nothin'. If anything, after seeing him and the control he had over others with his ability, I'm in awe of you. You're so fucking strong to escape a man like that. You fought for your life, and that's more than I could ever say for myself."

"That's not true." My palm wraps around the back of his neck. "You fought tonight."

"Only because of you." He brushes his thumb across my cheek, admiration shining from his deep garnet-tinged eyes. "If I didn't have you, I have no doubt that tonight would have been my last night."

"That would have been a travesty. You bring patience and kindness to a world where there is none. Chaos, hatred, greed, and power are just a few examples of what is causing the world to spin today. Everyone's doorsteps are darkened, but light always awaits. That's you."

"I can't change the world, Dru."

"Not true." I clutch his blood-soaked shirt and pull him closer. "You've changed mine. Isn't that enough?"

A barely there smile tugs at the left corner of his mouth. The tip of his nose brushes against mine. "That's the only world that matters to me." He turns his head, hesitant for a second before sealing his lips over mine.

His kiss is soft, careful, and not too deep. Electricity

shoots through my nervous system, tingling throughout my entire body. His emotions seep into me, showing me every layer Kentucky has ever hidden. There's no question about his love for me. The pure weight and bliss of how much he loves me almost has me crying.

Then, there's the bottom of his emotions, where he has kept all the negative, all the pleas for death, and I grab onto him harder. I deepen the kiss, showing him I don't care how dark his nights get.

I'll be here.

He breaks the kiss, a half-chuckle, half-sob, leaving him.

His hand warms my stomach. "You're pregnant, aren't you?"

I look down into my lap, not wanting to see the expression on his face. "I am. Lorcan just told me."

"Look at me."

I can't.

He forces me to by grabbing my chin and tilting my head up. "Look at me."

"I'm looking," I sass, needing a way to protect myself. "How did you know?"

"I can feel him or her. They add to your emotions. Why didn't you tell me when you knew? Darlin', I'm fucking ecstatic. Are you kiddin' me? I get to have a family. One I never thought I'd have. I can't remember the last time I had one. I don't remember my parents' faces. I have no siblings. We are alike in that way. And I want you to have the biggest family you've ever wanted—you've ever dreamed. You want ten kids? I'll happily give them to you. I want this with you. I want *life* with you. You've made me the happiest man in the world, and my plans for death? They died the second I smelled you for the first time. I knew you'd change everything for me, and I won't stand here and say that didn't scare me because it did. You did. I didn't know what having you in my life meant when I had convinced myself my plans were so much better than anything you could ever give me."

I can't hold in my tears from his declaration. "I was scared to tell you because of what happened tonight. I thought telling you would be too soon after..." I point to the pile of ash in his hat. "I didn't want you to dread becoming a father again."

"Again? Darlin'." He cradles my face in his hands, staring directly into my eyes. "This is the first time I get to be a father. Come here."

He wraps me in his embrace, leaving no room for me to go anywhere. My cheek is pressed against his chest, and I breathe him in, allowing his scent to calm me.

"I'm going to take care of you for all of our eternities. That's an oath. Let's get you home. Tomorrow, we will tackle where the nursery will go. What about names? Oh, our kids will have to learn how to ride a horse, you know that, right? I have to baby-proof the house—"

I lull his words to a peaceful quietude with a kiss. "We have plenty of time to plan all that. You still have to take me on that date, remember? So you can claim me in the way you dreamed about. That's step one."

"Yes, ma'am, Ms. Whitley."

"That's Mrs. Jones to you. Or did you forget we're mated?"

His smile fades while happiness shines in his eyes. "I could never forget the bond that saved my life."

I kiss the middle of his chest, relieved that a few aspects of this new path for me are coming together. Louisville is dead, so I no longer have to worry about my life, Kentucky's, or our child's. He's happy to build a family with me. Tonight's nightmare is over, for the most part.

There's still one heartache we will have to live with.

Romeo.

Three days later

I stare at Romeo's statue in his stall. I hate the fear frozen on his face. His head is reared back, his eyes are wide, and his fangs are lengthened. Instead of being in the front like mine, his fangs are more towards the sides of his mouth. His lips are peeled back, preparing for an attack, but he never stood a chance against Louisville.

Speaking of, his ashes are currently floating down the river. I decided that even though he was my son, he had no business on my property. I had a few days of grief to work through my emotions, and the more I came down to normal, I realized keeping him around was like a slap in the face to Dru after what he put her through.

Rubbing my hands down my face, I let out a sigh burdened with guilt for not being able to save him right away. Yesterday, I bought every horse, pig, cow, mule, and donkey that was at the slaughterhouse. I've saved them, and they will be brought to the ranch today.

All I can do is hope one of those horses is Romeo's Beloved. I need my best friend back. A man isn't a cowboy without the horse he trusts most.

"Don't worry, Romeo. I'll search every end of this earth for your mate, and if I have to look in other dimensions, then I will. I'll go to every nook and cranny in the universe." I pat his neck, and it's still warm as if he is alive under the sheet of stone. "I promise."

Locking his stall door, I walk back to the house with my head confounded with the hopelessness of not finding Romeo's mate. What are the chances that I can?

The sound of the rocking chair squeaking has me lifting my head to see my Beloved sitting down in one of them. She sips her coffee, then smiles at me with a big wave.

The heaviness in my chest lightens when her happiness soaks into me. All that happiness from seeing me. I don't think I'll ever get used to it.

"Hey, Beloved," she calls me, and right away, it brings a smile to my face.

I love that she calls me by that term of endearment.

Climbing the steps two at a time to be at her side, I bend down and place a quick kiss on her cheek. "Mornin', Darlin'. How are my girls doing?"

She giggles while shaking her head. "Kentucky, it's too soon to know if they are a girl or a boy."

"I think our baby is a little cowgirl. Imagine. We can get little pink boots to match yours. Oh, god. She'll be so damn cute in a little hat." Ever since I've found out Dru is pregnant, I've been daydreaming.

Imagining teaching our kid to ride a horse, to lasso, to barrel race, to do anything and everything on the ranch. Then my dreams turned into me being a girl dad. Protecting her, showing her how she deserves to be treated, and never settling for less than what she deserves.

And to teach her how to deal with the night when it enters her mind. No one should be alone in learning about this hard fucking world.

"Plus, I want her to have your eyes, your hair, your everything. Why wouldn't I want to bring another you into this world? Do you know how much better it would be?"

"You keep talking like that, we'll have to go back for round two today, Mr. Jones," she taunts, hiding her luscious lips behind the rim of her coffee mug.

I growl, thinking about how I woke her up this morning with my cock in her mouth. I'd love to toss her on the bed and have my way. I am sad about one thing when it comes to her pregnancy.

She won't have her period.

At least I got a little bit of a taste. I don't know when I'll get to experience that again. It all depends on how much time Dru wants in between having kids. Whatever she wants. I'm on board. Her wants, her needs, they all come first.

I find that my wants? My needs?

They take the shape of the woman sitting in the rocking chair. As long as I have her, I have everything I need.

"I got you a present. Stay right there. Don't move."

She cozies into the blanket she has thrown over her body. It's a cool, foggy day, perfect for cuddling outside. If we are lucky, the fog will clear, and we can go outside to stargaze.

I'll have to end our date just like that. Tonight, I plan on reclaiming her the way she deserves. Not in some dirt arena with holes in my body and a bull charging at us. I refuse to not try to make it right.

Instead of wishing I were part of the constellations, I can sit back and appreciate their beauty with the woman who saved my life by my side.

"I don't plan on going anywhere. I'm excited. What is it?"

"Close your eyes."

"Kentucky."

"Do it. Do it. Close them!"

She's skeptical, eyeing me with curiosity. Dru closes her eyes and holds out her hand.

"I'll be right back." I dash inside and swing open the closet door where I hid her gift. She probably won't be stunned or love it because it's more of a necessity these days.

That reminds me that I need to replace the screen door Dru tumbled through the other day. Actually, I need to install a security system too. I wonder if there is a paranormal one. I'm more worried about that now that I want to submerge myself into this life at last.

I want my little girl or boy to know everything there is about being a vampire. They shouldn't have to question anything because their father didn't know.

My boots pound on the porch when I rush outside, placing the box in her hand. "Open."

I hold my breath when she does.

"Oh my god, Kentucky. Is this a phone?"

Taking the chair next to her, I grab the mug from her hand to set it aside so I can take her hand. "I told you when you arrived that you could borrow the phone I had to call Carmen or your job. You've had no contact with your previous life, and that's not fair."

"Kentucky—"

I hold up my hand to stop her. "Let me finish." I kiss her fingertips one by one. "I know we had a lot going on lately, but I should have tried harder to get you what you needed. I was terrified that if you called your friend, you'd leave me. That wasn't right of me. Apologies, Dru. Forgive me?"

"There's nothing to forgive." Her hand is gentle as it rests against my cheek, then begins to stroke her fingers through my beard.

I love it when she does that.

"I tried to charge my old phone, but it wouldn't work. I threw it away. It was a flip phone with an antenna."

"Oh, wow. An antenna. No wonder it didn't work."

"Careful." I nip at her knuckles. "I'll take that phone back." She knows I'm teasing. There isn't anything I would ever take from her.

Besides her virginity. That is mine and mine alone.

The thought of her only being mine has a drape of burgundy igniting my vision.

"Your thoughts are in the gutter," she points out, waiting for her phone to turn on.

"With you around, it stays there, Darlin'. You know, I still haven't been able to count all those freckles on your body. I think I'll do that soon. Take my time. I don't want to miss one."

She blushes, nibbling on her bottom lip to the point the flesh turns white from pressure. I tug it free, rubbing my thumb over the spot.

"Don't make those pretty lips bleed. I'd hate to have to do something about that."

An aromatic dose of lust drenches the air, sweet and warm, just like her pretty pussy when I'm sinking into it.

"My home and lockscreen need pictures of you," she says. "You'll have to send me some." She looks me up and down, pretending to bite her nail, and flutters those hazel eyes at me. "Shirtless. Definitely shirtless."

"Shirtless?" This time it's me who blushes. "I ain't ever done anything like that, Dru."

Her hand drifts up the innermost part of my thigh, and I catch my breath.

"You'll do it for me, though. Won't you?" She stops before she grabs my aching cock pressing against my jeans.

God, it's a good thing I bought the same phone at the store this morning. I have no idea how to work a touchscreen, but I'll fucking figure it out if it means she sends pictures to me too.

Fuck everyone else needing to get a hold of me.

I lick my lips, nearly panting with need. All she has to do is lower the zipper and free me. She lights a growl within my chest, and all I want to do is reach for her phone to throw... somewhere. I need to have my way with her.

The squeaks of metal have me turn my head to listen. Tires roll onto the driveway, followed by the loud roar of mufflers.

Of course, we are interrupted.

Standing in front of Dru, I extend my black claws, readying myself for a fight. The first truck comes into view, and a trailer is attached.

Then another.

And another.

They line up behind each other, reaching the end of my driveway.

"It's the animals from the slaughterhouse, Dru. Think any of them will be for Romeo?"

She stands, clutching the blanket to her chest. Her head leans against my shoulder, watching as the first person climbs out of the driver's side of the brand new, deep green truck.

"Hey there," the guy shouts. "I'm looking for Kentucky Jones. I have the animals from the slaughterhouse. I think I have the right address." He flips a few pages on his clipboard to find it.

"Go inside, Darlin'. He's a vampire. I can smell it on him. Lock the door."

"Kentucky, he's delivering animals for goodness sake. I'm sure he is harmless. Stop being a man. Go up to him so he isn't shouting across the damn lawn."

"Yes, ma'am," I grumble with a pout of my lips.

She smacks my ass as I head down the steps. I look over my shoulder, brow raised, a sly smirk on my face.

"You wait until later, Darlin'."

"Can't wait." She forms her hand into a gun, kisses her index finger, aims it at me, and pulls the trigger.

I catch it, pressing it against my lips. I don't give a damn if I'm in front of another man, witnessing me paying attention to my mate.

"Are you Kentucky Jones?" he asks when I get close enough.

Wait a damn minute.

I know the driver. He was at the rodeo.

"I know you. You're Oklahoma Richards. Your partner, Cal, got terrorized by that bull. How's your friend?"

He hands me the clipboard to sign a few forms, the wind rustling them. His lips form a grim line. "He died yesterday. A stroke. There were too many injuries. I tried to give him my blood so many times, but he wouldn't take it."

"Damn, I'm so sorry to hear that. He was a great rider." Knowing this information twinges my gut with guilt, knowing his teammate died at the hands of my son. Do I offer that information? What good would it do? "Do you need anything? You're welcome to stay here and rest up. We have plenty of room."

"Thank you, and I appreciate that, but I have to travel across the country for another pick up. Besides ridin', this is my true love. Rescuing animals."

On the side of his truck in big white letters, it says, *"Oklahoma Rescue: bringing love to where storms are."*

"I appreciate you hiring us for a delivery this size. I'm outgrowing where I live at this point. I think I'll need to look into a piece of property, but donations only go so far."

"Get me out of this tin can!"

"I need to stretch my legs!"

"I hope this guy is nicer than the last owner."

"Me too. I hope we can have water."

"And food. Don't forget the food."

One by one, the horses and other animals sing their thoughts loud and clear.

"Don't worry. You're safe here. You have constant water, food, and shelter," I tell them in hopes they calm down.

"Who was that? Who can hear us?"

"Apologies. My name is Kentucky. I rescued you from the slaughterhouse. I can speak to animals."

They fall silent. I don't blame them. They probably think I'm full of shit after all they have been through.

"There's a piece of property in Oklahoma"—he chuckles at the irony —"that is perfect. It's around two hundred and fifty acres. It has one lake on it and smaller ponds scattered about. It has one big house on the lake with separate living areas for employees. A handful of barns. There's so much I could do with it."

I don't know what compels me. Maybe it's that I'm feeling generous, or maybe it's because I've been isolated for so long, I'm ready to do more with the life I have now. I have plenty of money from working on the ranch. Millions. Too much for me to spend by myself.

What if I decided to expand Dead Man's Ranch into other states? A place where anyone can be saved. Whether it's animals or paranormals. No humans unless they wander onto the property or a paranormal has a human mate like me.

It can be a ranch and a haven.

"Let's unload the animals. I have an idea to run by you that I think would make both of us happy," I say, tossing the clipboard through the open window of his truck.

"Alright." He turns to the line of vehicles, inserts two fingers in his mouth, and whistles. "Let's go!"

"Any horses, I want lined up outside the barn, please."

"Sure. Whatever you want. They're your animals." He lifts the lock on the trailer, swinging the back door open. "Our first horse is Juliette. She's a Grey Roan. Absolutely beautiful. She was sent to slaughter for being violent."

"Did you just say her name is Juliette?" I must be living in daydreams because there is no way the universe is being this good to me.

My heart finds a new beat, pounding more than three beats a minute.

"Yeah, she's around five years old. Still so young. Come girl. It's okay. He won't hurt you."

She neighs, her hooves slamming onto the metal floor of the trailer.

"There you go. Good girl. You're doing great, Juliette," Oklahoma praises her, and when she has all four hooves on the ground, emotion lodges in my throat when I see the deep scars on her sides.

"She was whipped for not doing anything they wanted. She hates being attached to anything, so no carriages or plows or whatever else."

My fangs lengthen at the senseless violence. I want to kill her previous owner. "Are they still alive?"

"They are," he confirms, stroking Juliette's neck.

I'll have to change that one day.

Juliette's dark eyes widen, darting her gaze over the pastures. Her attention lands on the barn, her black ears flickering forward, and her nose wiggles as she sniffs the air.

She rears up, kicking her front legs out.

"Whoa. Whoa. Juliette. It's alright."

With a high-pitched neigh, she bolts. Juliette runs straight for the barn. Her reddish black mane drifts in the breeze with every gallop. She's gorgeous. She has some healing to do, but that's alright. That's what the ranch is for.

Oklahoma raises his hand to stop the other employees from coming forward with any animals, a silent signal that has them stop in their tracks. Both of us jog to the barn to see what she's doing.

She's kicking Romeo's stall, whining to get to him.

"There's no way I'm this lucky," I say to myself. "My horse got turned to stone by Cemetery Ophids, and only his Beloved can bring him back."

"Wait, the horse you were on at the rodeo? I just saw him. He was fine. Interesting, he's a vampire."

"Another story for another time. I've been devastated about him. I decided to save every animal I could, so he had a chance. I never thought it would be the very first horse I brought home."

He slaps my shoulder. "Fate's funny like that."

I unlock Romeo's stall, hoping Juliette is the answer.

"You want to meet Romeo?" I don't open the door to his stall just yet.

She swings her head up and down.

"Be gentle with him. He's stone."

The hinges creak as I open the door.

"His name is Romeo? No wonder you were excited when you heard her name."

I smirk. "Romeo and Juliette is the love story that's always remembered, right?"

"If you want to call it a love story. It's sad to me." Oklahoma frowns.

"If anything happened to my mate, I'd make sure death was quick because living without her isn't an option. Romeo and Juliette's story is beautifully heartbreaking, and I hope these two"—I point to the horses—"don't have the same ending."

Juliette nips at Romeo's jaw. When that doesn't work, she

rubs her face across his and licks his cheeks and nose, whimpering for him to awaken.

"Come on, Romeo. Come on," I beg, staring at his statue without blinking for far too long.

The stone cracks and veins down his body.

"Yes! Come on, Romeo. Come on. You can do it. Come back for Juliette. She's waiting on you like many others. Come on, come on." I take my hat off, slinging it off to the side to run my fingers through my hair.

I'm anxious. I need this to work.

Another crack forms down his leg, small pieces of stone crumbling to the floor.

"Looks like it's working," Oklahoma says. "Congratulations. I'm glad you got your horse back. I'm going to start putting the others in the barn unless you have other directions."

"That's fine." I stretch my arm out to shake his hand. "I hope to see you back on the circuit one day."

"Afraid I'm not going back. My teammate and best friend died. I have no interest in competing again. I'm happy with rescues."

"You're doing a good thing. When you're done, come get me. I still need to talk to you about something."

Oklahoma nods, giving me a small two-finger salute. He jogs out of the barn to start helping the others.

The stone falls in big heavy chunks, showing his onyx hide. His coat changes by having life breathed into him again. From dull to pools of ink in the sunlight, he's coming back to me. The stone veins down his back, breaking the curse that was cast upon him. Little by little, Romeo is breaking free.

More stone shatters onto the ground.

"Come on, Romeo." I have tears in my eyes waiting for him to come back.

A few minutes pass with no cracks, no crumbles of stone

—nothing. Hope begins to fade, and I wonder if Lorcan didn't know the entire cure.

His ears flicker, and Juliette neighs with excitement, urging him on. Until she becomes impatient, nipping at his neck and pawing the ground.

More time passes without any movement.

Until burning cherry reds stare into mine.

DEAD MAN'S
RANCH

Chapter Twenty-Two

DRUSCILLA

Dru is in the kitchen, sitting on one of the stools, video chatting with Carmen. It's amazing how technology has advanced. I still haven't figured out this damn touch screen. My fingers are too fat for this damn keyboard. It's so fucking little. Every word I type, there's a typo in it.

"I promise, I'm okay. I'm so sorry I didn't call sooner. The ranch is in the middle of nowhere, and the cowboy who rescued me didn't have a phone that worked."

"Do you know how that sounds? It sounds like he lied to you to keep you there, Dru. I can't believe this. Do you have that Stockholm Syndrome?"

"Carmen, how could I have that when he didn't kidnap me? Another person did. I ran away, and Kentucky saved me." Dru reaches her arm towards me. "Come here, Beloved. Let me introduce you to my best friend so she stops freaking out."

In two large strides, I'm by my mate's side, waving into the little camera that somehow fits into this tiny phone. "Hey there, Carmen. It's nice to meet you. Dru has told me a lot about you, and I wanted to let you know that you're always more than welcome to come visit."

Carmen's face fills the screen. "Oh, you bet your cowboy ass I'm coming to visit. Actually, I'm coming to live there, and there isn't a damn thing you can do about it. You might be all tall and handsome with your little accent and big muscles, but I'm onto you, buddy." She gestures with two fingers, pointing them to her eyes, then at the camera.

A signal to say she's watching me.

"Don't be rude, Carmen."

"I'm not being rude. I'm being protective. I'm packing now. Send me your address."

"It was lovely meeting you, Carmen." I give her a slight wave and slowly back away, not wanting to be a part of this conversation anymore.

She's aggressive.

I slink away into the bedroom, peeking my head out into the hallway to see that her attention is still occupied.

"I can definitely do this," I say to no one other than myself to hype myself up.

Never in my life have I done something like this.

I tug my shirt off, grab my hat from the top of the dresser, and set it on top of my head.

I won't lie, I'm blushing.

"Good lord," I grumble under my breath. "For Dru. She wants this. You can do this for her."

Swiping the screen, the camera aims at my face, and I lift it into the air for a better angle.

Hooking my thumb into my belt loop, I lean against the wall, tuck my chin down, flex, and press the button.

"Absolutely not." I delete the image so it can never see the light of day and try again.

This time, I allow my fangs to show with the murderous color of my eyes.

I snap a few photos. I twist my body one way, then another, pinching the brim of my hat like I always do. I must take a hundred pictures. One of them has got to be good enough.

The mattress dips when I sit down as I swipe through the photos until I find a few I like. I smirk, knowing damn well she's going to love these.

Checking the time, I realize I've been in here way too long. We need to leave soon for our date night. I snag a black button-up and roll the sleeves to my elbows, spray a little cologne, shine my belt buckle a little, and make my way down the hall.

Dru has been ready for our date since before she called Carmen. She wanted to make sure time didn't get away from her while she talked to her friend. It was the right choice considering they have been talking for around two hours.

When she hears me, she turns her head, and her eyes hood with lust. Her arousal marinates the air, and I growl low in warning. She can't look at me like that when we have plans.

We won't make it out of the house.

She's wearing those shorts I love so much. The ones with the frayed hem. They show the slight undercurve of her cheeks, and I can never keep my hands off her when she's wearing them.

She's wearing her pink cowboy boots, of course, and a plum-colored crop top with sleeves that hang off the shoulder. God damn, she looks beautiful. Freckles pepper her shoulders, and she even has a few on her chest. My tongue flicks onto my lower lip as I imagine running my hands down her body and kissing that spot between her legs that will make her squirt on my tongue.

Fuck.

My mate is fucking sexy. I have to look away, or we are never going to leave this house, and I've promised her a special night. I have to keep my word. She tests my resolve. Her legs look so fucking soft as the light from the kitchen shines on them. In those shorts, she has legs for miles, and I'm ready for them to wrap around my waist.

Her eyes drop to the bulge in my jeans, nibbling that damn bottom lip again.

Tilting my head, I stare at her, thinking about all the ways I'm going to feed from her tonight. My gaze drops to every spot I'm salivating for.

The neck.

The breast.

The wrist.

Left inner thigh.

And right.

Pulling out my phone, I select a shirtless picture of me and type out a message.

"The sooner we leave. The sooner I can get you home and in bed. Remember, you gotta feed me, Darlin'."

I press send, crossing my arms over my chest as if I've just done the most impressive move known to mankind.

Her phone dings with the message, and when she sees it, she squirms in her seat by pressing her thighs together. The kitchen fills with the smooth spice of her arousal, nearly drugging me with how good she smells.

"Carmen, I need to go. Kentucky and I have plans, but I'll text you later, okay? I love you."

"You'll be seeing me tomorrow. I'll be on your doorstep first thing if you don't call me. Be safe. Take pepper spray," she whispers, so I can't hear her.

I do.

And I stifle a laugh.

"I don't have pepper spray, Carmen."

"Fine. Just be alert and use your head. I'm glad you're

okay, but if anything happens to her, Kentucky, I'm finding you."

"I don't doubt it, ma'am." I wrap my arm around Dru, plucking the phone from her grip. "Have a good night." Pressing the red button to end the call has never felt better.

"Darlin', you're mine tonight." I grab her ass, my fingers sinking into the thick flesh, and tug her closer to me.

I can't help but growl. Fuck, she's perfect.

"I'm yours every night," she purrs, drifting her finger across my chest.

I'll be damned if nights haven't turned into my favorite part of the day.

DEAD MAN'S
RANCH

Epilogue

One

DRUSCILLA

The music is loud at Rodeo's Way, a bar next to the arena we were at a few days ago. Every step I take, my boots stick to the floor from all the spilled beer from people dancing with a drink in their hand. In the far-right corner, cowboys play pool while their girls watch. To the left is a massive dance floor where the line dancers are.

I've never seen so many cowboy hats in my life. *Everyone* has one on.

There's a larger crowd congregating around the mechanical bull. It's in the middle of a wooden fenced-in area with big fluffy red mats on the ground, so the riders are protected when they fall off.

The bull itself seems huge. It has horns pointing forward and a silver ring hanging from its fake nose.

"Kentucky." I tug on his belt loop, keeping my finger curled into it so I don't get lost in the crowd. "Can we go over there?"

"Anything my mate wants, she gets. Come on, Darlin'." He takes charge, stepping in front of me to lead the way.

The crowd parts for him naturally, as if their instincts are screaming that there is a predator near. Men and women alike crane their heads back to look up at Kentucky, eyes widening when they see how tall he is.

Even though I'm holding onto him by his belt loop, he reaches behind to lace his fingers with my other hand.

The ceiling, the floor, the bar, everything is made of wood. Even the chairs are old and antique. A few of the legs have duct tape wrapped around the center to keep the pieces together. Can they not replace them? That seems like a hazard.

Kentucky pulls out a chair for me when we get to a table. A chair without duct tape.

This place is rough around the edges, but I love it already. There's an authenticity to it that not many other places have.

"Why, thank you. What a gentleman." I sit down, watching a guy jump onto the mechanical bull.

"Let's see if he can make it eight seconds, everybody!" The operator shouts into the mic so others can hear over the loud country music playing for the line dancers.

The crowd surrounding the bull begins to cheer, lifting their drinks in the air. Beer spills over the rims of their glass pints, splashing onto their arms and the floor. No wonder this place smells of beer.

When the operator flips the switch on the bull, its eyes glow red and fog drifts from its nose, clouding the rider in a faint sheet.

"What do you want to drink, Darlin'?" Kentucky has to raise his voice so I can hear him over the chaos of the bar.

"I'll take a Coke." I don't need to shout or yell. I know Kentucky can hear me with his advanced hearing.

Kentucky snags my chair, yanking me closer to him. Our chairs touch, and he wraps his arm around the back. Leaning in, he draws gentle circles in the middle of my upper arm and whispers, "If you want something sweet, I've got something for you to suck on."

"Kentucky," I scold him playfully.

We're interrupted by the waitress, and Kentucky snarls under his breath. "Hi, welcome to Rodeo's Way. I'm Patsie. I'll be your server this evening," she shouts, clicking the top of her pen.

"One sweet tea and a Coke, please," Kentucky answers by lifting two fingers. "And a blooming onion with steak sauce. A lot of steak sauce."

"Coming right up!"

"A blooming onion with steak sauce?" I scrunch my nose at how unappetizing that sounds.

"You have to try it. It's so good. I can't remember when I first had it. It was years ago, and it blew my mind. Please try it. For me. So we can enjoy my second favorite food."

"Second?"

"First place goes to you, Darlin'. Ain't nothin' that will ever taste better than you."

Heat pools between my legs, wishing we were anywhere but here so he can eat in private.

The cowboy on the mechanical bull gets flung off and lands on the mats. He lifts his arms into the sky, cheering to celebrate that he made it the full eight seconds. Someone hands him a drink, and he downs it in one gulp. Crunching the cup in his grasp, he throws it across the room.

"I want to do that so bad." I plop my elbow on the table and hold my chin in my hand.

I'm jealous of the next person who hops on the bull. I won't be able to ride it since I'm pregnant.

"We can do it together." Kentucky inhales my scent as he buries his nose into my neck. "I can tell the operator to go very slow, so my girls are okay." His hand flattens against my lower belly, causing my insides to melt with how sweet and thoughtful he is.

"We don't know if it's a girl." I lean into him, needing to

be closer. I want to feel him on every inch of my body. I've never felt so protected.

Usually when I'm at a bar, I have to be alert and focused. When I was single, I would cover my drink, and I'd never go to the bathroom alone. Even with all my precautions, Louisville got through all my defense systems. No system is perfect, but Kentucky is.

He won't let anything happen to me. He'll kill anyone who gets too close, and I find comfort in that.

"Your existence is my royalty." He kisses my shoulder, his beard scraping against me when he pulls away. "And I will always kneel at your feet. I am yours in any way you ever want me."

Our gazes find one another, attracting one another like magnets.

"Here you are." The waitress interrupts again.

How do servers always manage to come up to their tables at the worst times? Either mid bite or mid kiss.

"Thank you." Kentucky slides my drink in front of me. He goes as far as stripping the paper from the straw to shove it in my drink.

"I could have done that, you know," I tease.

"And? I don't want you to have to lift a finger for the rest of your life. Now, try my favorite snack." He plucks an onion petal, dipping it into the steak sauce, and shoves it into my mouth.

The crunch is just what I needed. "Mmmm," I moan in surprise. "That's...that's actually so good." I grab another piece, having to roll it into the sauce to get it covered. I bite into it, groaning again when the tangy zest bursts across my tongue. "I can't believe I've never tried that. People are missing out if they don't eat blooming onions like this." I can't help but moan again.

"You can't be making sounds like that wearing those shorts. That just ain't fair, Darlin'."

"Who says I'm doing this to be fair?" I suck a finger into my mouth to lick the sauce off, giving him an unnecessary show of what I can do with my tongue.

His nostrils flare watching me with a laser-focused, lustful gaze. "This night won't last long if you keep that up. I'm about to push you to your knees so I can experience you wrapping that tongue around my cock if you continue to test me."

"Maybe that's my goal."

His eyes shift into the brilliant crimson, and he ducks his head to hide his fangs from the crowd. Those long, calloused fingers dig into my thigh, his claws poking into my skin.

I am so proud of myself.

When he is calm, he relaxes, letting go of the tight grip on my thigh. "You just wait until later," he says. "You're all mine."

His.

I'm in love with that fact.

Kentucky grabs a few fried onion petals himself, and he dips them into the sauce too. "Damn, that's so good. We will need another basket. I'm going to demolish these."

"Another?" I squeal.

He chuckles, covering his mouth as he chews. "Darlin', if you wanted to order the entire menu, I'd have no problem with it. Taking care of you is what I live for." He leans forward, folding his arms on the table. The loud music dies down, and the DJ announces a fifteen-minute break. "Do you want to get on the bull?"

"You were serious? Do you think it will be okay? I don't want to cause any harm." I place a hand protectively over my stomach. "I'd feel terrible if anything happened."

"Like I said, I'm going to mystify the operator to go very slow. No quick turns, no spins, none of that. You won't be flying off. It will be a very easy ride, like going up and down a hill in a car."

"Do you need to mess with his mind to do that?"

"When it comes to you? Absolutely. I don't trust him to keep his word. He'd probably try to fling us off. I'm not risking that." He dips another petal into the steak sauce. "I don't care if he gives me his word. A man's word ain't enough these days. Actions are more important. Words can be lies. Actions are honesty—good or bad."

I sip down my drink, the carbonation hitting the back of my throat. It's so refreshing. The small bubbles fizz and pop in my mouth as I swallow, washing down the blooming onion perfectly.

"Come on." He stands, pulls out my chair, and offers me his hand. "Let's get you on that bull, Darlin'. And then I'm going to get you home, peel those shorts off you, and have my way."

"I don't know, don't you owe me a dance too?"

"You don't know what I have planned for the rest of the night." He clutches my hand, dragging me away from the table to the operator.

I loop my arm through his to hang onto him tighter. I crowd his space, so I don't bump into anyone.

"Excuse me?"

The operator peers down from his booth. "Want to ride the bull?"

"We do." Kentucky's tone changes. He's softer, speaking slower with an intensity I've never heard before. "You're going to go very slowly. My wife is pregnant, and we can't have any accidents. *Slow*. No fast turns, no whips to the left and right, and no trying to throw her off. If you do, I'll fucking kill you. Do you understand?"

"I understand," The operator's face is relaxed, his eyes

hooded, and his pupils blown from Kentucky's influence. "You'll be safe."

"How long is the line?" Kentucky asks.

"There are about ten people ahead of you."

"You're going to let us go first."

The operator grins. "Looks like you're up. Give me the thumbs up when you're ready."

Kentucky swings me into his arms and sets me on the other side of the fence.

"You just skipped so many people," I scold him.

Using the wooden post as leverage, he hops over the fence. I'm not sure why that turns me on so much, but I want him to do it again.

"I wasn't kidding when I said I was going to get you out of those shorts." He taps my ass with his hand. "Come on. Let's get you on this bull so you can ride me later."

Is this what it is like to be happy? To have someone love you? Like, truly love you? No wonder the world is obsessed with finding love. There isn't a better feeling in existence.

Kentucky grabs me by the hips and swings me over the bull. I grab the handle, scooting forward until I feel comfortable. My mate hops on behind me, proving he has done this a hundred times. His muscular arm wraps around my waist like he promised, tugging himself to my back.

My breath catches with him so close. His legs hug the back of mine, gluing himself to me. Kentucky reaches around with his free hand, placing his over mine to have a better grip of the handle.

"Ready?"

"Ready." My reply is breathless from being caged against him.

His nose is against my neck, and he nips at his claim, sending jolts of desire through every single one of my limbs.

He lifts his thumb in the air to the operator and wraps his arm around me again.

"We have to be careful with this one," the announcer says. "She's pregnant. Everyone cheer for the couple!"

The crowd is loud, everyone raising their drinks in the air to celebrate.

I grip the handle and keep a hold of Kentucky's arm when the bull tilts forward. I scream, worried I'm going to fall off.

"I got you. I ain't going to allow anything to happen to you, Darlin'. You're safe with me."

The bull rocks slowly, just like the operator promised. Kentucky slides back and forth. His arousal presses into me with every motion of the bull. We turn slow and steady. Warm breath puffs against my neck, the tease of his lips ghosting over my nape.

I lean into him, trusting him to keep me safe when the bull rocks back. Kentucky presses a kiss to his mark, a moan slipping from his lips. His control is slipping just as mine is.

A light sheen of sweat sticks to my skin. The air is full of humidity from our bodies, yet I'm hot for an entirely different reason.

Kentucky kisses my shoulder and neck before wrapping his hand around my throat to keep me secured to him.

"I'm taking you home. Right now."

Epilogue Two

KENTUCKY

Getting her home is all I can think and breathe about. She smells so good. Her blood, her body, her touch, it is calling to me. I can't wait another minute.

Those short fucking shorts are driving me wild. Her legs are smooth and toned. All I can imagine are those beauties wrapping around me while I thrust as deep as I can.

If she weren't pregnant already, I know tonight would be the night that she would be.

I'm fucking feral.

Only one more minute of her hand stroking my thigh, and she's mine. She doesn't know the night is young and we are going to spend it in the bed of the truck, looking up at the sky, and surrounded by wildflowers. I could fuck her in the backseat, boots on, spurs swirling, her shorts pushed to the side while I take and feed.

I want to.

I envisioned something special for the claiming night, and that didn't get to happen.

I'm going to make it happen.

And then, tomorrow I'm going to fuck her in the backseat of the truck.

I inhale a sharp breath when her fingers skim up my inner thigh, teasing my hard cock pressing against the rough denim.

A growl forms in my throat. "Darlin', I'm barely holding on to my sanity." I shake my head, trying to rid myself of the blood-colored hue tinting my vision.

I can't. I'm too far gone.

"I like it when you lose control."

When the driveway comes into view, I jerk the wheel and take a sharp left. The truck fishtails, sending us skidding across the pavement. I correct the wheel and slam on the gas.

Pressing the button I have connected to my visor, the gate to the pasture opens, and I slow, careful to make sure I don't hit any animals.

New horses, donkeys, and mules hang by the row barn while the cows are lying in the field.

Most of them are sleeping and choose not to speak to me, which is great because my attention is focused on Dru. The ride across the fields is bumpy and uncomfortable. Dru is holding onto the bar above the door. With every hole we hit, she bounces out of her seat a little.

"Sorry, Darlin'. The ride to where we are going will be rough, but I promise, it will be worth it."

"Well, I might as well make use of the time, then." She leans over the middle console and unzips my jeans.

I grab her wrist, nostrils flaring from how badly I want her to continue, but her safety is first. "Dru, your seatbelt. I'd rather you be safe."

"You'll keep me safe, won't you?" She frees my hard, leaking cock from my jeans. "You'll protect me."

"With my eternal life, Darlin'."

"Then, I'm not worried." She licks her plump lips, her

hand wrapping around the base of my cock to give it a firm stroke.

"Fuck," I groan, curling my hips to slip through her hand more.

She bends down, taking me between her lips, and I clutch the wheel with one hand while the other palms the back of her head.

"God, that mouth, Darlin'. I'm going to spill down your throat. Keep you full in every way tonight. Your cunt, your mouth, your stomach. All of it will be claimed. You'll taste me on your tongue all night and know who you belong to."

She hums around my cock in reply, the vibrations reverberate inside the throbbing muscle. Her mouth is wet and warm, causing me to pump the brakes every other minute. I can't focus.

The pasture is blurring together with every delicious suction of her cheeks when she hollows them. She slurps and moans, so audible, and those filthy erotic noises are heating my skin, fueling my body with the need to claim her.

"Fuck, Dru. Fuck, I love how you suck my cock. You make me feel so good. Do you like my cock in your mouth? You love being unable to speak, don't you?"

She answers me again, groaning around me as if she can't get enough. My hand roams down her back, gripping her ass in those little shorts. My fangs lengthen when I smell how wet she is. Her arousal is thick in the air, and it only gets stronger the longer she fucks her mouth on me.

I lift off the seat, pressing against the gas pedal, panting from my orgasm, gaining traction, and getting closer.

"Dru," I grunt her name between the strokes her tongue gives me around the crown.

The meadow is up ahead, the flowers glowing under the moonlight while the trees sway in the slight breeze.

"Ah, oh, damn it, Dru. You'd better swallow every drop of

me." I slam the truck in park in the middle of the meadow, pressing my hand flat against the ceiling.

I need to hold onto something. I have the urge to climb out of my seat and away from the orgasm because it feels too good, and I almost can't take it.

"Dru!" I shout her name on a snarl.

Jets of come fill her mouth. I paint her stomach as she swallows, loving that I can smell myself inside her body.

Fisting her hair, I lift her off my cock to see her eyes glazed. A string of spit and come drips from her bottom lip, falling onto my jeans.

Capturing her swollen lips with mine, I drink the saliva down, wanting her in my body too. My fangs nip at her bottom lip, cutting it open, and blood rushes into my mouth.

I kick open the door, and the sweet aroma of flowers rushes into the cab, reminding me of how good Dru smells every day.

"Trust me?" I kiss her bottom lip.

"With my life," she whispers against me.

"Stay right here." I kiss her again, wanting her to know I'm not leaving her.

Opening her door, I offer my hand for her to take, and the lucky man that I am, she slides her palm across mine.

I love the feel of her skin on mine. I'm enamored. Captivated. Obsessed.

And happy.

We stand in the field, the flowers to her waist, swaying in the breeze. The moonlight dances upon her dark brown skin, a serene glow added to her cheeks. She appears ethereal, a beauty from so far out of this world. I'm not sure how I am graced with a woman who holds the stars within her soul. She shines brighter than any constellation, any moon, any shooting star, and I'm honored to know the galaxy of her soul belongs to me.

"What do you have planned, Mr. Jones?" She turns to me, the left side of her face ignited by the moonlight, and for a moment, I forget what I have planned.

I'm under a spell. I want a hand-painted portrait of her just like this. Standing in the meadow, her hair in perfect voluminous curls, the hazel of her irises bright from the glow of the moon, and her fingers caressing the petals of the flowers as she stands there.

It's a perfect picture, and a camera would not do her justice. I want this moment of her painted, framed, so I can see my favorite memory of her anytime I want.

"Close your eyes and I'll show you."

She squeezes them shut, then peeks one eye open.

"Ah, ah, ah," I tsk. "No cheating, Darlin'."

"Fine." She covers her eyes with her hands in a huff.

I kiss her cheek, still able to smell myself on her breath, and it motivates me to hurry up.

Using my speed, I jump into the bed of the truck and unlock the cross-bed toolbox. Snagging the fluffy blankets and pillows, I line the bed with them, wanting us to be comfortable as we look up to the sky.

There are around four layers of blankets. I hope that's enough to keep her comfortable.

Pulling out a small cooler, I packed sodas, fruit, veggies, and other snacks for us. I plan for us to spend the night under the night sky. I want to hold her until the sun rises and a new day starts. I light a few candles, setting them on the edge to add to the ambiance.

She deserves the best.

Jumping from the truck and into the meadow, I swing Dru into my arms.

She screeches from the unexpected move. "Oh my god! Kentucky?"

"It's me. I'm here. You're alright. I didn't mean to scare you." I kiss the top of her head. "You're okay."

Her heart rate slows when she hears my voice. Damn, that does wonders for my mind—to know that I calm her in the wake of fear. We've come so far since the beginning, when she was afraid of being in the same space as me.

Her trust in me will be something I cherish and protect for the rest of our lives.

"A fast jump and you can open those pretty eyes I love so much, okay?"

She presses her head against my chest. "Okay," she says with complete trust.

In one leap, we are in the air and on the tailgate. "Open," I state.

She gasps, climbing out of my arms to stand. "Oh my god," her voice in riddled with awe. "You did this for me? This is beautiful."

"It's no five-star hotel but—"

She throws her arms around me, her lips taking mine in a passionate kiss, silencing me before I can finish the sentence.

Her eyes sparkle in the eternal glow of the moon, the tears causing them to glisten. It's wrong of me to say, but the way they shine reminds me of all the stars surrounding us. Even with tears, she's the most beautiful woman I've ever laid eyes on.

"It's better," she informs me with a grateful smile. "This is romantic, Kentucky. It shows you were thinking of me. I'm in the middle of a wildflower field, surrounded by their fragrant scents. The stars are out by the billions, watching us from afar. The moon is full, and it seems so close, it's almost as if I can touch it. I have you here, my mate, creating a night for me full of thoughtfulness and love. That's so much more than a fancy hotel, Kentucky. I'd choose this over a hotel any day, any night."

I've never felt more loved than I do in this moment. Grasping the back of her neck, I pull her forward, sealing my lips over hers again. With every motion of our kiss, I fall more in love with her. The plump clouds give and mesh with mine.

My arm wraps around her waist just as the crickets begin to sing, giving us our own music. Our tongues tease one another; the once-loving kiss has turned into a heated frenzy.

Her hands skim down my chest, then up, beginning to unbutton my shirt.

I growl into her mouth, yanking my arms through the sleeves without breaking the kiss. I toss the button-up somewhere in the field behind me, forgetting to take my hat off. It tumbles off and lands somewhere behind me.

In the distance, the new horses neigh, and her smile stretches upon my lips.

"I think they are happy." Her fingers begin to work on my jeans, unbuttoning and unzipping.

"Not as happy as me," I add, ripping her shirt down the middle with my claw. I growl when I see her plum-colored lace bra pushing up and cradling her breasts the way I wish my hands were.

Purple is by far my favorite color on her against her skin tone. I keep saying it, but she's so gorgeous.

"Your beauty goes beyond anything this world could create."

"So does yours," she whispers, kissing the middle of my chest with a type of affection I've never received before.

Her love takes care of me.

She goes to unbutton her shorts, and I stop her by placing my hand on top of hers. "Leave them on. They drive me fucking crazy."

Her brows rise, and she snickers, finding my addiction to those little shorts funny.

"Oh? That's funny? You driving me wild all night with

your long, soft legs, is funny to you?" In one swift motion, I place her on her back, her head resting safely against one of the pillows.

"A little bit."

"Well." I kiss her lips, cheek, and neck. "I'm going to show you what happens when you taunt me all night." Slipping a hand under her, I unhook her bra, then skim my fingers under the delicate fabric of the strap, hooking around her shoulders.

The moonlight shines onto her collarbone, illuminating the perfect place to kiss. Who am I to say no to the universe? I place a kiss there, her velvet soft skin a gift to my lips.

I kick my boots off, and she follows suit. Pulling away for just a moment, I tug my pants off, adding them to the field.

My cock slaps against my stomach, hard and smearing precome across my skin.

"Ready so soon?" she asks with wide eyes.

Her nipples bead from the mixture of the breeze and lust. Her hands skim up her body, goosebumps arising across every breathtaking inch of her.

"Darlin'. I'm a vampire. My recovery time is immaculate." I lift her leg onto my shoulder, kissing the side of her calf, drifting my blunt fingernails down the gorgeous dark skin.

"I could bury myself in the marrow of your bones and it still wouldn't be close enough." I pepper kisses down her leg until I'm at the crease of her thigh.

Pushing the small strip of denim covering her pussy to the side, I part her lips as my finger glides up and down. She's already so wet for me, so warm and ready.

I want to take my time, but my hunger for her blood, for her heat, is beyond the amount of control I have. I'm not disrespectful. Even though I want her more than my next breath, she needs to be ready for me.

She groans when I insert one finger, her arms stretching out beside her to reach for something to hold onto.

"That's a good girl," I praise when she becomes more wet, soaking my hand with her want. "I'm going to fuck you until I hear my name echoing over the hills. You're going to take every drop of me. I'm going to breed you over and over again, filling you to the point your womb can't take anymore."

"I'm already pregnant, Kentucky. You can't breed me more than that," she moans when I slip in another finger.

Curling over her, I nip her ear, dragging my lips down her neck where her vein is. My mouth waters when I smell the rush of blood. The scent is divine. It's sweeter and it has been for a few days.

That's when I should have known she was pregnant, but I didn't know. My entire life, I thought I was infertile. I never thought I'd have a mate or children.

"Every single day, I'm going to fill you. Every day, I'm going to push my come so deep into your womb that when you have our baby, you'll have enough of me inside you to become pregnant again. I'll breed you every fucking day. I want to smell my come soaking your panties every day. I want to smell your claim every waking moment of my life. Because if I can smell you, others can, and they will know you're bred by me."

Another gush of heat floods my hand, and I chuckle. "You love the sound of that, don't you? What a filthy fucking girl." I kiss my way down her chest, twirling my tongue around her nipple before licking my way up to her neck.

Bringing my lips to her ear, I whisper, "You're going to come for me, aren't you? You love being finger fucked. Show me how good it feels, Darlin'. Come for me."

She whines and whimpers, rocking her hips against my hand for more friction.

Wrapping my free hand around my cock, I stroke it in tandem with every thrust I give her with my fingers. My shaft burns for relief.

"Kentucky!" she screams, squirting all over my hand.

My name echoes across the pastures just as I wanted. "Good girl," I snarl.

She soaks the blankets beneath us, and I lower myself between her legs, cleaning up the mess I made.

"Too much. Oh, god. Kentucky. It's too much." Her body becomes warmer when another orgasm begins to build.

I'm too greedy. I need to feel her clench around my cock during her next orgasm.

"You taste so good. I could stay down here all night just feasting." I tease my fangs over her inner thigh. "I want to bite right here and leave another mark on you."

"Do it." She arches her back, kneading her breasts. "Please. I need you. I'm burning up for you, Kentucky. I can't wait. I need your bite. Let me feel you. Let me feed you."

Lifting her leg onto my shoulder, I don't ask her if she's sure. Faster than the speed of light, I bite, piercing her flesh with my fangs. Blood flows into my mouth, sweet and succulent. I growl, biting harder, my eyes bleeding scarlet, the more intense my need for her blood becomes.

"Kentucky!" she screams my name again, her orgasm drugging her blood with all the feel-good chemicals.

My head becomes light when my own orgasm shoots from my cock just from the taste of her. I soak the blankets under me with ropes of come, and I'm annoyed at myself for not saving it for her tight pussy.

Easing my fangs free, my vision blurs from my high. I lick the bite mark, gathering every drop of blood I can.

Parting her thighs, I grip my cock, and push her shorts to the side.

"Fucking love and hate these shorts. I've been driven crazy all night with these damn things. Hiding what I want yet showcasing what belongs to me."

In one hard thrust, I bury myself to the hilt. My vampire

nature takes over. My claws scratch down the back windows, and I roar into the night so loud, the truck shakes.

My pace is relentless. Our skin slaps together with every harsh thrust.

This. This is what I wanted. What I needed. This is what I dreamed about since meeting her.

"I can't wait to claim you again," I snarl while wrapping my arms around her body to bring her closer to me.

I thrust, driving my hips as hard as I can.

Flipping us, I'm on my back and she's on top. She grinds against me, using my chest as leverage for her palms.

She fucks me hard and fast. Her thighs shake, which has me losing my damn mind. My claws scratch down her hips, leaving more of my marks on her body.

Fireflies surround her, adding their blinking orange lights as a crown meant for a queen.

My Queen.

"Fuck, that's it, Darlin'. You take my cock so fucking well. You feel so good. You're going to make me come with how you fuck me. This is your cock. Use it. Claim me, Dru. Come all over me."

Much to my surprise, she bends down, yanks my head to the side, and bites my neck. Her blunt teeth morph, and the prickle of tiny fangs causes me to bleed. She has to apply more pressure than I would since her fangs are so much smaller, but I love the sensation of her sucking my blood down her throat. Her body is adapting to being my mate, preparing itself to feed and carry my child. That's all it takes for me to erupt.

She's still human until the day she comes to me to ask for more.

"Dru!" I call out her name for all to hear, filling her so much, my come begins to drip down my shaft. "Take every fucking drop of it."

She continues to chase her orgasm, her moans becoming louder the closer it becomes.

"Mine. You're mine." She licks my neck, sits up, and rolls her body.

My blood is smeared across her lips and chin, only adding gasoline to the fire that burns for her inside my heart.

"That's right. I'm all yours. Forever. For all eternity."

The words send her over the edge, her muscles tightening around my cock as her orgasm breaks her rhythm.

I'm more satisfied and at peace with her bite on my neck. Knowing I have something that can be shown to the world settles me. I hope it doesn't heal. It hasn't yet, which is promising. Maybe since she is my mate, her mark will scar like the one I gave her.

I catch her when she collapses, continuing to thrust so my come gets pushed as deep as possible.

My nose skims the side of her neck, where I press a kiss before I sink my fangs into my mating mark, claiming her all over again. With every drag, I taste her orgasm buzzing through her blood.

I don't stop drinking and thrusting into her.

Both are too much.

I can't last.

I growl into her neck, blood spilling from my mouth when my orgasm overflows her again.

Her fingernails dig into my chest, and she bites my pec as hard as she can, screaming at the top of her lungs. Her last orgasm tenses her body.

God, I love how she tastes when she comes.

"That's it," I whisper in between cleaning the blood from her neck. "Suck me deep, Darlin'. Remind your taken womb who you belong to and what awaits when it's empty."

Her lips find mine in a messy, tired kiss before she flops down next to me, placing her head on my shoulder.

We lie there in silence, catching our breath while we look up at the never-ending abyss of the star-filled night sky.

I sit up, leaning my back against the truck, which causes Dru to match my position.

"You're right, that was a much better claiming night than the first," she yawns, stretching her arms over her head.

"Tired? Dru, Darlin', I'm nowhere near done with you. Eat so you can have some energy." I hand her the bowl of fresh strawberries I cut up.

"Don't mind if I do," she says, popping a strawberry into her mouth.

Thunderous hooves capture our attention, and that's when I see Romeo and Juliette running through the field. The moonlight catches their eyes, and that's when I see it.

Juliette's eyes are red just like Romeo's.

"I'm happy he found his Beloved."

"Me too. He needed someone other than me." Just like I needed Dru.

"Skew-dang!"

I groan when I hear Lorcan. How does he always find the worst moments to interrupt?

I glance around, not spotting him until Dru points to the left. That's when I see him running through the field with the spine lasso I made out of Dru's enemies.

"Can I have this?" he shouts from across the field, practicing lassoing a wooden post.

Dru munches on a strawberry to stop herself from laughing.

"No! It's Dru's. You can't have it," I shout, covering most of Dru's body with my own so Lorcan can't see what belongs to me.

"Can I borrow it?" he yells again. "Please? I want to go to Purgatory with it."

"Just let him take it. I'm not using it."

"You give him an inch and he will take a mile," I warn.

"That's fine. He's a good friend. I trust him. As should you."

Well, her honesty has me feeling a little guilty.

"Fine. Take it. Go now and stop interrupting our date night!" I cup my hands by my mouth to make my voice louder.

"Oh, the other Voids aren't going to believe this." With a wave, he vanishes, finally leaving us alone.

After a few snacks, we lie down again, covering ourselves with a couple of blankets as we stare up at the stars.

"You know, you never told me where you got your name," she says. "Kentucky is very unique."

"I was named after the Kentucky Coffeetree you see in the front yard. I was born under it."

"I'll need to make sure nothing happens to that tree."

I grin, kissing her temple.

"Look! A shooting star. Let's make a wish. Wow, I've never seen one before. It's gorgeous."

I love to hear the excitement in her voice. I watch her follow the shooting star illuminating the sky, wanting to get every glimpse she can of it.

"My only wish to spend every Kentucky night with you for all eternity, Darlin'."

The end.

"I met Dru on August 18th, 2025. The day my life finally began."-Kentucky

Bonus Chapter
DAPHNE

"Lorcan, it's imperative that Kentucky never learns the truth about my sacrifice."

"What? Why? He deserves to know the truth, Daphne. He is struggling with the thought of being infertile, and on top of the secret that your lifespan got cut in half when you chose to be with him, isn't this something else he deserves to know?"

I watch Kentucky and Romeo move the herd of cattle to the next pasture; more content than I've ever been in my life.

"That is why he can't know. Promise me, you will never tell him the truth and if you tell his fated mate, which I know you will, I've seen it, she can't tell him either. You know his soul, Lorcan. He fights with the night entering his mind. If you tell him the truth, he will end his life sooner than he has planned. He will think he isn't deserving of such sacrifice, and that's not true. He's deserving of everything this world has to offer and more. I love him so much, but I'm only temporary. A stepping-stone to help him get to where he deserves to be. If we can get him there, he will be okay. His soul will be healed. He would never forgive himself if he ever found out I sacrificed my life and my ability to have kids. All the progress would be gone. I'll hold onto my lies if it means keeping him alive."

Lorcan sighs, rubbing a bony hand down the front of where his face would be. "Fine, I promise. But I don't like lying to him. He's too good a person."

"I know, but his heart and mind can be his enemy. We will lose him if we tell him the truth."

"I won't make his mate promise not to tell him. It isn't right for her to hold onto that lie for you."

"If she wants Kentucky to live, she will."

"I don't see Kentucky wanting to kill himself after meeting his fated mate. That's fucking dark, Daphne. Come on. I know you're used to seeing him in another light, but no matter how many glimpses of his future you will see, you won't know the future Kentucky."

"True. I'm just scared for him, I guess. I've seen too many alternative endings to his future. It's hard to decipher which one leads the way."

"I understand." Lorcan pats the top of my hand. "I'll keep an eye on him, and eventually, I'll get a matching hat to irk him. I live for that. Makes the sulfur in my dead soul pitter-patter."

The end.

ACKNOWLEDGEMENTS

First, I want to thank everyone who read my first vampire cowboy romance book. I hope you enjoyed it!

This book was so different for me to write than my other books. When I got the idea to write a vampire who is a cowboy, it was all due to JW Photography's photo of Tony Brettman—Thank you both for the amazing image!

The cover photo inspired an entire story. Kentucky Nights is definitely a lighter romance—lighter than what I typically write—and it was something my soul needed

Thank you to my team, Tiff, Bryckk, and Carolina. None of these books would happen without any of you. No matter what, you're there, supporting me through all my ups and downs. I don't know how you all deal with me, but I thank you for it.

Thank you to my Alpha Team: Tee, Rocki, Makayla, Greta, and Bryckk for helping me make Kentucky Nights the best it can be. You all gave constructive feedback to help better the story.

And of course, thank you to my amazing, supportive, loving, thoughtful husband. I have no doubt I wouldn't be where I am without you. Your belief in me keeps me going. When I don't have faith in myself, you have faith in me. I love you so much and thank you for your support over the last few months. You mean the world to me.

I love you with all my insides,
January

About the Author

January Rayne is a paranormal fantasy romance author who lives in Buffalo, NY with her husband, son, two dogs, and two leopard geckos. Buffalo is freezing, but January loves when it snows as it gives her the perfect atmosphere to write a book for you to get lost in.

Scan here for easy access to follow me
on social media: